CHEERS FOR R. D. ROSEN AND
*STRIKE THREE, YOU'RE DEAD:*

**"Mr. Rosen has hit a home run**.... His dialogue is smart and sophisticated and his characters altogether three-dimensional. An entertaining and well-written book."
—Newgate Callendar, *The New York Times Book Review*

**"A fastball**.... You'll be promising yourself just one more page of this whodunit, even though it's after bedtime."
—*Boston Globe*

**"The literary equivalent of a home run."**
—*Newsday*

**"Fresh and feisty:** a triple-homer for baseball/mystery fans and no strikeout even for those ignorant of the game."
—*Kirkus Reviews*

"A plot that keeps you turning pages ... full of bright banter that resembles the laconic lingo that enlivens Robert B. Parker's Spenser novels."
—*Sports Illustrated*

SIGNET MYSTERY

# STRIKE THREE, YOU'RE DEAD

## R.D. ROSEN

A SIGNET BOOK

NEW AMERICAN LIBRARY

## PUBLISHER'S NOTE

This novel is a work of fiction. Names, characters, places, and incidents either are the product of the author's imagination or are used fictitiously, and any resemblance to actual persons, living or dead, events, or locales is entirely coincidental.

SIGNET TRADEMARK REG. U.S. PAT. OFF. AND FOREIGN COUNTRIES
REGISTERED TRADEMARK—MARCA REGISTRADA
HECHO EN CHICAGO, U.S.A.

SIGNET, SIGNET CLASSIC, MENTOR, PLUME, MERIDIAN AND NAL BOOKS are published by New American Library, 1633 Broadway, New York, New York 10019

First Signet Printing, April, 1986

1  2  3  4  5  6  7  8  9

PRINTED IN THE UNITED STATES OF AMERICA

In memory of Ann Hall

# THE PROVIDENCE JEWELS

Owner and President: Marshall Levy
Manager: Felix Shalhoub
Public Relations Director: Buzzy Stanfill
Stadium: Rankle Park (seating capacity—37,000)
Colors: Emerald green, black, and white

## Coaching Staff

Timothy Bayman, pitching coach
Anthony Cantalupa, third base coach
Campy Strulowitz, first base coach and batting instructor

Arky Bentz, trainer
Duncan Frye, clubhouse manager

## ROSTER

| No. | Name | Position | Age | Birthplace |
|---|---|---|---|---|
| 14 | BATTLE, Cleavon | IF | 29 | Bakersfield, CA |
| 49 | BLISSBERG, Harvey | OF | 30 | Boston, MA |
| 6 | BYERS, Lester | IF | 33 | Syracuse, NY |
| 15 | CHARNESS, David | C-OF | 23 | Cloquet, MN |
| 10 | EPPICH, Randall | C | 26 | Allentown, PA |
| 22 | HOSMER, Robert | OF | 21 | Spanish Fork, UT |
| 12 | LUGO, Luis | IF | 22 | Fajardo, P.R. |
| 9 | MANOMAITIS, Charles | IF | 24 | Fairlee, VT |
| 7 | PENZENIK, Charles | IF | 24 | Sacramento, CA |
| 3 | RAPP, John | OF | 29 | Pueblo, CO |
| 11 | SALTA, Rodney | IF | 25 | Cali, Colombia |
| 19 | SMITH, Clyde | C | 34 | Belleville, IL |
| 25 | STILES, Richard | OF | 29 | Lima, OH |
| 8 | VEDRINE, Angel | IF | 23 | Barquisimeto, Venezuela |
| 24 | WILTON, Steven | OF | 27 | Bessemer, AL |

**Pitchers**

| No. | Name | Position | Age | Birthplace |
|---|---|---|---|---|
| 17 | VAN AUKEN, Daniel | LHP | 26 | New Britain, CT |
| 39 | CROP, Stanley | RHP | 25 | Rosenberg, TX |
| 29 | FURTH, Rudolph | LHP | 28 | Palmyra, WI |
| 40 | MARLETTE, Marcus | RHP | 25 | Lumpkin, GA |
| 48 | O'DONNELL, John | RHP | 24 | Cambridge, MD |
| 32 | OTHER, Donald | LHP | 31 | Moline, IL |
| 55 | POTTER-LAWN, Andrew | LHP | 26 | Bishop's Stortford, England |
| 50 | STORELLA, Edward | RHP | 22 | Manhattan, KA |
| 52 | WAGNER, Robert | RHP | 27 | Roanoke, VA |
| 34 | WEATHERHEAD, James | LHP | 22 | Los Angeles, CA |

It's when you're going good that they throw at your head.

Harvey Blissberg had been starting center fielder for the Boston Red Sox for five seasons, had two years left on a new three-year contract, and had just engaged the services of an interior decorator for his recently acquired Back Bay condominium when the team abruptly left him unprotected in the expansion draft over the winter. As a direct result of this insult, he became the property of the Providence Jewels, the latest addition to the American League Eastern Division. At an age when most of his contemporaries were winning their first big promotions, Harvey was obliged to pick himself up and start over with a team composed largely of cast-offs, players of proven mediocrity, and a few arrogant rookies thrown in just to remind him that, as far as baseball was concerned, he was no longer a young man.

Last year, with the Red Sox, he had considered himself in his prime. Now he felt like someone detained at the border before being allowed to pass over into the rest of his life.

Providence, Rhode Island, looked like a place you ended up when they kicked you out of everywhere else. It was too small and not nervous enough to be a city, as Harvey understood the term, but it was too big to be anything else. It seemed to consist entirely of outskirts—a sad city where a Mercedes or a tuxedo

was as incongruous as a camelia bush in a vacant lot.
At night, the streets of Providence were as empty as
Rankle Park's upper deck on any game day.

Actually, the lower grandstands were never that
crowded either. The Jewels' aging brick and concrete
home, built in the twenties and enlarged a few times
for a succession of short-lived minor league teams,
dominated a drab neighborhood that discouraged traffic, let alone baseball fans. With its odd assortment of
gray facades, turrets, and archways, Rankle Park re-
sembled a rusting battleship docked among shoe fac-
tories, textile mills, and warehouses whose tenants
had migrated in the seventies to the more congenial
Sun Belt.

The fans weren't the only ones who thought they
deserved better. When visiting clubs first saw the
park, the players tended to react with the polite dis-
may of people invited to dinner at a house that hadn't
been cleaned in weeks. The proposed new stadium
outside town didn't look as though it would material-
ize for another two years, if at all. That the team
playing in so tarnished a setting was called the Jewels was an irony seldom lost on the sportswriters who
fought for elbow room in the battered press box over
home plate. Still, there was logic to the name: the
team's owner and president, Marshall Levy, was the
founder of Pro-Gem, the biggest costume jewelry concern in a state that had the biggest costume jewelry
industry in the country. Levy had ignored the argu-
ment that "Jewels" was an unfortunate name for the
team of a town where most of the gems were phony.

Even though you had to wonder—and Harvey Blissberg was among those who did—what the baseball
commissioner and team owners had been thinking
when they awarded a franchise to Providence, the
Jewels had exceeded expectations. It was August 28,
and with their 63-and-66 record, the Jewels could

glance down in the Eastern Division standings and see Detroit and Toronto.

As for Harvey, at the age of thirty he was somehow enjoying his best season ever. His .309 batting average was more than 40 points above his modest career average, and he led Providence in batting, doubles, and—his legs felt five years younger than the rest of him—stolen bases. He was throwing around a lot of leather in center field. And as a bonus, he and Mickey Slavin—some said she was the best and most attractive television sportscaster in Providence—were finally an item.

These unexpected blessings made Harvey slightly uncomfortable. Having been burned once, he had the distinct feeling that someone was bound to start throwing at his head again. But as he stood with bat in hand behind the batting cage an hour before Tuesday night's game with Chicago, the only threat to his well-being came in the form of a vaguely familiar voice.

"Hey, Ha'vey, whaddya say, guy? Come ova heah a sec." It was one of those New England accents that produces *r*'s when they aren't called for, and drops them when they are.

Harvey turned toward the box seats. Ronnie Mateo stood in his usual pre-game spot in the first row by the Jewels' dugout, one spindly leg poised on top of the low wall separating the seats from the field. He was a thin man in his thirties with tightly curled black hair, a long face that looked like a blanched Brazil nut, and a taste for colorful double-knits and two-tone imitation snakeskin casuals. He was well known to many of the Jewels, to whom he tried to sell dubious merchandise from time to time. Occasionally he succeeded, which was why Chuck Manomaitis, the Providence shortstop, had shown up in the clubhouse a month before with a dozen digital traveling alarm clocks—still in their boxes next to the Desenex on the shelf of his locker.

Ronnie had never approached Harvey before. Harvey liked to think of himself as the kind of person who didn't look as if he needed a lot of cheap traveling alarm clocks.

"Professah! Hey, Professah," Ronnie shouted. "Come ova heah."

Harvey, who owned five Harris tweed sports jackets and read hardcover books on road trips, had been slapped with the nickname in his rookie year. It amused him because his older brother Norman was a real professor—of English, at Northwestern. "Professor" implied a clubhouse intimacy that Harvey was not aware Ronnie Mateo enjoyed with him. He finally ambled over to the box seats, not looking at Ronnie until he was standing in front of him.

"What can I do for you?" Harvey said. "You're a little too old for autographs."

"It's not what you can do me, Professor. It's what I can do you." Ronnie bent over the leg up on the wall and smoothed a tan sock with both palms. "You interested in a gross of necklaces, real nice merch, the kind that every month's got a different stone?"

Harvey narrowed his eyes. "Have we met?"

"We need an introduction? I'm pretty friendly with a lot of the ball players."

"All the same. Harvey Blissberg," he said, extending his hand.

Ronnie shook hands, pronouncing his name so it sounded like "raw knee," then flicked something that wasn't there off a brown and gold shoe. "A hundred forty-four necklaces, twelve of each month, each month a different stone. This is a very nice item." He pulled a handful of necklaces out of his jacket pocket and held them in Harvey's face.

Harvey rubbed some pine tar on the shaft of his bat with the rag. "What the hell would I do with them?"

"Now that all depends. If I was you, Professor, I'd

give 'em to your lady friends." His smile showed a fringe of tiny teeth.

"Yeah, well, I'm about a hundred and forty-three-and-a-half girlfriends short. Besides, all the women I know were born in February or October."

"So give 'em to your fans. Look, this is quality merch." Ronnie ran a thumbnail coated with clear polish over a red stone. "I wouldn't make this offer to anybody."

"And I don't blame you," Harvey said, starting to turn. "See you around."

"I wouldn't make this offer to anybody but you, Professor," Ronnie said again. In the row behind him, an elderly usher in a jacket with torn epaulets was showing a couple to their box seats.

"Where'd you come up with a gross of necklaces, anyway?"

"Here and there," Ronnie said.

"That wouldn't be the kind of junk Marshall Levy makes, would it?"

Ronnie's face dimmed at the mention of the Jewels' owner, and he carefully put the necklaces back in his pocket. His little black eyes wandered off behind Harvey toward the batting cage. "Gee, that kid Wilton can sure hit," he said. "You're hitting good, too, this year, Professor."

Harvey pivoted away from him again. "I'll see you around."

"They warned me you was a standoffish guy," Ronnie said to his back.

Harvey kept walking, but the voice stopped him after a few yards.

"Hey, Professor. What month your mother born in?"

Harvey turned to him. "February," he said.

Ronnie produced a glittering tangle of necklaces, extricated one, and lobbed it at Harvey. "That's an ametist, Professor," he called out. "For February. Tell your mother it's from Ronnie Mateo, who's a big fan of her son."

Harvey walked back toward the cage. When you wore a major league baseball uniform, sooner or later everyone wanted a piece of you. It was a matter of pride to Harvey that after six years of being approached by hustlers, hot-shot investment counselors, and all the shades of manipulators in between, there weren't any pieces of him missing.

When Rudy Furth, the Jewels' relief pitcher and Harvey's roommate on the road, came up to him at the batting cage, Harvey was idly running the necklace through his fingers.

"I've jerked off in front of more people than this," Rudy said. He was twenty-eight, but he looked like a senior in high school.

Harvey scanned the stands. The gate this evening would be lucky to hit the dismal average. "Yeah," he said, "and here I am playing the best ball of my career."

"At least someone on the team is." Rudy blew a pink bubble with his gum and sucked it back noisily into his mouth. "A gift from Ronnie Mateo?"

Harvey looked at the necklace in his fingers as if surprised to find it there. "Yeah, he tried to sell me some. What's his story?"

"He tried to sell me some color TVs once."

"What is he—some kind of low-grade fence?"

Rudy shrugged. "Who knows? I told him to buzz off. Even I know enough to stay away from him."

"Normally you don't have such good judgment."

"Thanks, roomie," Rudy said, pulling on his ear a few times. He was always moving, pulling his ear, snapping his fingers, thrusting out his lower lip. Harvey kidded him about belonging to the Tic-of-the-Month Club.

Harvey bobbed his head in the direction of a paperback book poking out of Rudy's back pocket. "I see you picked up the novel finally." In the Kansas City airport on their last road trip, Harvey had bought him the book with the intention of improving a mind whose severest tests came in the form of *Sporting News* and *People* magazine.

Rudy patted his pocket and jiggled his hand. "Well, it's kind of rough going for a farmboy like me. No pictures." He grinned boyishly. "But I like this guy Gatsby. Had a damned nice life-style, didn't he?"

"I can see you haven't read very far."

Rudy rotated his head a couple of times, like someone with a stiff neck. "If Wagner doesn't need any help from me on the mound tonight, I'll promise to get some reading done in the bull pen. That is, if the other guys don't mind me moving my lips."

Harvey returned Rudy's smirk. "Believe it or not, Rude, when you're through with baseball and out there in the big bad world, you're going to have to know how to read and write." Harvey wondered who the hell he was to pontificate about the big bad world out there.

"Yessir, Professor." Rudy flipped him a military salute.

"Yo-yos," Harvey said. "Nothing but yo-yos on this club."

"You worry too much." He tugged down on the bill of Harvey's cap and jogged out toward right field.

At the batting cage, Steve Wilton, the Jewels' right fielder, and Roger Kokis of the White Sox were discussing a woman who was sitting in the boxes behind third base.

"I'm telling you," Wilton was saying, "it's a law of nature. The bigger their tits, the closer they sit to the field."

Harvey stepped into the cage against Stan Crop, who was pitching batting practice. He popped up the first two pitches, cursing the little hitch that had lately developed in his swing.

"Hum babe, Harv babe, come to the pitch, you're the one," chanted Campy Strulowitz, who was leaning against the cage. Campy was the Jewels' bowlegged, sixty-year-old first base coach who did double duty as the team's batting instructor. A weak hitter in his own distant playing days, Campy had devoted long hours on the bench to studying his superiors at the plate. Harvey credited Campy with at least 20 points of his .309 batting average.

"You're the hum babe, Harv," he said. "Glide it and ride it, bring those wrists, babe, bring 'em and fling 'em, settle down, hum-a-now, you're the kid." He hunkered down in an imitation of Harvey's batting stance, his fists raised to grasp an imaginary bat.

Steve Wilton stood next to Campy, peeling off a batting glove. "Shut up already, will you, Campy?" he said. "The Professor's already hitting three-something. Stop hum-babing him."

Campy fired a thick brown stream of tobacco juice close to Steve's left spike. "I don't see you hitting top ten, Steve kid, don't see you ripping off the big hits."

"Whyn't you just choke on your chaw and die," Steve said, stalking off.

"Hum kid, hum kid, hum-a-now," Campy said.

Harvey sent Stan Crop's next pitch through the humid dusk of August into Rankle Park's utterly empty left field upper deck.

By game time, there were only six thousand people in the park, and the Jewels ran out on the field to thin applause. In center, Harvey adjusted the bill of his cap with a tailor's curt flourish and winged the warm-up ball back and forth with John Rapp, in left field. He snapped off his throws with a deliberate motion, glancing down to make sure his stirrup socks were pulled tightly over his calves. Being alone with all that grass calmed him. Even as a kid, when other Little Leaguers wanted to play only shortstop, or pitch, Harvey had played center field. Green, spacious, removed from the crowded, dusty infield, center had all the virtues of a desirable suburb.

When Chicago's Scott Dykes sent Bobby Wagner's first pitch high over Harvey's head toward the 447 FT sign in right center, Harvey surrendered to familiar instinct. He registered the trajectory of the ball, then turned and put his head down and sprinted toward the wall. Thirty feet from the dirt warning track, he looked up to see that he had beaten the ball to its destination by a split second, allowing him to catch it with an effortless twitch of his glove. Over his head, Rankle Park's new electronic scoreboard commended the play by flashing "A GEM" in rapidly increasing sizes.

On the mound, Bobby Wagner, who had been struggling for most of the season, heaved a sigh. The flame-thrower from Virginia had been one of the American League's premier right-handers when the Baltimore Orioles left him for dead in the off-season because of alleged calcium deposits in his arm. The Jewels, who needed a big name on their pitching staff, had traded four players for him even though he was now playing out the last year of his old Baltimore contract and would be eligible to become a free agent in the fall. His record stood at 8 and 14, the worst showing of an otherwise brilliant career.

Harvey's catch seemed to have settled him down, and the White Sox were scoreless after seven innings. Providence picked up two runs along the way, one of them on Harvey's fifth inning double. But in the top of the eighth, Chicago's right fielder, Dave Shingle, lined a home run off the auxiliary scoreboard on the facing of the right field pavilion, cutting Bobby's lead to 2–1. When Bobby proceeded to walk Abbler, and Dykes followed with a single to left, Felix Shalhoub, the Providence manager, walked slowly to the mound, his body bent forward slightly at the waist. He lifted his left arm desultorily to signal the bull pen for Rudy Furth. Bobby Wagner slapped the ball into Felix's extended right hand and headed for the showers.

In deep center, the bull pen gate opened in the fence, and a compact figure with long, blond hair emerged, sliding his emerald green nylon warm-up jacket over his left arm. He walked across center field toward the mound, pulling abreast of Harvey, who accompanied him part of the way.

"How's the arm?" Harvey said.

Rudy jutted out his lower lip. "It's been better. I can't get my fastball to lay down where I want it tonight." He stroked his sheathed left arm nervously with his glove, as if to encourage it.

"Then go with the slider. It's been looking pretty good to me.

"You think so?" Rudy said with his way of giving too much credit to obvious comments. "But this guy creamed the slider last time I showed it to him."

"That one was up in his wheelhouse, Rude. Keep this one down."

"Yeah, okay," Rudy said, a little glumly.

"Now you're the one who's worrying too much. Just go out there and get 'em."

"Sure," Rudy said, and they walked a few more yards before he squinted up at the press box and asked, "Seen Slavin tonight?"

"I don't think she's here. I think she's out covering women's soccer or something."

Rudy spat. "When're the three of us going to get together again? I have fun with you guys."

Harvey looked straight ahead.

"I tried to call you last night," Rudy said. "Were you at Mickey's?"

"Could be."

"She's pretty good in bed, huh, Professor?"

Harvey turned to look his roommate in the eye. "You tell me."

Rudy pulled twice on his ear. "Did I say something wrong or something?"

They walked a few more yards without speaking. Then Harvey said, "Go get 'em, and keep the goddamn slider down, will ya?"

Rudy warmed up on the mound. Dean Levine of Chicago promptly stroked his first pitch deep in the hole at second. Rodney Salta couldn't make a play on it, and the bases were loaded for Mac Bodish, who swung and missed on a slider, then picked on a fastball at the knees. From Harvey's perspective in center, the pitch didn't tail, it didn't rise, it didn't sink; all it did was jump off Bodish's bat and rattle off the wall in left. By the time Rapp chased it down on the warning track, three runs had scored and Bodish was standing on third. The White Sox now led 4–2, and it stayed that way.

In the clubhouse, the Jewels stripped off their white double-knit uniforms with the depressing black and green trim. Chuck Manomaitis, the shortstop, was once again trying to sell Steve Wilton his digital alarm clocks at a small margin over what he had paid to get them from Ronnie Mateo. Wilton once again suggested to Chuck an unsavory use for the clocks that quickly ended the negotiations.

Half a dozen reporters trying to corner a few quotes scurried underfoot. The dean of the local baseball writers, Bob Lassiter, of the *Providence Journal-Bulletin*, accosted Les Byers, the Jewels' third baseman.

"Les," Lassiter said, wagging his pencil. "I make twenty-nine thousand a year. You make one forty-five, and I'm not even going to mention the bonus on signing and deferred annuity. Now, if you ask me, you're getting paid enough to swing at that called third strike in the ninth."

Les stepped gingerly out of his jockstrap, held it for a moment in front of Lassiter's nose, and let it fall to the floor like a coquette releasing her handkerchief.

"Man," he bellowed, "you expect me to do ever l'il thing? The game's hard work. Shucks, sometimes we put in six, seven hours a day."

Lassiter, who did not excel at getting jokes, stammered, "Well—well, that's not exactly slave labor." But Les was already showing him his back.

"Hey, Furth," Steve Wilton yelled across the locker room. "Way to handle Bodish. Next time, why don't you throw it to him underhanded?"

It was one thing to ride a teammate like that when reporters were *not* around. "Shove it, A-hole," Rudy yelled back.

Harvey caught up with him at the long table in the middle of the locker room where the post-game meal was laid out—hamburgers, fried chicken, french fries, and tossed salad provided by the owner's, Marshall Levy's, sister, who operated a catering outfit in nearby Attleboro, Massachusetts.

"I hear the fried chicken's good here," Harvey said.

Rudy was wearing nothing but shower clogs. He picked up a hamburger, tossed his hair off his face, and said, almost carelessly, "He's right, you know. I couldn't have done any worse throwing underhanded." He took a bite out of the hamburger, handed the rest to Harvey, and shuffled toward the showers.

Harvey pushed a few french fries into his mouth and followed Rudy, passing the open door to Felix's tiled office on the way.

"Gentlemen," the manager was explaining to a trio of reporters, "we stopped hitting after the fifth inning, the bull pen was not in a positive posture tonight, and at the end of nine we were behind by two runs. And that's the whole six flavors."

Of the five most popular topics of locker room conversation among ball players—hunting, fishing, cars, real estate, and women—only the last interested Harvey, and even then he found there was little to be gained by subjecting his views to clubhouse scrutiny. Yet clubhouses were the closest thing he had known to an office in his life, and he felt protected by their walls. It was with a feeling of returning to his natural habitat that the next morning, on Wednesday, August 29, after dropping off his Chevy Citation for a tune-up, he had a taxi leave him in the players' parking lot at Rankle Park. Nine-thirty was early to show up for the afternoon game against Chicago that would close out the series, but Harvey felt he needed some extra work against the pitching machine under the left field stands. He liked the ball park early in the morning. Only Dunc would be in the clubhouse. When Harvey swung open the door, Dunc was standing just inside.

Contrary to the unwritten law that all major league clubhouse managers had to be seriously lacking in human qualities, Dunc was better-natured than twenty years of catering to the whims of young athletes would seem to warrant. He was short, amiable, and had a taste for apricot brandy. Harvey, who occasionally supplied him with a pint, found that in exchange Dunc was more than willing to load baseballs into the pitching machine.

At the moment, however, Dunc was wearing the

distorted expression of someone who had inadvertently swallowed his chewing tobacco. His jaw hung open—revealing that in fact his tobacco was still there, in a mouth full of brownish kernels that had once been his teeth. He stood there in his white duck uniform staring somewhere to the right of Harvey's face.

"What gives, Dunc?"

Dunc said nothing, but raised a stubby arm and pointed behind him toward the center of the locker room.

"Well, what is it?"

Dunc didn't speak, or wasn't able to, and Harvey went past him into the empty clubhouse.

The Providence Jewels' clubhouse was a collection of unattractive rooms beneath the stands along the right field line. Nauseating green indoor–outdoor carpeting had been laid down over the original cement floors; given a choice, however, Harvey would much rather get dressed on an artificial surface than play on one. The lockers, open cubicles, took up three of the locker room's four walls, and in front of each was an orange or powder blue molded plastic chair like the ones found in Greyhound bus stations; given the team's operating budget, there was no reason to believe the management hadn't found them in an abandoned Greyhound bus station. The fourth wall, a stretch of gray plaster, featured various calendars, schedules, bulletin boards, equipment lockers, and a large blackboard for personal messages such as "Stan—call your wife" and "You suck, Rodney," as well as for inspirational memoranda like "Winners Are People Who Never Learned How to Lose," usually scrawled by Felix Shalhoub in palsied capital letters.

By the door to the trainer's room was a bat rack and next to it stacked cases of soft drinks and beer, which were fed regularly into an ice chest against a pillar in the middle of the room. A long wooden table supported a Cory coffee machine. Elsewhere, a canvas clothes hamper, piles of newspapers, and a portable television set on a folding table gave the locker room a tenement feel that Dunc and his crew of teenage assistants were unable to reform.

To the left as you entered was a door to the runway that connected the clubhouse to the dugout. It was a badly lit corridor with exposed steam pipes, and it was littered with balls of used tape, discarded Red Man foil pouches, and generations of tobacco juice. Halfway down the runway on the left was a metal door leading to a system of dark tunnels that ran under the grandstands to several storage areas and the visitors' clubhouse. The catacombs, as they were called, were home to a colony of brown rats. Impervious to the poisons used by the occasional exterminator, they had lived in he bowels of Rankle Park for as long as anyone could remember, surviving on unfinished hot dogs, peanuts, popcorn, and old lineup cards. The rats rarely ventured into the seats, at least not during games, and only once since the Jewels had moved in had one of the grayish brown creatures wandered into the clubhouse during working hours. The reserve catcher, Happy Smith, had clubbed it to death.

Harvey saw nothing unusual in the locker room and turned impatiently to Dunc, who was still at the door.

"C'mon, Dunc," he said. "What's going on?"

Except for a barely perceptible jerk of his head in the direction of the trainer's room, Dunc did not move.

The noise was like that made by a motorboat on the other side of a lake.

"Why's the whirlpool on?" Harvey said, walking in the direction of the noise. Then he stopped.

Over the rim of the stainless steel tub, a man's hand was draped, palm down, as if waiting to be kissed. Harvey took two steps toward it and reached out to grab a corner of one of the trainer's tables.

The churning water was the color of rosé wine. Harvey went to the whirlpool and stooped to switch off the motor. As the water settled, it revealed the form crammed into a fetal position at the bottom of the tub. The head was bent over between the knees; its blond hair fanned out and swam along the surface, mingling with flecks of blood and mucus.

Harvey closed his eyes. He did not have to see the face to know who it was. He lurched to one of the sinks and vomited, clutching the faucets with both hands. When he was through, his face wet with tears, he vomited again.

Dunc now stood behind him in the doorway to the trainer's room. He hid his mouth behind the crook of his upraised elbow.

"It's Rudy," Harvey said. "Call the cops."

Dunc disappeared, and Harvey plunged his hands into the hot red water and hooked them under Rudy's arms.

"Oh, Jesus, Jesus, Jesus," he said, and with all his strength hoisted Rudy's naked body out of the tub and laid him on his back on the floor. His pale knees would not go down.

His half-open eyes seemed to watch Harvey warily. Harvey closed them. Straddling Rudy's stomach, he began pumping his chest furiously. Thick bloody water bubbled out of Rudy's mouth and ran in trails down his cheek.

"C'mon, you bastard!" he shouted. He pried Rudy's jaws apart and breathed into his mouth. "Oh, Jesus," he said and moved his left hand around to the back of Rudy's head to steady it.

He immediately jerked his hand away. Above Rudy's ear, the skull was sticky and soft, not like a skull at all.

"He's gone, Harvey," Dunc was saying over him, holding a sheet. He was crying, too.

The next hour passed in a haze. Two uniformed cops arrived first, then two more, then a plainclothes de-

tective in an ill-fitting seersucker suit. He snapped
back the sheet as if he meant to surprise the body,
examined it with a few efficient movements, and asked
Harvey to make an identification. Then he asked Dunc
and him to wait outside in the locker room. The cop
who ushered them out remained there, thumbs hooked
importantly on his belt. Harvey and Dunc slumped in
two chairs. A lanky young man with a doctor's bag
passed through the locker room, followed by two more
cops with a stretcher, a red-faced man in a brown suit,
and after him, two mobile lab technicians with black
cases.

Through the open door to the trainer's room, Harvey saw the man from the medical examiner's office
touching Rudy's body here and there and conferring
with the detective. Flashbulbs went off, and one of the
mobile lab men scraped away at the indoor–outdoor
carpeting while the other used large tweezers to pick
up rolls of adhesive tape and a pair of snub-nose
scissors and drop them into manila envelopes. The cop
chaperoning Harvey and Dunc went over and closed
the door.

"I take it you guys found him in the whirlpool,
huh?" the cop said. When neither of them acknowl-
edged the question, the cop smacked his lips, said,
"Rudy Furth—my kid brother played against him in
the minors," and resumed his post near the bat rack.

By the time the two ambulance men brought Rudy
out on a stretcher in a green zippered body bag and
carried him out to the players' parking lot, the locker
room had filled up with members of the team. They
stood around in their street clothes with shocked faces,
like worshipers discovering the desecration of their
shrine. The clubhouse no longer belonged to them.
The place was silent except for the crackling of
walkie-talkies.

Felix Shalhoub came in with his wife, Frances. She
tried to force her way past the cops into the trainer's

room, where the detective was holed up with the M.E.'s man and the technicians.

"Officer, would you mind explaining—" she began.

A cop interrupted her in a voice louder than necessary, "Lady, I don't know what you're doing here in the first place, but you'll have to wait with the others."

The door opened at last, and the man in the seersucker suit lumbered out to introduce himself in a bored, gravelly voice as Detective Sergeant Linderman of the Providence Police. He had a graying crew cut and a heavily stubbled face. Under his jacket, he wore a yellow and maroon paisley shirt. He wiped his hands on a handkerchief and stuffed it in a pants pocket, from which he pulled out a small notebook.

At this gesture, several voices erupted. The detective held up both hands in front of his face, as though protecting himself from flying objects.

"The way I understand it," he began, "Rudy Furth's body was found in the whirlpool by"—he consulted the notebook —"Duncan Frye and Harvey Blissbaum." Those latecomers to whom it was news gasped in unison, then produced a trickle of Oh-Jesus's.

"Blissberg," Harvey heard himself say. "Harvey Blissberg." They were the first words he had spoken in an hour.

"Yeah, yeah, yeah. Blissberg," the detective said. "You found him in the whirlpool?"

"Dunc found him first."

"Please, Detective," Frances Shalhoub blurted, "will you just tell us what you know?"

"Patience," Linderman said. "Where's Duncan?"

Dunc rose, the front of his white duck shirt splotched with pink stains from the whirlpool water. He steadied himself against the ice chest. "I saw somebody in the whirlpool when I opened up the clubhouse at nine. That's what happened. Then Harvey came."

"Yeah, yeah, yeah, so who took him out of the whirlpool?"

"I did," Harvey said.

"Why?" Linderman said.

"I thought he might be alive, I guess."

"My guess," said Linderman, "is that he'd been soaking in there since last night. Who saw him last, alive?"

Apparently Dunc had been the last—or next-to-last—person to see Rudy alive the night before. After the rest of the team had cleared out, Dunc explained to Linderman, Rudy remained in the whirlpool. He liked to soak for a long time after he'd pitched; he had a bad back, and Felix had authorized him to have his own key to the clubhouse. At eleven-thirty, Dunc had turned off the lights in the locker room, poked his head in the trainer's room to remind Rudy to lock up, and fetched him a beer from the ice chest. Dunc remembered nothing strange. He locked the clubhouse door behind him and told Jack Fera, the uniformed guard in the players' parking lot, to knock off; Rudy would let himself out. The only cars left in the lot were Dunc's, Rudy's, and right fielder Steve Wilton's, which had been there for days with a dead battery.

"Who's in charge here?" Linderman finally asked.

"Me," Felix said, running his hand through his strands of silver hair.

Linderman was pacing a little, biting on his pen. "You let all the players have their own keys to the clubhouse?"

"Maybe two or three," Felix said. "I'd have to think about it. It's not a common policy, but—"

"That's all right; it can wait." Linderman closed his notebook. "You gentlemen have a game today?"

When Felix nodded, Linderman added, "You plan on playing it?"

Felix looked around at the faces in the locker room. "That would probably be a bad idea," he said.

The M.E.'s man came out of the trainer's room, spoke briefly in the detective's ear, and left. "Then maybe you should put in a call to the commissioner's office, or whatever you're supposed to do, and explain that there's been an accident," Linderman said.

"You think this was an accident?" Felix said.

"Not unless the man just happened to club himself over the head with a blunt object, knocking himself unconscious, and then drowned." He stroked the plane of his crew cut. "What about his next of kin? Does he have a wife?"

"He's single," Felix said. "But he's got foster parents somewhere in Wisconsin, I think."

Felix's wife, dressed in a skirt and blue blazer, hopped off the ice chest. "I'll take care of it," she said.

"Okay, then," Linderman resumed. "Now, as long as I've got most of the team here, I'd like to ask you to bear with me and stay here until me and Detective Bragalone've had a chance to talk to each of you. Briefly. Just routine." He ran his hand over the butt ends of a few bats in the rack. "That is"—he threw a thumb over his shoulder—"unless someone already knows what went on in there and is just keeping us all in suspense."

Linderman clapped his hands and disappeared with Felix into Shalhoub's office off the locker room. Harvey sat in front of his cubicle and watched one of the mobile lab men clear everything out of Rudy's locker, a few down from his. The man gingerly placed the garments, Rudy's glove, a bottle of Selsun Blue, and a package of sugarless bubble gum in bags and envelopes. When he was through, the only thing left was a strip of adhesive tape on the metal frame above the locker that read, "FURTH #29."

Before long, Tim Bayman, the Jewels' pitching coach, came out of Felix's office, where Linderman was conducting his interviews. The detective stood in the doorway looking at the team roster in one of the official programs. "Blissberg," he called out and showed Harvey in. Linderman perched on the edge of Felix's desk and waited until Harvey settled into a chair.

"I've got a shirt like that," Linderman said, pointing at the dark green Chemise Lacoste from which Harvey had painstakingly removed the alligator. "Mine's red."

Harvey surveyed the detective. One of his legs was hooked over the desk corner, baring a pale patch of hairless shin above a thin white sock. He wore a big Timex. An extensive collection of Bic pens was jammed in the breast pocket of the seersucker jacket. Harvey was blearily staring at the pens when Linderman spoke again.

"I know this is tough," he said. "You feel like talking?"

Harvey wondered what it was like to be a guy who was about to spend an afternoon telling thirty people how tough it was.

"So," Linderman said. "You got any ideas about Rudy Furth?"

"Okay," Harvey said in a daze.

"Okay? Yeah, I like that. But it's not much of an answer."

"We were roommates."

"You were?"

"Yeah, I guess I knew him pretty well."

"Do you know anybody who would want to kill him?"

Harvey shook his head. "No, no," he said. "It's unbelievable."

"Was he in any trouble?"

Harvey just looked at him.

"Let's see," Linderman said. "There's gambling, for starters. How's that? Or maybe he ran around with the wrong people. Woman trouble? Maybe he was sleeping with somebody's wife. Am I making any sense to you? Did he ever tell you somebody was after him?"

"No. I can't see any of that."

Linderman waited for Harvey to continue, which he didn't. "I mean, your roommate's been murdered. You must know something about him."

"I know he was one of the few guys on the team I really got along with."

Linderman pushed himself off Felix's desk and began circling it. "What's wrong with the rest of the guys that you didn't get along with them?"

"I didn't mean it like that."

"How'd you mean it, then?" The detective stopped behind the desk to thumb through Felix's desk calendar. He was working his mouth as if he had something lodged under his gum.

"I just meant that Rudy and I—you know, roommates grow on each other. Can I have a cigarette?"

"Take this one," Linderman said, tossing him the unlit Marlboro he had been holding since the beginning of the interview between his thumb and middle finger. "It's not doing me any good." He fumbled another cigarette out of his pocket and began playing with it.

"He was a funny guy," Harvey said. "Like a big kid."

"Rest of the team get along with him?"

"As far as I know." Harvey glanced around the tiny office, trying to recall that he was at the ball park.

"But not like you got along with him?" Linderman craned his neck to look at Harvey.

"Maybe not. One thing about Rudy, he had a mouth on him. Some players don't like that."

"You mean he talked too much?"

"More like at the wrong times. He could get on a guy."

"Look," Linderman said, walking again, "I know there're about seven or nine things you'd rather be doing, but bear with me, will you? What do you mean, he could get on a guy?"

Harvey struggled for an anecdote. "Oh, I don't know," he said. The questions themselves fogged his memory. "Well, one thing he'd always do was if some guy complained about something, Rudy liked to say, 'B.F.D.' It didn't matter what you were complaining about; it was just his way of getting attention, I guess. He was an orphan; he wanted people to like him, but he could rub them wrong. Rudy didn't always wear real well."

"Am I supposed to know what B.F.D is?"

"Big fucking deal," Harvey said.

"I get it. But you don't know who could've been rubbed the wrong way hard enough to kill him for it?"

"No, I'm telling you, this whole thing doesn't, it's—"

"You mean he had a mouth on him, but he never used it to give you, his roommate, any clue as to what he was doing in the whirlpool this morning?" Linderman heaved himself up on the desk and finally lit his cigarette with an 89-cent lighter he ferreted from his pants pocket. "There was no special tension between Rudy and any of the others?"

"I don't know of anything out of the ordinary."

"What's the ordinary?"

"Look, I don't know. One guy doesn't like another guy's attitudes or his politics, or the way he borrows your shampoo and doesn't give it back, or the fact that he gets more playing time. Do you like all the guys on the force?"

"Did he carry a lot of money? Cash?"

"He wasn't broke."

"I mean, a lot of money. Like try a thousand dollar bill."

"A thousand?"

"We found one in there with him."

"Where?"

"In the whirlpool."

"I didn't see it."

"No reason why you should've. They don't float. There was a crumpled thousand dollar bill at the bottom of the whirlpool."

"That's interesting."

"Sure it's interesting. If it belonged to Rudy, then robbery probably wasn't the motive. And if it didn't belong to him, I'd like to know who." Linderman tapped some ash into his palm, bounced it once, and let it fall to the floor. "Harvey, do you have your own key to the clubhouse?"

"Yeah, as a matter of fact, but that doesn't—"

"Doesn't mean anything. I'm just asking. My keen deductive mind tells me that whoever killed your roommate didn't have to have a key to get to him. See, Furth could've let his killer in, or he could've been in there all along and no one knew it. I might even entertain the thought that Furth could've been killed somewhere else and then put in the whirlpool."

Linderman spotted Felix's ashtray, a ceramic piece in the shape of a hollowed-out half-baseball, and poked out his cigarette. Harvey did likewise. "See," Linderman said, "the field's wide open. I just thought you might want to narrow it for me."

Harvey shook his head.

"All right," Linderman said, pushing himself off the desk and walking to the door. "Why don't we take this up again some other time?"

Harvey got out of his chair. "You'll find the bastard who did this," he said.

"Yeah, yeah, yeah." Linderman took the rolled-up roster out of his inside jacket pocket and moved his finger until he found the name after Blissberg.

"Les Byers," he said thoughtfully. "Isn't that the black kid who homered in extra innings a couple of nights ago?"

When Harvey left Linderman, he still had the eggy taste of vomit in his mouth. He went over to the ice chest and pulled out a root beer.

Happy Smith detached himself from a clutch of teammates standing nervously by the coffee machine and approached him.

"You're the smart one, Professor," he said with the air of one old-timer consulting another. "You tell me since when they murder guys in the clubhouse." Happy was thirty-four and had spent the last twelve years of his life as a second-string catcher for five different teams, like a seldom needed spare part kept in the trunk of the car.

"I don't know, Happy," Harvey said between pulls on the soda. "I don't know when they started doing it." The door to the equipment room opened and Cleavon Battle, the Jewels' first baseman, came out ahead of Bragalone, the other detective. "I need some air," Harvey told Happy.

"You're lucky your name's Blissberg," Happy said.

"How's that?"

"They're going alphabetically, aren't they? I'll be here all day before the cops get around to me."

"I feel for you," Harvey said and made for the clubhouse door.

Frances Shalhoub was at the wall phone attached to one of the peeling pillars, her slender hand pressed to her forehead. "No, no, no, of course," she was saying into the receiver. "I understand. You are his only family, though. . . . No. . . . Yes, as I said, we'll be happy to take care of all that at this end. . . ."

In the players' parking lot, a couple of newspaper reporters were talking to Campy Strulowitz. A van from one of the local stations had pulled up, and a television reporter in a Dacron blend suit stood next to it, grooming his hair in the sideview mirror.

On the sidewalk, a nut vendor in a canvas porkpie hat glanced up from his cart. "What's up, Harvey?" he called.

"Knock off, Sam. No game today."

The old man ate one of his own pistachios. "No game? On account of what?"

Harvey decided to walk home and took the enclosed pedestrian crosswalk over the expressway into the Portuguese neighborhood. Suddenly, he felt his stomach surge again, and he retched under a tree by the curb.

The thought occurred to him that he hadn't told Linderman about Rudy and Mickey when the detective asked if Rudy had any woman trouble. It sickened him to have to fight off thinking about the one time he had really hated Rudy. Of course, it had really been Harvey's woman trouble, anyway, not Rudy's. Soon after Harvey had met Mickey Slavin, while she was shooting a feature story about the team in May, he had introduced her to his roommate, and the three of them quickly formed a trio for occasional dinners out, movies, short trips. From the beginning, Harvey felt he had a claim on Mickey, but she clearly enjoyed the company of the two roommates too much to risk jarring the symmetry of her affection. Gradually, though, Mickey warmed up to Harvey, and when the two of them started sleeping together in June, Rudy took it in stride; as it was, he certainly got enough on his own. Then came the night at the Boston Sheraton, when somehow or other—in any case, Harvey didn't blame himself—Mickey ended up in Rudy's bed. Harvey and Mickey soon picked up where they had left off, but Rudy, who was pleasantly indifferent to the complexities of their threesome, had never mentioned the night at all.

Harvey made his way down the brick sidewalks of Hope Street, past clapboard houses of yellow, ocher, turquoise, and pale green. They were set, without yards, directly into concrete. An old man in slippers was hosing down his car in a driveway. On a street corner, a few teenage boys in T-shirts and girls in tube tops and red toenail polish silently smoked. One of the boys recognized him: "Hey, Ha'vey, youse guys gonna win de pennet?"

Harvey raised a noncommittal hand at him and kept walking. He was wondering what it said about him that Rudy had been as good a friend as he had on the ball club, even though just about the only thing they had in common was a fascination with Mickey Slavin.

That Harvey was a baseball player at all, let alone a major leaguer who was batting .309 with just over a month to go in the season, still struck him as bizarre. He had grown up in a Jewish family outside Boston, where his father owned an Italian restaurant. Neither Al nor Mary Blissberg felt that baseball was the proper career for a child only two generations removed from a Polish shtetl. "My childhood," he had quipped to a magazine writer back in the days when he talked freely to reporters, "was colored by a deep historical prejudice against wearing spikes to work." Nonetheless, his aptitude for playing baseball attracted several pro offers, and he signed with Boston after his last year at the University of Massachusetts. His mother was able to overcome her opposition to his choice of career—death had by that time rendered his father's opinion academic—when Harvey pointed out how vulnerable he would be to invitations to Sunday brunch once the Red Sox brought him up from the minors, which they did after a single minor league season.

However, Harvey had never shaken off his inherited ambivalence toward the game; he continued to feel that he had somehow missed his proper calling, although he had no idea what that calling might be. For Rudy, on the other hand, the game was an all-day sucker. Baseball rescued him from a life of raising veal calves on his foster parents' farm in southern Wisconsin; he had lost his parents in a car accident as a teenager. Now he always behaved like someone on furlough. "I love this game," he once told Harvey, actually grabbing Harvey's shirt to make his point. "I love it even when I lose."

Rudy wore fifty-dollar designer jeans and boots with three-inch heels, and he told all the tasteless jokes that had made the rounds the year before. He wore a gold I.D. bracelet on his right wrist and ignored his agent's advice against making risky real estate investments. Rudy and the Minnesota Twins had parted company the previous winter shortly after he announced to the press that the Twins were "the horniest team in baseball and the guys want to get laid so bad they don't have time to think about fundamentals."

Harvey liked Rudy for the very traits that some of their teammates regarded as bush league. Even when Harvey was angry at him, it was with the affectionate disdain of an older brother. At the same time he knew, even if Rudy didn't, that their friendship would never have existed outside of baseball.

Harvey stopped into a neighborhood tavern on Hope called the Nip 'n' Tuck. At noon, the only other customer was a woman in a floral housedress conversing with herself and stubbing out menthol cigarettes almost as soon as she lit them with a trembling hand. Harvey drank a bottle of Narragansett, slid off the stool, and went to the phone booth by the men's room.

Harvey dialed his older brother's number in Evanston, Illinois. "Hi, Norm," he said when his brother answered.

"What's the good news, Harv?" Norm said. "You calling from a submarine?" The connection was bad, and Norm's voice sounded metallic.

"I'm calling from a bar in Providence."

"You guys get rained out today?"

"No. Rudy Furth was murdered last night."

There was a slight pause on Norm's end. "You called to tell me that? C'mon, Furth hasn't been able to get anyone out all season."

"Someone killed him last night. Dead."

A longer pause this time. "Wait a second. You're not kidding, are you?"

Harvey supplied what he could of the details. "I had to call someone," he said.

"Christ, that's really horrible." Another pause. "Born Racine, Wisconsin," Norm said suddenly. "Lifetime record of forty-four and fifty-nine, two years with the Reds, four with the Twins. Are there any suspects?"

Norm was a compulsive student of baseball and its statistics; Harvey thought Norm got more pleasure out of his baseball career than he himself did. If Norm didn't know exactly how to respond to the news of Rudy's murder, it was because he saw ball players less as human beings than as lines of agate type in *The Baseball Encyclopedia*.

"Harv? You there, Harv?"

"I'm here."

"Look, I know how you must feel."

"Good, because I don't. I shared a hotel room with the guy in every city in the league. I know what color his goddamn toothbrush is—" He broke off.

"You going to be all right?" Norm said.

"Yeah. I'll call you soon. Say hi to Linda."

"Harv, if you want to talk about it—"

"I'll talk to you soon, Norm."

Harvey walked along College Hill, where the streets have reassuring names like Hope, Friendship, Beneficent, and Benevolent. He lived on Benefit, halfway up the hill, where most of the buildings were Federal or Victorian or Greek Revival. The beauty of the neighborhood seemed to be trying to atone for the dreariness of the rest of the city. He had a few immense rooms on the second floor of a rambling red brick Victorian mansion, owned originally by General Ambrose E. Burnside, who served as governor of Rhode Island after the Civil War. This fact interested Harvey, who had written his undergraduate thesis on the Army of the Potomac. He didn't particularly like Burnside—neither had President Lincoln—but he was willing to forgive him his mistakes in return for an apartment with high ceilings, a bow window, and a reasonably flattering view of Providence.

Once inside, he flipped on the air conditioner and stood in the middle of his living room looking at his two mismatched club chairs, his horsehair love seat, and the swaying stacks of paperbacks on the floor next to the windows. Two neglected scheffleras and a framed poster for a Philip Guston exhibition constituted his only attempts at interior decoration. It was no way for someone who made $150,000 a year to live.

He went to the kitchen and reviewed the contents of his refrigerator: Frank's Louisiana Red Hot Sauce, calamata olives, Vitarroz green tabasco peppers, Zatarain's New Orleans remoulade sauce, Lan Chi Brand Chili Paste with Garlic, Sanju's South Indian Lime Pickle, Bolst's Sweet Mango Chutney. A fondness for condiments was one of the few things that tied him to his dead restaurateur father.

Eventually, he discovered the makings of a meal. He boiled some linguini, opened a can of minced clams, and, applying a culinary lesson he'd learned from Al

Blissberg, made a clam sauce with the remains of an American chablis. He carried his lunch to the kitchen table, sat looking at it for five minutes, walked over to the sink, and dropped the meal down the disposal.

Bob Lassiter of the *Journal-Bulletin* called that afternoon to ask what Harvey thought about the murder.

"I thought it sucked," he said.

Even under ordinary circumstances, Harvey was not what reporters called a "good quote." It irritated him to be the object of grown men's trivial speculations. His reputation had preceded him to Providence, and Lassiter had approached him at the beginning of the season to propose a truce. Harvey explained that he'd be glad to type up a long list of inoffensive remarks that Lassiter could use freely, as he wished, during the year. Lassiter was not amused.

"You knew him, Harvey," Lassiter was saying.

"What kind of comment is that, Bob? Of course I knew him. You know, you guys've got the world's greatest job, don't you? Calling me up five minutes after my roommate's been murdered."

"Don't chew my head, Harvey. Just tell me if you've considered the possibility that someone on the team might be involved."

"No, I haven't considered it," he said, and hung up.

The phone rang again—Doug Leboutillier of WGNT radio. Harvey was more civil to him, but no one was going to mistake it for a lesson in telephone etiquette. When the phone rang a third time, he left to pick up his Chevy at the garage. The mechanics there hadn't heard the news. Harvey listened uncomprehendingly to the status report on his carburetor, paid the bill, and drove around the city until it was time to pick up Mickey at the television station.

He was afraid he'd have to break the news about Rudy. She had been in New York all day for a job interview with ABC Sports. When he had called her last night after the game, and she had told him about the interview, he had replied, "Really?"

"C'mon, Bliss," she said, "you're supposed to say how happy you are for me."

"I'm very happy. But it would mean you'd be moving away."

"Don't jump the gun. They're just sifting the sands for a woman who can do play-by-play, and my only credentials are two years of radio play-by-play in Glens Falls."

"You're good. They'll hire you. You'll throw me over for your career."

"If I thought you were really serious, Bliss, I'd deliver a withering feminist tirade right now. But since you're not—"

"I am too being serious."

"As I was saying, since you're *not* being serious, I'll simply suggest you pick me up at the station tomorrow night for dinner."

"Only if you promise you'll start mentioning me on the air." She had too scrupulously avoided saying his name on the evening news—even when the game-winning hit had been his.

"You know I feel funny about it, Bliss. This is a small town; people know we're seeing each other."

Harvey could never tell whether the relationship was taking a wrong turn or whether they had never quite been on the same street to begin with. At six-thirty, he sat in his car in front of the portico of WRIP-TV's low yellow brick building just beyond the Providence train station. She emerged in a loose lavender blouse and pleated pants. She walked briskly, rolling her shoulders like an athlete. She had carotene-rich skin that gave her complexion a slight orange tint, not sallow, but perpetually radiant, as though she had just returned from a week in Barbados. Her lips were the color of smoked salmon. There was a faint band of freckles running across her cheeks and nose.

She got into the car without saying anything, threw her handbag at her feet, and looked straight ahead through the windshield. Harvey had been winding up to throw her the bad news, but she exhaled loudly and said, "Oh, boy. I've been a very good girl since I heard about it an hour ago. I even made a couple of phone calls, like a good reporter." She turned to Harvey. "I think I'm going to have my cry now."

She cried with her hand over her face and her shoulders heaving. Harvey reached over and laid his hand on the back of her neck. She made a small choking sound and then found a tissue in her bag and dabbed at a smudge of mascara. "All right," she said with one last sniffle. "I'll be all right now." She leaned toward Harvey and kissed him lightly on the mouth. He kissed back, thinking, She's competent even when she cries.

They drove a few blocks to Atwells and passed under the cement archway that marked the beginning of the Italian section. A large bronze pine cone hung from the apex of the arch.

"Any idea who could have done it?" she said.

"No," he said. He backed into a parking place in front of Angelo's restaurant. The exterior had new fake fieldstone and stucco facing, but inside, the latticework-patterned wallpaper was peeling in the corners. It was the kind of Italian family restaurant that would have an awkwardly executed oil painting of its original location on the wall, and it did, directly over the vinyl-upholstered booth where Harvey and Mickey sat holding hands across the table.

"The food would taste better if we had a little conversation to go along with it," Harvey said.

"I'm not hungry."

"Let's talk anyway."

"Okay, I'll tell you about New York."

"I forgot about that."

"Yeah," she said. "It seems far away now." She cut a wedge out of her veal chop and, without eating it, put down her knife and fork. "They showed me part of an NBA basketball game on a monitor and wanted me to do play-by-play for them, just like that. It was horrible. I kept confusing Cedric Maxwell and Robert Parish, and I couldn't think of the word for 'lane.' I used a lot of other lingo, though—'nothing but net,' 'transition game,' stuff like that—but I don't know if they were fooled. Christ, did they cross me up. I thought they wanted me for baseball. But let me tell you, it was great fun doing play-by-play in a tiny room with two guys wearing eight-hundred-dollar suits."

She picked up her fork, scrutinized the veal impaled on it, and put it back down. "He's really gone, Bliss. Oh, Jesus, just like that."

"Let's get out of here, Mick."

"Okay," she said. "It's just—it sounds so selfish, Bliss, but you never think of yourself as someone who knows someone who gets murdered. Jesus, not a guy like Rudy, anyway."

Their waiter was suddenly standing over them. "You don't like?" he said, observing the barely touched plates.

"No, no," Harvey said. "It's all fine. We've got to go, though. Something happened. Can we have the check?"

The waiter glanced at Mickey, who held her face in her hands, and looked back at Harvey. "No check," he said. "You don't eat, you don't pay. Next time you pay."

They drove back in silence to Harvey's apartment and took off their clothes as matter-of-factly as two people removig their coats at a party, and faced each other in the dark living room. Her body was well-tanned except where her bikini had left two pale lozenges across her breasts and a scarf of white across her groin.

"Do I still look good to you?" she said.

He held out his arms. "Come here."

She moved across the floor, her breasts nodding, and they held each other in the hot apartment, saying nothing, and then, as if it had been a ritual now completed, they turned and walked hand in hand to Harvey's bedroom.

"You're the best one I ever had." She smiled, pulling him down on top of her.

Harvey smiled back. "I'd say you're in my top ten. But moving up quickly." He had still not grown accustomed to her jaunty references to past lovers, even though he suspected the motivation. She had come into physical beauty, as if it were an inheritance, only in her twenties, and she always needed to reassure herself that she was no longer the gangly teenager whose intelligence, to say nothing of her irritating knowledge of the male world of sports, had not made her one of her prep school's most sought-after dates. She had told Harvey once about a prep school boyfriend, a pitcher for his school team, who lost interest in her soon after she advised him to mix up his pitches and start more batters off with the curve. Heartbroken, she ran to her father, an athletic New York lawyer, who respoded by saying that her boyfriend's curve was probably not good enough to start batters off with anyway; her father thereby proved himself a doubly cruel parent—insensitive to Mickey's disappointment in love and skeptical of her baseball judgment. At twenty-six, she was now dating another baseball player.

"Hey, you," she said beneath him. "Pay attention."

"I can't, Mick. I'm too depressed."

"Sure you can. Like this."

She was right; they made love, then peeled away from each other and lay on their backs.

"What're you thinking about?" she asked. He was drifting away, and she was reeling him back in.

"You really want to know?"

"I'm game."

"I was thinking about that night at the Sheraton in Boston. Last June."

"Hunh," she said. "So was I."

Harvey had gone 3-for-4 against Dennis Winston in Fenway Park that night, one of those hits giving Providence a one-run lead in the eighth. Rudy came into the game and gave up a three-run homer to Tony Jallardio. It cost Bobby Wagner a win, the Jewels the game. Rudy and Harvey took a cab over to La Hacienda in Somerville, which, its name notwithstanding, served the best pizza around. They had a few beers back at the Sheraton Boston bar, where they drunkenly accommodated an autograph seeker by scrawling their names in felt-tip pen all over her bare arm. At one in the morning, they stumbled up to their room and fell into their beds.

There was something in Harvey's. It was Mickey, and she wasn't wearing much. "What a pleasant surprise," Harvey said.

"The station sent me up to cover the game tomorrow," she said, pulling the covers up just under her eyes. "You know, Boston and Providence, natural rivalry. My crew's driving up tomorrow morning, but I thought I'd surprise you. You're not angry, are you?"

"Do you always hide in other people's beds?"

"Don't you?" Mickey said. "You're drunk."

"How'd you get in here?"

"I told some nice fellow down at the desk that you were expecting me for an interview, and I showed him my press credentials."

"And he gave you a key?"

"The power of the press," she said and laughed. "Why don't you get out of your clothes and come to bed so Rudy and I can get some sleep? Hi, Rudy," she called out.

Rudy was lying on his bed with his arms folded behind his head. The smoke from his cigarette curled up into a shaft of blue light thrown up from the street below. "Hi, Slavin," he said.

"Tough luck with Jallardio tonight," she said.

"I threw dumb."

"By the way, Rudy, what's with Charlie Penzenik?" she asked. Charlie had started the season at second base, but lost the job to Rodney Salta in June because Charlie was rapidly winning the race for lowest batting average in the American League. At Rankle Park, they had stopped flashing his batting average on the scoreboard when he came to bat after Charlie had threatened, only half in jest, to file a defamation-of-character suit against the club.

"What's wrong with Charlie," Rudy replied, "is that the league doesn't have a designated-hitter rule for second basemen like they got for pitchers. See, like it is now, if you play second base in the majors, you also have to hit. It's not legal to have someone do it for you." Rudy chuckled, dispersing a smoke ring over his head. "Outside of that, he's a great little ball player. But this is off the record, Slavin."

"Will you settle for not-for-attribution?"

"To tell you the truth, Slavin, I'd settle for a good-night kiss. Ball players get lonely on the road."

"Gee," Harvey said, "since when are you two such good friends?"

"Hey, it's only fair if she's sleeping with you these days that I get kissed and tucked in," Rudy pouted. "You got to look after your roomie, don't you?"

"I didn't know that included sexual favors," Harvey said.

"C,mon, Slavin," Rudy said. "My lips are puckered."

"Oh, all right," she said and got out of Harvey's bed. She was wearing a bra and a pair of pink panties with a white lace border. "But only if you've already made pee-pee. I don't want to have to take you to the toity in the middle of the night."

"I already made," Rudy said.

Mickey bent over Rudy and planted a soft kiss on his lips. Rudy threw his arm around her neck and held her there for a moment.

"Naughty boy," Mickey said. "No tongues."

"C'mon, cut it out, you two," Harvey said.

"Hey, it's no B.F.D., Professor. Tell me, how did an ugly outfielder like you land a beautiful television personality like Slavin?"

"Wait a second," Mickey said. She sat down on Harvey's bed. "Nobody's landed anybody."

"What do you call hiding in my bed?" Harvey said, too piously.

"Jesus, Bliss, will you lighten up? What is it?"

"Why don't you get a little less light?" he shot back.

"You know, you don't own me."

"Fine," Harvey said. "And I'm not going to sublet you to Rudy."

"That's real cute." They stared at each other for a moment. "C'mon, Bliss," she said, holding out her hand to him. He ignored it. "Damn it, Bliss!"

Rudy faked a loud snore. "Children, please. I'm trying to rest. Show the bull pen some consideration. And, roomie, why don't you pull the piano wire out of your ass?"

"Screw yourself," Harvey said. "You too, Mick."

Mickey turned to Rudy. "Do you get the feeling I'm not welcome in his bed?"

Rudy put out his cigarette. "It's not the only one in the room."

Harvey went down to the hotel bar. It closed half an

hour later, and he walked along Boylston Street and sat in the deserted Boston Common. When he got back to the room, he quietly pushed open the door and looked in. Rudy and Mickey were asleep side by side under the covers, his blond hair mingling with her red on the pillow.

5

Now she was in Harvey's bed and Rudy was dead.

"I never thought we'd get back together after that night," Harvey said.

"Why not? Everyone's entitled to act like an idiot once in a while. It comes with the dinner."

"All I meant was you didn't have to sleep with him."

Mickey jolted up on one elbow and stared at him. "I cannot believe you," she said tightly.

"Believe what?"

She fell back on the bed and pressed the heels of her hands to her eye sockets. After a moment she said, her voice wobbling, "Number one, my dear: Rudy has just been murdered, and all you seem to care about is if I slept with the guy. What's wrong with you? You were his best friend. At least he thought you were." Her voice broke.

"You're right, Mick. I'm sorry."

"I mean, what is it with you?" She glowered at him. "The guy is dead, and you're angry at him and—"

"I said I'm sorry, Mick—"

"Let me finish. Number two: there was never anything to be angry about."

"What do you mean?"

"I mean I never slept with Rudy."

Harvey squeezed his eyelids together. "Wait. . . . You mean you got into his bed, and then the two of

47

you just fell asleep? Like a couple of puppies or something?"

"I can't believe you thought I'd—what'd you take me for anyway? I was just pissed at you. And what'd you take him for?"

Harvey said nothing.

"I see," she said. "You simply assumed the worst and then never bothered to say anything. Now I know why Rudy felt you weren't always the friend you could've been." She snorted. "The guy really liked you, Bliss. He looked up to you. So you turned him into a rival. I guess boys will be boys. That's just great, Bliss."

"I cared about him. I did. I just—" He felt no emotion at all right now.

"Well, if you'd cared about him a little more, you'd have given him a little credit. He wouldn't do something like that to you, any more than I would."

Harvey tried to hang on to what she was saying, but all he could do was lie there looking at the oak dresser in the shadows. He felt her turn away from him and draw into herself at the far edge of the bed. Ten minutes later, she turned halfway toward him.

"He never had a lot of breaks in the first place. At least you could've given him this one," she said. "Look, if you'd cared a little more, maybe you'd know who his enemies were."

"He didn't have a lot of friends, but I don't think he had any real enemies."

"That seems a bit optimistic."

"For a guy who talked so much, he didn't say a lot," Harvey said. "What do you know about him?"

"I know he was in love."

"Mick, *all* the players are in love with you. You shouldn't take it so personally."

"Bliss, I know this is hard for you to absorb, but not only did I not want to sleep with Rudy, he did not want to sleep with me. He was in love with someone else, for God's sakes."

"It's very difficult to believe Rudy was serious about a woman."

"So he never told you about her?"

"No. Who was she?" Harvey asked.

"I don't know. He never told me, either. All I know is that he said he loved her."

"So when did he tell you all this?"

"Remember our little excursion to Maine?"

He thought back to the time in June, before the scene in the hotel, when the team had had an off-day. Rudy called Mickey and Harvey at eight in the morning and told them to be ready in half an hour, without saying why. He came for them in his MG, drove to Green Airport, and put everyone on a twin-engine plane to Bar Harbor, Maine. By two in the afternoon, the three of them were drifting in a rented motorboat, fishing for pollack and squid off Northeast Harbor, and drinking bottles of Grolsch beer from a Styrofoam cooler. By four, they all had their arms around each other in the boat and were singing show tunes. At six, they were eating dinner at the kind of roadside lobster pound where they throw lobsters, steamers, and corn-on-the-cob into a net and lower it into a trash can filled with seaweed and boiling seawater. Rudy talked about his brief marriage, in his early twenties, to a dental hygienist. Mickey did impersonations of the anchorpeople on WRIP-TV's "Eleven O'Clock Edition." After dinner, Rudy checked them into the Asticou Inn, and they trooped down to the deserted beach and stripped for a moonlight swim. Rudy slept in one room that night while Mickey and Harvey, too sunburned to make love, slept nine hours in the next. By eleven the next morning, they were back in Providence, in time for an afternoon game against the Detroit Tigers.

"When we were skinny-dipping," Mickey was saying now, "you stayed out in the water longer than we did, and Rudy and I wrapped ourselves in towels and sat talking on the rocks. I asked him if he had a girlfriend, and I remember he said, 'Thousands,' and I told him to be serious, and then he said, 'Yeah,' and he got all wistful. Then he said, 'It's not working out.' I asked him if the problem was that he didn't really love her, and he said, 'I love her, all right. It's just that I'm not the only one who does.' "

"He could've been talking about you, Mick."

"That's what Ms. Modesty here thought, too. I said to him, 'You're not trying to tell me something, are you, Rudy?' And he said, 'Slavin, if I thought I had half a chance in the world, but I don't, so I'm afraid you're not the lucky girl. Besides,' he said, 'the Professor'll take better care of you than I ever could.' "

"Maybe it was someone in the Providence chapter of the Rudy Furth Fan Club," Harvey said.

"You're going to make me cry again," Mickey said. She glanced at the alarm clock over Harvey's shoulder. "Oh, Jesus, I've got to go." She rose to her knees on the bed. "I'm doing the eleven o'clock. Let me take your car, will you?"

She dressed in the living room, where they had discarded their clothes, and came back in, plowing a brush through her thick hair. "I know when things are sinking in and when they're not," she said, kissing him too maternally on the forehead. "And this isn't sinking in yet."

At eleven, Harvey sat naked in the living room watching the news. The first story was Rudy. They ran some videotape of him in action during a recent game, some shots of the clubhouse and the whirlpool, and a pro forma interview with Detective Linderman. Harvey's attention wandered during the reports of the tax cuts, the debate over a forthcoming vote on the sale of arms to a tribal Middle Eastern nation, the local run on air conditioners, and five minutes of a man in a red sports jacket standing in front of a map that had a picture of a thermometer with a face. Finally, Mickey appeared in her lavender blouse, her hands folded neatly in front of her. A slide of a smiling Rudy Furth was chroma-keyed on the screen behind her shoulder.

"When they talk about violence in professional sports," she began reading off the TelePrompTer at a somber, easy tempo, "they almost never talk about the game of baseball, and they almost never talk about murder. But today witnessed a violent tragedy in baseball that will be remembered and mourned long after all the football injuries and ice hockey brawls have been forgotten. Providence Jewel relief pitcher Rudy Furth was found murdered this morning in the team's clubhouse at Rankle Park."

Harvey cringed at the memory of the whirlpool, of how unfair he had been to Rudy. "Sadly," Mickey continued, "other athletes throughout the years have died as a result of the sports they played, and a few have even been murdered. But the death of Rudy Furth is different: it was brutal, and so far it appears to have been meaningless. I knew Rudy Furth, and I grieve at the untimely death of a fine man and a fine athlete. Let us all hope there is a swift solution to this ghastly crime."

Harvey had to hand it to her. She must have composed the commentary in her head on her way to the studio. Now she turned to camera two.

"In light of today's event, other sports news seems insignificant, but here are the scores in major league baseball action." And then Mickey Slavin, not looking in the least like she had left the bed of the Providence Jewels' center fielder little more than an hour before, spoke of Reds and Cubs and Dodgers and Phillies, Twins and Royals and Yankees and A's.

"Put Felix on, will you?" Harvey said when Dunc answered the clubhouse phone the next morning. It was an off-day on the schedule, and Harvey didn't know if Felix expected the team for practice.

Felix's voice had the consistency of hot cereal. "I thought we'd take some B.P. at noon. Just a light workout. It might do everyone some good, but if you're not in the mood, Professor, take the day off and I'll see you tomorrow."

"I'll see you at noon. How're you holding up, Felix?"

With him, it was never an idle question. After nine consecutive losing seasons managing five different major league teams, Felix Shalhoub was not a well man. In May he had disappeared from the club for three weeks. Buzzy Stanfill, the Jewels' public relations director, had informed the press that Felix was home with a severe pulmonary infection, but anyone who had played under him had the right to speculate that Felix's ailments were located not in his lungs, but in his head and his liver.

Marshall Levy had handed the reins over to Campy Strulowitz in the interim, but Campy was soon joined in the dugout by Frances Shalhoub. Levy liked her—and her master's degree in business administration from Columbia—and apparently, as a courtesy to Felix, he had agreed to let her be closer than usual to the team in Felix's absence. The press reacted with amusement, then indignation, and for a couple of weeks stories on the order of "First Woman Manager in Major Leagues?" enlivened the sports pages in the cities where Providence played. But since Frances had been in the public relations business for many years, the prevailing rumor was that her presence in the dugout was nothing more than a badly needed publicity stunt. She denied, to all who asked, that she was even remotely connected with any managerial decisions.

After Felix returned to the team, looking gaunter than usual and complaining pointedly of a lingering cough, Frances remained in the dugout during the games, charting pitches on a clipboard. The commissioner, who fancied himself something of a feminist, was unbothered by this breach of protocol, and only a few of the players were indiscreet enough to kick about it, and none of them to the press. There was no reason to believe Felix found in his wife's presence in the dugout anything but consolation.

Felix's spinelessness, an object of concealed scorn among the ball players, was the quality that had kept him in the majors so long, despite his penchant for losing; front offices liked a man they could push around. Harvey enjoyed a closer relationship with Felix than most of the players did, and he was afraid that Rudy's murder would unhinge him.

"I'm in a distressed posture, Professor," Felix was saying. "How could anyone do such a thing? I've seen some sick things in my years in baseball, but this is the sickest. I can't take it, Professor. I haven't had an easy time of it in the majors. Nine seasons, I won five hundred six games and lost nine-fifty-two. It's a miracle I'm still here. For that I can thank a lot of people. But that's beside the point. The point, Professor, is that in those nine seasons, I've never known anything like this. Someone murdered my goddamn relief pitcher. It's sick. I ask myself, why did it have to be me? Why me? I'm fifty-three years old. I'm too old to have my

goddamn relief pitcher murdered in my clubhouse."
He caught his breath. "How're you holding up?"

"I'm sick about it, Felix."

"I can't sleep, Professor. I've been in a baseball
posture my whole life. Why couldn't it have happened
to a manager with a winning record?" He was shout-
ing, and Harvey held the receiver away from his ear.
"This team doesn't get along too good as it is. Until
they find who murdered Rudy, everybody's going to be
running around looking at everybody else sideways."

"Felix, take it easy. Don't take it personal. You're
talking like you were to blame."

"You think I had something to do with it? Is that
what—"

"Felix! I said it's got nothing to do with—"

"That's all I need, Professor. My mind can't take
anymore."

"Listen to me, Felix. It had nothing to do with you.
The cops'll take care of it. Life'll go on. Get a grip on
yourself."

"Okay," he said, his voice subsiding. "All right. I'm
getting a grip on myself. Let's reach down and play
them one at a time. All right, let's bear down."

When Harvey arrived at the clubhouse half an hour
later, Dunc was sitting at the long table in the middle
of the locker room where the players sat before games
to play cards or autograph balls for disadvantaged
children and men at the V.A. hospital. He was ironing
strips of black tape on the left sleeves of the Jewels'
uniforms. While Harvey slipped into his practice uni,
three teammates were talking behind him. The conversation smelled of agents and lawyers.

"I was talking to a friend of mine on the White Sox,
who shall remain nameless," Happy Smith, the Jewels' backup catcher, was saying, "and he was telling
me that his agent got him a clause in his contract that
every time he gets an extra base hit in the last three
innings, it's a cool five grand. That's what I need, an

agent like that, so I can get a little gravy when I re-sign."

"You'll be lucky to re-sign, period," Steve Wilton, the right fielder, said. "Don't you ever get tired of riding the bench and wish you were doing something useful in life?"

"When I re-sign," Happy said, "I know one thing I'm going to get in my contract. I'm going to get a clause that says I don't ever have to be within fifty feet of you."

"Man, this organization just nickels-and-dimes you," Les Byers, the third baseman, broke in. "When I send my shirts out with Dunc, they come back with heavy starch and broken buttons. I'm gonna call my agent and tell him I want a clause next year that says *light* starch, man, and no broken buttons. Those shirts don't come back right, I want them replaced. Then I want me some incentives like this guy on the Sox, but I mean real incentives. I want it in writing that any time I got to leave my feet to make a play at third, it's a couple thousand bucks right there. Hey, man, if I'm going to dirty myself up, I want to be compensated, hear? And then, like if I get hit with a pitch, man, risking my life up there, I want a new car with a quadrophonic tape deck. I'm serious about this."

"You're forgetting the masseuses, Lester," Happy said, laughing. "We got to have masseuses in every hotel room on the road. How they expect us to play good ball if we don't have masseuses?"

Harvey stood next to them, shaking his head. "What's the matter, Professor?" Steve Wilton said. "You need some incentives, too?"

"You guys are really something," Harvey said, pulling a terry-cloth sweatband on his wrist.

"Hey, man, everyone deserves a spoonful of the gravy," Les said.

"I mean, one of your teammates was murdered two days ago, and you guys are throwing a party."

"We were just goofing around," Les said. "No harm, my man, no harm."

"I didn't kill the guy," Steve said.

Harvey bent down to tie his spikes. "You guys are assholes."

"We didn't mean anything," Happy said.

"Look," Harvey said, "I know you guys didn't think Rudy was the greatest thing since free agency, but the man was murdered in our clubhouse. Do any of you guys find that weird, let alone a little disturbing?"

"Yeah, man, I find that weird," Les said, "and that's why I'm trying not to think about it. Look, Professor, I'm sorry your roomie was killed—"

"My roomie? Les, you really surprise—Look, it's not like Rudy was some total stranger. The least you guys could do is—Oh, screw it."

"We told the cops everything we know," Steve said, with his hands out. "What do you want us to do, wear black?"

When Harvey stepped into the batting cage to take his cuts off Tony Cantalupa, he wanted something to be different. But the park was the same, the pocking of wood against horsehide, the smacking of horsehide against leather, the pitchers running wind sprints along the warning track, their spikes kicking up small clumps of dirt behind them. There was no sign that Rudy was missing. Harvey stroked a couple of Tony's pitches to center and watched them tail lazily.

Campy Strulowitz leaned on the aluminum frame of the cage behind him. "Bring it to him, Tony," he yelled to Cantalupa on the mound. "Come to this guy with some heat, Tone, hum-a-now, be a hitter, Harv, be a stick up there, you're the kid." Harvey slammed one through the hole at short. "Way to come to the ball, way to come." Harvey flattened a couple more to left, then lofted one into the left field seats. "Just a bingle, babe, just a bingle." Harvey moved over to the left side of the plate and sliced one down the left field line. He jumped on the next one, too, and the ball arched down the right field line, climbing as if under its own power, and curling around the 339 FT sign at the foul pole. He was smoking. Tony mopped his face with the back of his glove and reached into the basket for more baseballs. Carnpy was still at it. "That's the sweet," he said, "that's the stroke, babe, way to be, you're the kid."

Harvey topped the next two pitches feebly toward the mound and turned to Campy. "Not today, Campy," he said. "I'm not in the mood."

"All right, babe," Campy said, "no chatter, big batter, no chatter, you're the one," and then he fell silent.

After Harvey took a few more of Tony's pitches— big, fat, sweeping curves now—and hoisted them deep against the fences, Les Byers called out, "Hey, man, don't hurt the fences. Save something for us two-thirty hitters, hear?"

On his way back to the dugout, Harvey was startled to see Ronnie Mateo in a first-row box seat, eyes closed and sallow face tilted toward the midday sun. He was wearing a muted green leisure suit with five-inch lapels and chrome buttons. It looked more like a '58 Buick than an article of clothing.

One of Ronnie's eyelids eased open, and Harvey heard him say in a low voice as he passed, "That was a horrible thing happened to your roommate, Professor."

Randy Eppich, the Jewels' starting catcher, was sitting on the bench with Bob Lassiter, babbling about the effect of the murder on "the team as a whole." He sounded as if he could have been speaking about the effect of groin pull to a key player.

At the end of the bench, filing her nails, was Frances Shalhoub. She was a tall woman, in a navy skirt, white blouse, and spectator pumps. Her long brown hair was streaked with blond and her face had a fine, disdainful beauty, something designed to be admired rather than touched. Her wide green eyes were set above severe cheekbones. Her nostrils, thin as shells, always looked flared. She reminded Harvey of a well-groomed Afghan hound with earrings.

To explain her thirteen-year marriage to Felix, you had to believe that Frances at twenty-seven had been a naive or desperate young woman, neither of which seemed likely, or that Felix at forty possessed charms no longer apparent. Because she looked younger than her years and Felix older, together they gave the impression of a kindly father with his stunning oldest daughter proudly in tow. They had no children. All the men on the team guessed much more about the Shalhoubs' marriage than they actually knew.

She was a businesslike woman. For the last three years, while Felix managed the New York Mets, Frances ran a public relations firm in Manhattan, selling it over the winter in order to accompany her husband to Providence. She had helped Marshall Levy and the public relations director, Buzzy Stanfill, devise some publicity gimmicks for the team. On Ring Night, the first five thousand fans to pass through the turnstiles received a Pro-Gem ring with black and green stones—the team colors. Fifteen thousand had shown up, but after that, attendance dropped again.

Twice during the summer, the Shalhoubs had invited the players and their wives to barbecues at their rented home in Barrington. At the first, in May, Frances and Harvey had found themselves alone in the garden. Harvey, indicating her simple black dress and thin gold belt, had said, "You look like an expensive Dunhill lighter in that outfit."

"That's a better line than I expect from a baseball player." She smiled and swirled the ice in her gin and tonic.

"That's what college will do for you."

"You know, Harvey," she said, "I just want to say that we're glad to have you."

"I'm glad to be here," he said. "It's a nice house."

"No," she said, grazing his arm with her free hand, "I mean on the team. I can't for the life of me understand why the Red Sox didn't protect you in the draft. How many years were you with them, five? All right, for them you may not have been the hitter you've turned out to be for us, but you had consistent RBl production, you know how to advance a baserunner, and you've got a gun for an arm out there in center field. You weren't having problems with the owners, were you?"

Harvey shook his head and finished chewing a boiled shrimp.

"You're good for at least four, five more years, barring injury, of course," she continued. "This is what I want to say. We're an expansion team, and frankly, I don't care much if we win a whole lot of ball games this first year. I'd be happy with sixty, tickled with seventy. Now, what I want to see is Felix begin building a solid franchise for next year and the years after that. We need a solid nucleus. Every winning team has that. And you're a big part of the nucleus. If you ever lose a step or two in center, we can always move you to left, and when you're old and gray"—she actually winked at him—"we can always keep first base open for you. You know, I can almost see you as one of baseball's elder statesmen, bringing along the younger guys."

Harvey picked at the deviled egg on the cocktail napkin in his left hand. It was before Felix's absence from the team, and since Harvey had only the vaguest idea about her interest in baseball or in the Jewels in particular, her speech came as a refreshing surprise.

"All right," she said, "you're part of the nucleus. You and a few others. I can level with you, can't I? I like what I see of Chuck at short—I can never pronounce his last name. I think Randy is a major league catcher. We have to be strong up the middle. Every winning team is strong where it counts. Dan Van

Auken is part of the nucleus. What is he, twenty-four, twenty-five? In a year or two, he'll be one of the premier lefties in the league. We've already got Bobby Wagner. They're all part of the nucleus.

"Of course, we've got to hold on to the nucleus. Wagner's in the last year of his contract, and he'll go free agent over the winter, so we've got to do everything possible to keep him here. Same goes for Randy. You, Harvey, if I'm not mistaken, have another two years to go on your current contract, which I'm sure you'll want to sit down and renegotiate with Marshall, the way you've been playing. Felix and Marshall want everyone to be happy here." She took a lusty drink of her gin and tonic. "We'll make a trade or two in the off-season. We'll strengthen our left-handed hitting. We'll pick up a long reliever. We're building, Harvey, we're building for next year. You're wondering why I'm telling you all this."

"I'm wondering why you're telling me all this," Harvey conceded.

"I want you to be patient. Felix is tired of losing; underneath, he's a winner. I know it's not easy for veterans like you to start over with an expansion team. But we're going to be a winner."

"I hope so, too," he said. "You know, I didn't realize you were so involved with the team."

She lifted her glass to her mouth, cracked an ice cube between her teeth, and swallowed it. "Your wife probably doesn't like being left alone," she smiled.

"I'm not married."

"Oh. Then who's that lovely brunette over there in the white pants?"

"That's Randy's wife, Karen."

"How odd of me," she said, pressing a finger to her lips. "I thought you were married. Oh, well, what do you say we go over and try the poached salmon?"

That had been three months ago. Now, as he bent

over the dugout water cooler, he heard her say, "Hello, Harvey."

He wiped his mouth. "Hello. How are you?"

She stroked her nail furiously with the emery board. "How would you expect me to be?"

"Yeah, I guess that didn't come out right."

"Felix and I were up all night." She didn't look it. "We racked our brains to make sense of it. It's frightening. And the publicity—it's not the kind we need."

"To say nothing of the effect this'll have on the team."

"By which you mean?" she said crisply, raising her eyebrows. She had the capacity to make you feel as if you hadn't brushed your teeth.

"By which I mean no one seems to have any clue, and for all we know, someone on the team may've been mixed up in this, and everyone's going to be eyeing everyone else, as if enough of that doesn't always go on around here."

"I don't know why you say someone on the team may have been involved. But I suppose anything's possible. It just doesn't make sense. That detective was here again this morning. Maybe they'll find some fingerprints or something. You roomed with him. Do you have any ideas?"

"No, not unless Rudy was mixed up with gambling. Is that guy Ronnie Mateo a bookie or something?"

"You mean that tacky fellow who comes to all the games?"

"Yeah. In fact, he's here right now."

"He looks absolutely harmless."

"Who is he?" Harvey said. "What's he doing at a team practice?"

Frances shrugged. "Let me know if you find out. By the way, Harvey, I'm having Marshall set up a scholarship in Rudy's name for a deserving Providence orphan. I just wanted you to know."

"That's nice," he said and trotted out to the field to

shag some flies. Steve Wilton was standing about twenty yards away in right center with his cap turned around, the better to tan his face. At the plate, Les lofted a fly ball that landed fifteen feet away from Wilton and rolled toward the wall. Steve didn't make a move to get the ball, and Charlie Penzenik had to run over from farther away in right to retrieve it. It was just like Wilton. The Cubs had always considered him a head case, a good athlete only from the neck down. In a couple seasons, he'd wake up and find himself back in Bessemer, Alabama, uncrating produce at his daddy's supermarket and wondering what went wrong.

"They can't always hit 'em right at you, Steve," Harvey hollered at him.

Steve turned his head slowly, like a lizard. "Mind your own fucking business," he said.

After practice on Thursday afternoon, Harvey drove down the redeveloped section of South Main Street in the direction of Rudy's rented town house. He picked up a *Journal-Bulletin* at the corner drugstore on a block of boutiques and hair salons with names like the Opulent Owl, Nature's Comfort, and Diego's. A frontpage story about the murder told him the little he already knew and none of the things he wanted to find out. Detective Linderman was quoted as saying that despite the recent city budget cuts that had trimmed back even the homicide division, the Rudy Furth case was of course being accorded top priority. In search of more reassuring news, Harvey turned to the sports pages and found the box containing the American League's top ten batters. Mark Gaffney of the Texas Rangers had moved ahead of him into eighth place with two hits the night before in Seattle. He checked the standings: Providence was still in sixth place in the eight-team division. If he had a choice in the matter, he would gladly trade in his .309 batting average for the chance to play for a winner again.

He tucked the newspaper under his arm and crossed the street, to Rudy's place. It was in the middle of a row of new, terraced town houses in alternating gray and mustard clapboard that didn't quite belong in a neighborhood of old red brick. Like the others, Rudy's town house was a baldlooking two-story building on a sodded knoll. He knocked on the door, waited, then tried the doorknob. It was locked. He circled around behind the row of houses and found a squat man in a sleeveless undershirt pushing a power mower across the backyard next door.

"You live here?" Harvey asked.

The man cut the motor and said, "In a way. I'm the manager of this complex. I'm just taking care of the yard here while the Beckwiths are away." He wiped his hands on work pants coated with a fine spray of mown dry grass. "Something I can do you?"

"I was wondering if I could get into Rudy Furth's place for a minute. I left something there. Number four."

The man sized him up for a moment while Harvey tapped the folded newspaper against his thigh. Behind the man, Harvey could see the Burnside mansion where he lived, two blocks away and up College Hill beyond a parking lot.

"Guess you didn't hear the bad news," the man finally said. "Mr. Furth is dead. Murdered, if you want to know the—it's right there in your paper."

"I know," Harvey said. "He was a teammate of mine."

The man inspected Harvey's face. "I thought you looked familiar. You're that catcher they got, Randy Eppich."

"My name's Harvey Blissberg. I play center field."

"Yeah, that's right. I recognize you now. You know, I catch a few games on the tube, but I haven't been out to the park yet. Guess I should, though, new team in town and all."

"I was wondering if you could let me into Rudy's place for a minute. He's got a few things of mine in there I want to collect."

"I don't know about that," the man said, dragging a hand across his furry jaw. "The cops were already here yesterday, you know. Went through the whole place and told me to keep everyone else out of it. Now, maybe I could go in for you and get what you want if they haven't already taken it, but I just don't know about letting you walk in there yourself."

"He was a close friend of mine. I'd appreciate it."

The man leaned down and brushed some grass off the housing of the mower. "You know how it is," he said. "I've got my orders."

"A couple of box seat tickets to tomorrow night's game says you sometimes have trouble following them," Harvey said, smiling. "The club's playing good ball right now. I'll have them hold the tickets for you at the press gate."

The man thought about it, wiping his hands some more, and said, "Come to think of it, I've got a couple of boys at home who wouldn't mind seeing a major league ball game."

"Then why don't we make it four tickets? Just in case you know someone else who wouldn't mind. All I need is your name." Harvey took out a pen and scrawled "Joseph Katavolos" in the margin of his newspaper.

"Like I say," the man said, getting his massive key ring out, "new team in town and all. Just don't make a mess, hear? I've got to rent that place out." Katavolos showed him into Rudy's old town house, gestured at the door, said, "She'll lock behind you when you leave," and went back to his mowing.

The town house had a modern, open interior with an atrium in the living area that rose all the way to a skylight in the sloping roof. There were a lot of oak floors and heavy beams and unfinished pine surfaces, and there was a woodburning stove with a pipe that ran right up the middle of the atrium. It was perfect for a single relief pitcher whose idea of a night in was drinking Asti spumante with an airline stewardess.

There was a butcher-block sofa upholstered in oatmeal Haitian cotton, where Harvey and Rudy had gotten smashed drinking Grolsch beer only a week before, a Scandinavian leather chair and ottoman, a teak coffee table on a small blue shag rug, and lots of track lighting. He walked over to the kitchen area and opened the refrigerator, where he found some beer, three cartons of orange juice, a can of high-protein powder, a few plastic containers of coleslaw and macaroni salad, and some knockwurst. There were also a couple of steaks, as though Rudy had been expecting someone for dinner. On the floor by the stove was a plastic bowl filled with crusty cat food. The cops had probably taken Wanda, Rudy's Siamese cat.

He went upstairs, where he had never been before, and found a room with a television set and more butcher-block furniture, an elaborate wicker chair suspended from the ceiling, and a few hanging plants. It looked like a double spread in *Apartment Life*. In the bedroom, Harvey found a water bed covered with a bamboo-patterned comforter, a dresser, and a couple of canvas director's chairs. He opened the sliding closet door to find a multicolored row of slacks and sports jackets. On the shelf above, Rudy's sweaters were arranged neatly in color groups, like swatches of fabric. On the floor below, two dozen pairs of shoes stood in strict formation, facing the wall. No one would have guessed that the town house's tenant had spent even a single day—much less his boyhood—on a farm.

Harvey ran his hand across the sports jackets hanging on the closet rod. A thin cream-colored garment fell from between two jackets. He picked it up and studied it, a lacy thing with a snap at the crotch. Harvey knew there was a name for it, but couldn't remember what it was. The label said it was all silk, and it also said, "The Bare Essentials, White Plains, New York." He threw it on top of the sweaters.

There was a faint sound, a rustling, in the far corner of the closet, behind Rudy's suits. Harvey waited a cold moment for the sound to come again. It did, and was quickly followed by the appearance of Wanda, picking her way through the shoes. She raised her dark brown face toward Harvey and emitted a reproachful meow. Harvey picked her up and draped her over his shoulder, where she remained while he looked through Rudy's dresser drawers; they contained neat piles of professionally laundered shirts and Gold Cup socks. On the glass on top of the dresser was a jewelry box with some cuff links and rings in it. Next to it sat a bowl of coins, a bottle of Aramis cologne, and a stack of back issues of *Sporting News*. Rudy had a place for everything, and Detective Linderman and his men had managed to leave everything in its place.

With one hand on Wanda's back, Harvey riffled through an issue of *Sporting News*. As he did, he noticed a photograph under the glass on top of the dresser. He pushed aside the stack of newspapers to get a better look.

It wasn't a photograph. It was Harvey's baseball card. The photo on the front, from a few seasons past, showed Harvey in a Boston Red Sox uniform. He had a bat slung over his shoulder, and the face looking roguishly at the camera was more youthful, less angular. Harvey remembered how the photographer from the bubble gum company had coaxed him. "Don't look so grim," he had said. "You don't want to frighten all those millions of kids, do you?" Harvey knew that on the back of the card, along with his statistics, was a simple cartoon of a man wearing a mortarboard, with the caption: "Harvey has a degree in history from the University of Massachusetts."

He put Wanda down and lifted the edge of the glass and slid the card out. The thought of Rudy with his baseball card sent a tremor of grief and pity through him. He slipped the card into his shirt pocket, then noticed something else under the glass—a piece of stationery folded into eighths. He worked it out and opened it. It was a sheet of personalized stationery with a Pawtucket address, and it read, in a careful turquoise hand:

> *Dear Rudy, Well I feel like an idiot writing you, but I had to tell you how much I adore you. Every time I see you, it makes me want to jump up and dance, which is really saying something. As it is, I just sit and daydream about the future we'll never have. It's not that I want everything, it's just that I wish I could have you.*
> *Oh, well. . . .*
> *Love,*
> *Valerie (Carty)*

Even if her prose left something to be desired, Harvey admired her taste in lingerie. He folded the letter and put it in his pocket with his baseball card. Wanda meowed angrily at him from the floor. "Yeah, I know how it is," he said, and fed her a can of Friskies Buffet Mixed Grill from the kitchen before taking her back to his own apartment.

Harvey hadn't fallen asleep until three in the morning. At five he had been jolted awake by a nightmare in which he had pulled a corpse out of a whirlpool, to discover that it was Mickey. She had opened her eyes and said, "I'm only kidding." He sat up in bed. Rudy was gone, Mickey might be going, and he didn't know how much longer he wanted to play the game of baseball.

He did not remember the point at which anxiety deferred to sleep, but at ten Friday morning the phone rang inside his brain. Wanda, who had been sleeping on his head, leaped to the windowsill. Harvey's hand sampled several objects on the nightstand before finding the pertinent one.

"It's Linderman," the voice barked.

" 'Scuse me?" Harvey mumbled.

"Wake up. I'm down at the ball park, but I'll be through soon and I thought you might meet me for a drink in half an hour."

Harvey located his tongue. "At ten in the morning?"

"Yeah, yeah, yeah. So have a cup of coffee with me. Plan to be there."

"I was planning to spend the morning trying to figure out who killed Rudy."

"Good. That's exactly how I plan to spend mine."

Harvey suggested Mandy's, a bar on the Brown University campus with plastic Tiffany lamps.

"Nice place," Linderman said. "We pinched a couple

hookers there last month. Imagine that, taking advantage of young college boys."

"Imagine," Harvey said.

Harvey had been at Mandy's for twenty minutes, seeing how many sips there were in a Bloody Mary, before Linderman lowered himself into the booth, beer in hand. The butt of a police Magnum rode up under his armpit, beneath a red and green plaid sports jacket. An archipelago of grease stains ran down the front of his white polo shirt.

"Something keep you at the park?" Harvey asked.

"I was over there," Linderman said, indicating a booth in the far corner of the lounge. "Watching you."

"That's just great."

"It's interesting what you can tell about a guy, watching him like that."

"So what'd you learn?"

"That you don't like Bloody Marys very much and that the service in this place is lousy. Your waitress never came over to see how you were doing."

"What'd you really want to know?"

"Some guys get nervous," Linderman said.

"About?"

"About knowing something about who killed Rudy Furth and not saying."

"You've been watching too many old movies, Linderman."

"Yeah, yeah, yeah, but you seem a little nervous now, Harvey."

"Some guys get nervous about being told they know something about who killed Rudy Furth and are not saying. I expected you to have all the goods at this point."

"I've got some." Linderman pulled daintily at his beer.

Harvey waited, then said, "Maybe you'll tell me someday."

"It's your move, Harvey."

"I don't know anything."

"I was hoping something might've come to mind since we talked the last time."

Harvey spread his hands.

"All right," Linderman said, bringing both palms down on the table. "Maybe this'll jog your memory. The preliminary report from the coroner says that Rudy was killed by a combination of asphyxiation by drowning and Cleavon Battle's bat."

Harvey's head jerked at the name of the Providence Jewels' first baseman. "Cleavon Battle?"

"Cleavon Battle's *bat*," Linderman corrected him. "We don't know who was holding it."

"How do you know it was Cleavon's bat?"

"That one was easy. The soft spot in Rudy's skull was perfectly consistent with the sweet part of a Louisville Slugger. It could've been someone else's bat, but Battle used it in the game that night, and it was gone by the morning, and no one can find it."

Harvey felt ill.

"Your fingerprints were all over the place," Linderman said.

"Now wait a—"

"Don't have a seizure. So were everyone else's. There must've been two dozen sets of pawprints around the whirlpool, none of them much good. And there was enough hair lying around to weave a bath mat. Head and pubic. Looks like the whole damn team sheds. The only blood we found was Rudy Furth's. Don't tell anyone I told you, Harvey, but a clubhouse is a nice place to commit murder."

"My lips are sealed," he said sourly.

"The M.E.'s people say there was a slight bruise under Rudy's eye, probably fresh, though God knows what ten hours in a whirlpool'll do. He didn't have a mouse when you saw him after the game, did he?"

"No. I would've remembered it."

"So let's say there was a struggle before someone

beaned him with Battle's bat. But we're still nowhere unless we can figure out who wanted to pick a fight with him."

"Not Cleavon."

"If it was him, he'd have to be pretty stupid to use his own bat and then tell us he can't find it. You know a sharp dresser named Ronnie Mateo?"

"Funny you should ask. On the night Rudy was killed, he spoke to me for the first time."

"Did he say anything of lasting value?"

"He tried to sell me some necklaces."

"Figures," Linderman said. "I hope he didn't make a sale."

"So you know something about Ronnie Mateo?"

"We've become pretty well acquainted over the years."

"How's that?"

"You ever hear of Bunny Mateo?" Linderman asked.

Harvey made the connection for the first time. "He's a gangster."

"Correct. In Providence, Bunny's *the* gangster. Now here's your bonus question: What's Ronnie's relationship to him?"

"I pass," Harvey said.

"Ronnie's his half brother, and he's sort of a simpleton. He's the guy the other guys send out for espresso, get the idea?"

"How dangerous is he?"

"As far as we know, he's not a leg-breaker. Shoplifting is more his speed." Linderman sipped his beer again. "He's the kind of guy we pick him up, we let him go, we pick him up, we let him go. He's small time, and there's never enough evidence to book him, anyway. He covers his tracks, or someone else covers them for him."

"You think Rudy was mixed up in gambling or something?"

"I don't think so. We checked around, and there's been no funny betting action on Jewels games. Nothing in Vegas, either." Linderman found a Marlboro, lit it, and just held it in his cupped hand. "Anyway, Harvey, you know as well as I do that a relief pitcher can't throw a game. Think about it. A starting pitcher can do it; he's scheduled to pitch, and he controls the game. But a reliever doesn't know when or if he's going to get in the game, so he can't control it. If Ronnie Mateo's in there somewhere, it's not gambling. Which is why I want to ask you about typewriters."

"Typewriters?"

"We found three IBM Selectrics in Rudy's house. The kind of machines that certain people have a habit of removing from offices without permission and selling on the street for five or six bills a pop. Any reason you can think of why there were three typewriters in his place and three thousand dollars in his pocket?"

"You said there was one thousand dollar bill."

"There were two more just like it in his pants pocket. We found them when we went through his clothes."

"Jesus," Harvey said. He pulled the celery stalk out of his drink and snapped it between his teeth.

"Three thousand bucks is a lot of money to be carrying around, even for one of you glamour boys. Now let's say that the money is tied to the typewriters. What I can't figure is why a guy pulling down big league money would want to get involved with a penny-ante operation in hot typewriters. What do you think?"

Harvey shrugged. "What does Ronnie Mateo think?"

"Thinking is not something he does real well. He says he doesn't know anything about typewriters, doesn't know anything about Cleavon Battle's bat, doesn't know anything about anything. Meanwhile, I'm holding nothing in my hand." Linderman looked at his cigarette, which had yet to reach his mouth, and put it out. "Do you know anything about Rudy and Ronnie I need to know? Rudy and Ronnie—gee, sounds like a nightclub act."

"All I know is Rudy said Mateo once tried to sell him some color TVs."

"What was Rudy planning to do, open a department store?"

"*Tried* to sell him. Ronnie tries to pitch everyone on the team. And you don't know for sure where Rudy got those typewriters."

"I'm thinking your roommate didn't live up to his end of some deal," Linderman said.

"You're guessing."

"It's more fun than waiting for the killer to come to your home and turn himself in." Linderman cocked a forearm and glanced at his Timex. "What else? Was Rudy sleeping with any of the players' wives or anything like that?"

"You asked me that in the clubhouse."

"Is it a crime to repeat myself?"

"You're the one in law enforcement. But the answer is no, not that I know of."

"Then let me ask you about another nightclub act— Rudy, Harvey, and Mickey."

"Mickey Slavin?"

"No. Mickey Mouse," Linderman said. "I understand both of you were planking her."

"You understand wrong," Harvey said, wincing at Linderman's choice of words. "Who told you that?"

"A teammate of yours, and which part do I understand wrong?"

"Both parts. Rudy wasn't 'planking' her, and I'm not either. We have a relationship."

"Oh, a relationship," Linderman said. "Well, how come this teamate of yours told me that both you and Rudy were in her drawers?"

"I did tell Bobby Wagner that, because I thought it was true once. I was wrong."

"What makes you so sure?"

"Because Mickey told me two nights ago I was wrong."

Linderman fixed him with a weary look, giving Harvey time to realize he'd just admitted that he hadn't learned the truth about it until after Rudy's murder.

"Okay, but give me a break," Harvey said.

"You can tell me if the two of you were fighting over the same broad, Harvey. I'll find out, anyway."

"Are you trying to tell me that if Rudy had been sleeping with Mickey I would've killed him?"

"I'm not telling you anything. I'm just asking."

"You're out of your mind if you think I had anything to do with this. Is that why you got me here this morning?"

"Now hold on—"

"If I'm the best suspect you've come up with, I don't know how the hell you're ever going to find out who killed him." Harvey downed the watery remains of his Bloody Mary and slammed the glass on the table.

Linderman was busy tugging a few singles from his wallet to pay the bill. "Tell me," he was saying as he searched his pockets for change, "does she look as good in bed as she does on television?"

Early Friday afternoon, Harvey watched from a window in the passenger waiting area as Rudy's body was put on a flight to Milwaukee with his foster parents. By coincidence, the Milwaukee Brewers flew in at about the same hour for a four-game series with the Jewels.

At seven that evening, when the Rankle Park lights went on, turning the grass a sudden green, the sea gulls that had been roosting on the struts of the huge light standards rose in waves and banked over the field. There were already twenty thousand fans in the stands, and more were arriving—groups of teenagers, solitary old men, girls in their boyfriends' athletic jackets, kids clutching Korean-made gloves in one hand and their fathers in the other.

"You don't think all these folks came out just to see us play, do you?" Harvey said to Felix, who was holding a fungo bat in foul territory and watching the Brewers take B.P.

"They came to see the team Rudy used to play for," Felix said sadly. "Violence is a big draw, Professor. We may still be in sixth place, but we suddenly lead the league in murders."

Harvey tried to sort out the little that he knew. If Rudy had been in trouble with Ronnie Mateo, then the typewriters would have to have been part of a bigger racket; otherwise, why would someone with a six-figure salary bother? And if Ronnie had been mixed up in Rudy's death, would he have been hanging out at the team practice yesterday? If, as Linderman believed, Rudy wasn't throwing games for gamblers, then what was he doing with all that money on him the night he was killed? Who was Valerie Carty? *Could* the killer have been someone on the team? He searched his memory for incidents and could only come up with one. In June, Rudy and Les Byers had quarreled over the last hamburger at a post-game meal. Rudy had playfully flicked a spoonful of ketchup at Les. Before the game on the following night, Rudy discovered that his favorite pair of spikes had been filled with ketchup, which prompted Rudy to shampoo Les's hair with mayonnaise after the game, whereupon Les ambushed him with a mustard squirter. The Great Condiment War, as Harvey called it, was amicably settled after a final flurry of pickle relish, and if there had been something more behind it than conflicting claims to the last hamburger, Harvey did not know what it was.

Of course, there was Steve Wilton, who was angry at everyone, but he was more likely to destroy himself. Marcus Marlette, one of Rudy's bull pen colleagues, was a religious fanatic, a product of something called the Church of the Wisened Up, in Birmingham, Alabama, but apart from his habit of referring to his knuckle curve as "God's pitch," he seemed a personable young man. Harvey proceeded mentally down the roster and came up empty.

Out in the stands, some fans were lowering a crudely lettered sign over the right field wall. "So Who Did It?" it asked. Harvey hawked at the ground near his feet. This was Linderman's job, anyway, not his. At least he had found a place for Wanda; Dunc had volunteered to take her home for his daughter.

The dugout was quiet before the game. Rodney Salta and Chuck Manomaitis were up on the grass throwing easily to each other, but most of the players sat on the bench, working their chaws or bouncing baseballs off the top step.

"All of a sudden, man, there seems to be a law around here against talking," Les Byers said. His hand was deep in his pants trying to get his protective cup to sit right.

Harvey didn't answer. He thought Les was just trying to make it up to him for the scene in the clubhouse yesterday with Happy and Steve. The scoreboard in center flashed the Jewels' starting lineup. He wondered if Rudy's murderer was on it:

| Manomaitis | SS | .273 |
|---|---|---|
| Blissberg | CF | .309 |
| Battle | 1B | .298 |
| Eppich | C | .270 |
| Stiles | DH | .257 |
| Wilton | RF | .264 |
| Rapp | LF | .255 |
| Byers | 3B | .231 |
| Salta | 2B | .219 |

**Van Auken (12–8)  P**

"See?" Les said. "Even you aren't talking, Professor."

"I'm willing to talk, Les. I just don't have anything to say."

"You think someone up there knows something about it?" He thrust his chin out at the scoreboard.

"I think if anyone up there does, going out there and playing ball tonight won't be the easiest thing he's ever done."

"Man, just to prove that I didn't have nothing to do with this shit, I'm going out there tonight and bust some babies." It was Les's phrase for getting some base hits. "With my batting average, I *better* start busting some. But look at you, man, you doing okay."

"Yeah, I decided I'm not going to worry anymore about my hitch," Harvey said, but became annoyed with himself for letting the conversation drift away from Rudy. "You know what Campy said to me? He told me that bad hitters have hitches; good hitters have rhythm."

Les laughed. "No, man, it's my people have the rhythm. *Your* people got 'most everything else."

Felix trotted back from home plate after exchanging lineup cards with the Milwaukee manager, and the Jewels took the field, trying not to appear unaccustomed to the applause of some twenty-five thousand fans. Before the national anthem there was a moment of silence for Rudy, and then, for the first time in three days, Providence was playing baseball. By the time the Brewers' second batter went to the plate, it was clear they were not playing it well. Les didn't get his butt down on a ground ball, and it rolled between his legs. Dan Van Auken, one of the protons in Frances Shalhoub's "nucleus," threw a flat curve to Kevin McQuilken, who sailed it far into the bleachers. By the end of the first, it was 5–0, Milwaukee in front. By the bottom of the eighth, the Jewels were down 11–0, there were only about ten thousand left in the stands, and there was bickering in the dugout.

"Why didn't you come to third on the play?" Les was saying to Steve Wilton. They were bellying up to each other by the water cooler. "Man, you know Stuckey's got no wheels left. We could've had him."

"No way," Steve said. "We're down by ten runs and you want me to gun down a guy who's halfway to the bag by the time I've got my hands on the ball?"

"Great winning attitude, man."

"You're one to talk," Steve yelled. Les had committed two errors already and gone hitless at the plate.

"Back off, man."

"Hey, bag it, you guys," Randy Eppich said.

"Yeah, shut up, Steve," Rodney Salta chipped in. "When you start to hitting the cut off man, maybe then you have a right to be bitching."

"Rodney," Steve said, "when you start lining yourself up with the bag like you're supposed to, maybe I'll think about it."

"C'mon," Harvey said, "just cut it out."

"Well, well," Steve said. "I figured we'd hear from you eventually, Professor."

"Steve," a voice said from the end of the bench, and everyone turned toward Frances. "Why don't you sit out the ninth? Rick? Where's Stiles? Rick, you go to right field, and Happy, you DH next inning."

Steve picked up a batting helmet and flung it at the water cooler. It bounced off and spun slowly on its crown at Frances's feet.

"That'll cost you, Steve," Frances called after him as he stormed off to the runway leading back to the clubhouse.

"Yeah, that'll cost you," Felix said next to her.

The Jewels lost it a dozen to zip. Half an hour after the last out, Harvey was driving with Mickey to her place.

"There was trouble in the dugout tonight," he said.

"It's always that way with you guys," she said, pulling a pack of Camel Lights out of her bag.

"It's worse now. And since when did you start smoking?"

"I stopped before you met me. Rudy's murder's got me going again." She lit a cigarette and blew a thin jet of smoke against the windshield. "Detective Linderman swung by to see me at work today. I never saw a man with so many Bic pens in one pocket."

"Well?" Harvey turned onto Washington Street. Even on a Friday evening, the city seemed barely alive.

"I gathered he went over the same ground with you this morning. Boy, the typewriters and that three thousand dollars. It doesn't sound like Rudy." Then her voice grew edgy. "I also told him he was wrong about Rudy and me and that you'd been wrong about it, too, although I don't know how that concerns

Linderman. I appreciate your spreading lies around about Rudy and me."

"I didn't spread lies. Bobby Wagner got it out of me in a bar one night on the road. I'm sorry, Mick. I feel worse since I found this yesterday." He took the baseball card out of his wallet and handed it to Mickey. "Rudy kept it under the glass on top of his dresser."

She studied it with a half smile and turned it over. She took a last, petulant drag on her cigarette and snuffed it in the car ashtray. "I think I'd like to hold on to this," she said and slipped the baseball card into her bag. "Sentimental value, if you don't mind."

"You were right the other night; maybe if I'd been a better friend I'd know why he ended up in the whirlpool."

"Maybe not. Maybe there was nothing to know, or nothing that he ever would've told you, anyway."

Harvey turned on the car radio, punched a few buttons, then switched it off. "Mick, am I crazy to think the guys in the club should be reacting more to Rudy's murder? It's weird. I've seen guys more shaken up when someone's traded."

"Unless they're really covering up for someone, it's probably just that no one really liked him that much. Rudy could be a pain in the ass."

"We didn't think so."

"Oh, I like pains in the ass," Mickey said. "You, for instance."

Harvey pulled into the parking lot of the Beaumont West, twelve stories that were 70 percent glass, 30 percent poured concrete, and 100 percent ugly. The only ornament on it was a ring of widely spaced white lights that circled the building above the first floor and looked like after-dinner mints.

"Let Linderman handle it," Harvey said, mostly to himself.

"I wanted to tell you something about Linderman," Mickey said. She explained in the elevator on the way up to the tenth floor. One of her co-workers, a veteran reporter at the station named Judy Martinez, had taken Mickey aside after she had seen Linderman questioning her. In the late sixties, when she was a crime reporter for the *Journal-Bulletin,* Judy had covered the story of two Providence patrolmen charged with being the bagmen for a local bookmaking operation. One of them was Linderman. They were suspended without pay following an internal investigation. While the DA's office prepared for trial, Linderman happened to learn through a friendly police informant that the son of the Providence deputy mayor was dealing hard drugs out of an East Side flat. The mayor himself was facing stiff opposition in his coming re-election bid. The DA, also a Democrat, had political ambitions of his own. And so it came to pass that a single late-night phone call hushed up the deputy mayor's son's East Side activities, caused the DA's office to find insufficient evidence to prosecute Linderman, and restored Linderman to the force, this time wearing plain clothes in the Homicide Division.

"That's just great," Harvey said as the brushed chrome elevator doors opened.

"No, that's just Providence," Mickey said. "But it happened a long time ago. Maybe it doesn't mean anything now."

"I always thought integrity was like virginity," Harvey said as they got to her door.

Mickey's hand swam about in her shoulder bag, searching for the key. "You don't think they'd put a guy they thought was a whore on an important case like this?"

"I don't?" he said, and they went in.

 Her apartment was a series of cold white compartments without moldings or baseboards. It reminded Harvey of the inside of a refrigerator. The ceilings were white stucco with recessed light fixtures. Mickey had tried to overcome the sterility by deploying Indian print cushions around the cinnamon wall-to-wall carpeting in the living room.

Harvey threw himself on her camelback sofa while she opened a German *spätlese*. By the time they were on their second bottle, the mood had lightened considerably.

"By day," Harvey announced in his best imitation of Bob Bolington, the orotund anchorman on WRIP-TV's "Eleven O'Clock Edition," "she's a reporter. She's tough. She's smart. She plays by her own rules . . . and she plays for keeps." He sipped his wine dramatically. "But by night . . . by night, she's a seething, lustful, savage beast."

"We'll see about that." She laughed from her end of the sofa and began unbuttoning her blouse.

"Let me help you with that."

"No, sir. Don't you know that in this day and age women can unbutton their own blouses?"

"Well, excuse me."

She wriggled out of her blouse and threw it over the lamp. "However," she said, "getting out of this skirt is a different matter altogether."

"Let's live together," he said after they had made love.

"And if I said no?"

"Why would you say something as annoying as that?" Harvey said.

"Do you want the long answer or the short one?" She had her hand on the side of his face.

"The short one. It's late."

"All right," she said, reaching for her glass of wine, "let me put it this way. Due to certain emotional upheavals in my childhood, I have intimacy anxieties that make me skittish about commitment. I seduce men into expectations I can't always fulfill—"

"You mean I'm not the first you've disappointed?"

"—On top of which, my father robbed my mother over the years of vital self-esteem. As a result, I associate cohabitation with a threat to my independence."

"Is that all?"

"No. I'm afraid I'll destroy any man I get too close to. Either that, or I'm afraid any man I get too close to will destroy me. It's one or the other." She jumped on top of Harvey and began tickling him.

"There's always the nunnery," he said.

"I don't look good in black."

"Then you'll have to settle for me."

"It's true," she sighed. "There's always you. Tell me again why a good-looking lug like you isn't already married."

"You want the short or the long answer?"

"The true one."

"My mommy won't let me," he said.

She rolled over on her back, giggling. "Be serious."

"Okay. Where'd you get all that stuff about yourself, anyway?"

"Dr. Lovett," she said.

"Some shrink of yours?"

"No, my dentist." She giggled again, bringing her hand up to her face.

"You mean he can tell all that just by looking in your mouth?"

"My molars are a dead giveaway."

"You be serious," Harvey said.

"All right. What were you doing in Rudy's apartment when you found the baseball card?"

He watched the sweat collect in the depression below his sternum. "I'm not sure what I was doing," he finally said. "Did Rudy ever mention someone named Valerie Carty to you?"

"Valerie Carty? No. Why?"

"Under the glass on the dresser, next to my baseball card, he kept a love letter from someone named Valerie Carty. There was also some kind of nightgown hidden away in his closet. One of those short things that snap under the crotch."

"A teddy?"

"That's it."

'You think this Valerie woman had something to do with it?"

"Be sure to let me know if you have a better idea."

On Saturday morning, they ate Rice Chex with sliced bananas on the vestigial balcony outside Mickey's living room. Thick gray clouds were wadded up over the skyline, and the air was hot and heavy. There was no more news about Rudy in the paper, and Harvey turned to the sports section. The headline on Lassiter's account of last night's game read: "Jewels Lack Luster on Diamond, Tarnished by Brewers." Harvey allowed himself a contemptuous laugh. When they won, the *Journal-Bulletin* always said, "Jewels Sparkle" or "Jewels Shine" or "Jewels Prove Priceless." When they lost, it was "Jewels Prove Counterfeit in Loss to Pale Hose" or "Jewels Only Semiprecious."

They walked down to a bookstore where Harvey bought a new biography of U. S. Grant. He didn't know what he was going to do when his playing days were over—a time he judged to be not so far off—so he tried sporadically to keep up with the latest Civil War scholarship. Harvey knew this was a charade. The prospect of returning to school for a graduate degree depressed him. Like baseball, college would be a kind of protracted adolescence. Well, he thought, there were always endorsement contracts.

"How do you think I'd look modeling Jockey shorts?" he asked Mickey at the cash register.

"In the privacy of my bedroom, I've been impressed."

"I was thinking more along the lines of a national audience, Mick."

"I suppose they could always airbrush that little roll of fat around your waist."

It reminded him that he and Bobby Wagner were scheduled to shoot a television commercial for a local insurance company at the park that morning before the game.

When Harvey walked onto the field at noon, Wagner was standing on the mound next to a man who wore a bird's nest of blond hair and a plaid shirt open to the navel. A cameraman and an audio man were setting up in front of the mound while a young woman with a clipboard kept glancing up at the cloudy sky.

"Burt Elias," the man with the permanent said to Harvey, offering a hand burdened with rings. "I represent Regional East Insurance."

"My favorite insurance company," Harvey said. "Sorry I'm a little late."

"No problem. I was just explaining to Bobby what we want to do."

"Welcome to Hollywood, Professor," Bobby said, speaking with a slight drawl. He was a couple of inches taller than Harvey, and he had the lean, symmetrical face of a male model, with strong black eyebrows that threatened to merge into a single one. They were arched in an expression of boredom. If Harvey was considered aloof, Wagner verged on arrogant. But since he was a bona fide star—he had come in second in the voting for the Cy Young Award twice in his career—his cockiness was credited as a kind of authority. That his talent had been less evident this season only increased his defiant pride. "Let's get on with it," he said to Elias.

Elias put on a pair of aviator sunglasses. "First we're going to zoom in on Bobby on the mound," he said to Harvey. "He'll pretend to throw a pitch that gets hit deep to center field, and he'll say, 'You know, folks, every once in a while something goes wrong when I'm pitching. And when it does' "—he grabbed the script from the young woman and consulted it— " 'and when it does, it's nice to know someone is backing me up.' We cut to you, Harvey, in center. You catch the ball, see, then turn to the camera and say, 'That's right. I like to think of myself as Bobby's insurance policy when he's out there pitching.' Cut back to Bobby on the mound, mopping his brow in relief. Then he says, 'On the field, I rely on Harvey Blissberg. Off the field, I put my trust in Regional East.' Then, Harvey, you join Bobby in the frame and say, 'Me, too. When it comes to my family, my home, my car, I count on Regional East. We know how important teamwork is. And in the game of life, it's good to know that Regional East is on your team.' That's it, gentlemen. Take a few minutes to study your lines. I want this to come out nice and natural."

"You're talking to a man who sold deodorant coast-to-coast for two years," Bobby said impatiently.

"As I recall," Harvey said, "you have very photogenic armpits."

"You guys should be glad to get me out here for the peanuts you're paying," Bobby told Elias.

"Of course," Elias said, "of course. I didn't mean to imply. . . .

When they were finished and walking to the dugout, Harvey turned to Bobby. "You're in a good mood today."

"For five bills and a year's car insurance, I don't need it," Bobby said.

"Wags, what do you know about Rudy?"

"Nothing."

"I thought he might've told you something, you know, trouble he was in. You pitchers hang together."

"Rudy hung alone."

"Did you know a girlfriend of his named Valerie Carty?"

"No. What is this, Professor? You some kind of cop now?"

"No, Wags, I just—there's—I don't know."

"Look, the guy probably had something going on the side, and he got burned."

"Yeah," Harvey said. "Maybe that's it."

Bobby got his warm-up jacket off the bench and put it on, mumbling, "A year's car insurance. Christ almighty."

Harvey picked up a leaded bat and was swinging it over his head in an arc when Cleavon Battle, the Jewels' mountainous first baseman, came up and said, "Let me ask you something."

Cleavon was the only player on the team about whom it was generally felt that you spoke to him only when spoken to—and Cleavon rarely spoke to you. After ten years in the majors with a healthy .289 career batting average, he was playing out the string in Providence.

"Ask," Harvey said.

Cleavon reached out and grabbed the end of Harvey's leaded bat. His fingers were the size of egg rolls. "You know it was my stick killed Rudy," he said.

"Yeah." Their hands were holding different ends of the bat. "I know about that."

"You know I didn't have nothing to do with it."

"I know that, too," Harvey said. Cleavon went six-three, about 220 pounds, and Harvey wasn't going to stand there and tell him he didn't like the way he wore his batting glove, much less accuse him of murder.

"I believe you when you say that."

"That's good, Cleavon."

The first baseman pursed his lips and nodded slowly, like a man dozing off. "Because I've got one bad-ass reputation around here."

"I don't know who killed Rudy," Harvey said, "but I know it had nothing to do with you."

"That's right," Cleavon said and let go of the leaded bat.

Harvey waited until he was out of earshot before releasing a sigh.

Andy Potter-Lawn, a young left-hander and the only major leaguer born in England, pitched for the Jewels that afternoon, but not with any great distinction. Behind Sammy Arguelles, Milwaukee coasted to a 7-1 win. Harvey was blow-drying his hair when Bob Lassiter came up to his locker after the game with a fried chicken wing in one hand and a reporter's notebook in the other. He waited for Harvey to snap off his Conair Pro 1000.

"Bob, you know I don't like to talk with wet hair."

"Just talk with your mouth, then." Lassiter laughed until he saw that Harvey wasn't going to join him. "Now look, don't chew my head again. I've just got one question, and I'll make it quick. You guys have played two miserable games in a row." He looked at Harvey.

"I think that charge would stand up in court, Bob," Harvey said.

"Do you think it has anything to do with Rudy's death?"

"Now, how did I know that question was coming?"

Lassiter tossed his chicken wing into a wastebasket behind him. "What I mean is," he said, poised to write, "it's got to affect your play in some way."

"No, I don't see why a team that's hiding a murderer shouldn't go out there every day and give it everything it's got."

Lassiter looked at him for a moment. "Wait. What you're saying is that—is that you think the guy who killed Rudy is on the team?"

Harvey realized immediately it was one of the dumbest things he'd ever said. The players who always talked to the press rarely said anything more provocative than "I really think the team's jelling now." It was the players who rarely talked who said too much when they did.

"That was a stupid thing to say," Harvey said. "Forget I said it." He pointed his hair dryer at Lassiter's face. "Keep that one out of the papers, all right? Look, I have no idea who killed Rudy. For all I know, it was the mob."

Harvey drove down Hope Street toward Pawtucket early that evening. Each block was like the one before, only slightly worse: an endless march of clapboard three-deckers with peeling bays and little half-balconies and chipped stoops. Neighborhood groceries called Tony's Spa and Marie's Spa sulked behind grated windows. It was hard to believe that Pawtucket had once been a hub of the textile industry, the source of the first machine-spun cotton yarn. Now it looked like the world capital of abandoned Impalas and busted screen doors.

He looked at the address on Valerie Carty's stationery on the seat beside him. Was any woman crazy enough to kill Rudy for love? In the clubhouse? Not even Rudy was that captivating. Was any woman's husband crazy enough to do it? Harvey hadn't thought of husbands until now. He hadn't thought of much, except that any woman who wore a teddy around Rudy's town house probably knew something he didn't.

At a red light, he rolled down his window and asked a man in a soiled Boston Red Sox cap for directions to Armbrister Road. He followed several more streets bordered by buckled buildings to a faded pink three-decker next to a lot filled with bakery trucks. A dumpster in the lot had spilled some of its contents onto the sidewalk. Harvey parked in front of the building, waded through the trash, climbed three steps to the porch, and found Valerie Carty's name on a black metal mailbox next to the door of the first-floor apartment. Above her name was the name Albert Carty.

The front of the building was covered with pitted pink aluminum siding, and the windows of the first-floor bay were shielded by thick yellow canvas shades the color of calluses. Harvey swung open the screen door, rapped on one of the small beveled glass panes, and waited with his back to the door. The orange sun had fallen behind the buildings across the street, silhouetting a serrated row of rooftops. Two boys raced minibikes with oversized wheels down the sidewalk and disappeared, whooping, into the lot. The air had grown chilly, and he pushed his hands into his pants pockets. Someone leaned on a car horn down the block. Harvey hawked over the porch railing. Pawtucket was having a bad effect on him.

"Yes?"

The man in the doorway wore an unbuttoned short-sleeved shirt that hung outside his pants, and at his side he held a bottle of Narragansett by the neck. He had thin sandy hair combed back in greasy streaks over his scalp, and wild sandy eyebrows. Other than that, he had the kind of sullen, unemployed face you could see ten times and still not remember.

Harvey had not expected the husband. "Uh, I should've called first," he stammered.

"About what?"

"I'm, uh, looking for your wife."

"I don't have a wife anymore," Albert Carty said. "Who are you?"

"My name's Harvey Blissberg." The man's eyebrows moved, but he showed no sign of recognition. "I'm wondering if—I'm looking for Valerie Carty."

"Then you're looking for my daughter."

"I guess that's right, then."

"My daughter doesn't get many visitors. What do you want to see her about?"

"It's kind of hard to explain."

"Try to find a way. It's nippy out here."

"Okay. I'm a baseball player, the Providence Jewels." Harvey raised his eyebrows expectantly.

"I've heard of them. I don't follow the game."

"I wanted to speak to Valerie about one of the other players. Someone she knew."

"She doesn't know any baseball players," Carty said.

A woman's voice called out from deep inside the apartment: "Who is it, Dad?"

"I'm trying to find out, honey," he called. He turned back to Harvey and repeated, "She doesn't know any baseball players."

"I'm pretty sure she knew this one."

"And I'm saying she doesn't. She's a baseball fan, but she doesn't know any baseball players."

"Okay, look. I'm sorry to bother you, but if you could just tell her that Harvey Blissberg of the Providence Jewels would like to talk to her for just a minute—about Rudy Furth."

Carty lifted his beer bottle, checked the contents, dropped it to his side again. "You wait here."

A minute later, Carty came back to open the door and say, "Well, she certainly knows who you are." Harvey followed him into a bleak hallway and living room with a low, veneered coffee table whose surface was ringed with glass stains, a mahogany highboy with polyurethane blisters all over it, and an assortment of easy chairs. Three small still lifes in dimestore frames dressed up the side wall between two windows with cracked sashes, and a tarnished light fixture in the shape of four tulips cast the room in a bad light.

Albert Carty went to one of the easy chairs, picked up a folded *Journal-Bulletin* off the rug, and sat down. "She's in her room," he said. "Second door down the hall, on the right."

Harvey walked slowly to the door and knocked. A

voice said tentatively, as if asking a question, "Come in?"

The room was square and stuffy. The curtains and bedspread were of the same ruffled blue-checked gingham. The large chest of drawers was painted white and scattered with bottles of perfume and stuffed animals. Above the bed were collages of pictures from sports and women's magazines and a Providence Jewels felt pennant tacked up at an angle. On a stamped-tin TV dinner table to the left of the door was a portable television set tuned to *The Love Boat*.

In the middle of the room, facing the television and also Harvey, sat Valerie Carty. Crinkly red hair, parted in the middle, fell on either side of a sweet face now set in a timid smile. She had a low forehead, wide brown eyes, and a fresh coat of pink lipstick that ran off her lower lip a bit. She wore a cotton T-shirt, and her legs were covered with a red blanket that fell in folds around the bottom of her wheelchair.

Harvey returned her smile.

"So it really *is* you!" she said. "I don't believe it!" She brought both hands up to her face and took them away, like a child playing peekaboo. "It—it's like a dream or something!" She was quite pretty, but Harvey couldn't tell if she was closer to fifteen or twenty-five. She breathed deeply and said, "I don't believe this! I just saw you on TV this afternoon. I can't believe Dad didn't know who you were! He doesn't know anything. Go on, go sit on the bed. I wish I had a chair, but"—she giggled—"I don't have much use for one. I mean, we could sit in the living room or something, but I think my room is the nicest one in the house. The rest of the place is sort of crummy. Oh, I don't believe this!"

Harvey sat uncomfortably on the bed, and Valerie pulled her wheelchair forty-five degrees around to face him. "You know, you look a little smaller in person. I don't know why I say that; I don't mean you look small or anything, but—but smaller." She covered her face again. "What, am I dreaming? *What* are you doing here? Look!" She pointed to the wall over Harvey's head. "I've even got your picture there, right next to Rudy's. Oh, this is ridiculous! I'm so excited!"

"This is a very nice room," Harvey said.

"Well," she laughed, "it's not exactly Bloomingdale's." Harvey figured her closer to twenty-five.

"Well, look," he said, "I guess I should explain why I'm here, but, well, Rudy—"

"Rudy," she pronounced. The giggle went away, and she lowered her eyes to the blanket on her lap. "I've been so depressed about it. I'm usually pretty cheerful; I guess you noticed. Even Dad started to worry about me." Her eyes brimmed. "Rudy was fantastic."

"He talked about you."

"No, he didn't!" She blushed even more now.

"Sure." Harvey slapped his hands on his thighs. "Why do you think I came here? He talked about you a lot. He told me there was a girl named Valerie Carty who wrote to him, and it was such a good letter that he said he was going to visit you someday." Harvey remembered a line from her letter—"Every time I see you, it makes me want to jump up and dance"—as he looked around at the little television set. "You know," he told her, "baseball players don't get as many letters as you would think. So I guess yours meant something special to him. So I figured the least I could do for him was to look you up and tell you that it meant a lot to him and that he was going to visit you sometime. And so here I am."

She was crying now, without making a sound. Harvey didn't know whether she really believed him; but what else could she believe? She pulled up a corner of the blanket and wiped her cheeks, revealing two slippered feet, lying thin and dead on the footplates of the wheelchair.

"And here I am," Harvey said. "He was quite a guy,

Rudy. You know, we were roommates, and we used to do a lot of things together." He wanted to get her a tissue, but didn't see any in the room. "They don't make too many like Rudy."

Valerie sniffed back her tears. "He always looked like he was having fun out there. Why did he always tug his ear before he pitched? Was that a sign?"

"Just a nervous habit," Harvey said.

"They don't know who did it, do they?"

"No, they don't." Harvey got up and kneeled next to her and put a hand on hers. She put her other hand on top of his.

"I still can't believe you're even here!" she said when he released her hand and stood up. "I can't believe Rudy told you about me! I mean, he didn't even write back. But it's true. Why would you be here if he didn't tell you about me?"

Harvey looked down at her and asked, "Do you need anything?"

She processed the question. "No," she replied with a slight stiffness, "I don't need anything. Are you going?"

"I'm in no rush."

"I mean, I feel like I should—I don't know. I've got a lot of *friends* who don't even come visit. Ha! Now I can tell them Harvey Blissberg was here in this room." She smiled the way she had when he first came in. "Could you just do me a favor? Could you come in the front room and let me explain to Dad who you are? Could you? He can really be dense sometimes."

"Sure. Should I push?"

"No," she said. "Just get the door for me."

She wheeled herself in front of Harvey down the short hall and stopped on the edge of the gray living room rug. Albert Carty put down his newspaper.

"Dad." She said it with mock reproachfulness. "I want you to apologize to this person. This person's a famous baseball player, and when famous baseball players come to the door, you shouldn't stand around asking them a lot of questions."

Valerie's father rose from his chair and beamed protectively at her. "Let me make it up to both of you," he said, without eagerness. "How about a beer?"

"No, please," Harvey said.

Valerie turned her wheelchair toward him.

"You sure?" her father said.

"No, really. I'd love to, but thanks, I've got to get back." Somehow it had been all right in the room with Valerie; now that the most awkward moments were over, he sensed how much he had trespassed, how preposterous his mission had been.

"You're sure, now?" Albert Carty said.

"Yes. I just wanted to pass on a message from one of Valerie's fans." He smiled at her.

She smiled at him. Her father smiled at her. The room was filled with bad smiles.

"Maybe next time, okay?" Harvey said to her.

"Okay, next time," she said.

He wanted to bend over and kiss her good-bye, but shook her little hand instead. Albert walked him outside and stood with him under the porch light.

"She doesn't get out much," Harvey said.

"If you mean dining and dancing, no."

"How long has she been in that thing?"

"Since she was four. She's used to it."

"I know it's none of my business, but—" Harvey began.

"She didn't look both ways," he said, almost brusquely.

"Do me a favor," Harvey said.

"I gather you've done her one."

"Naw, forget it." Harvey stared out at the street.

Albert Carty extended his hand. "I'd ask you to come back and see Val sometime, except I'm not that dumb. Thanks for coming this time."

He shook hands. "You're lucky to have a daughter

like that," he said and went down the porch steps as fast as he could without appearing to be in a hurry.

On the way home, he got lost and hit a dead end street, which put him in an even worse mood. He had wanted to ask Albert Carty to bring his daughter to a Jewels game. Harvey would leave them a couple of tickets. He knew an usher who would take good care of them. With the ball park ramps, it would be easy. But it was the sort of thing that only worked in the movies.

On Sunday morning, Harvey ground some Brazilian beans in his Salton Quick Mill and was sipping the result when the phone rang.

"So you didn't have time to call and tell about Rudy Furth?" a voice said.

"Hi, Mom. I was going to, but it's been too crazy around here."

"What kind of sport is that, a person gets murdered?"

"I don't know, Mom."

"Play something less dangerous. Not baseball."

"Too late, Mom."

"Harvey, he was murdered just like that? What do they do now, give you a new roommate?"

"From now on I think I'll take a single room on the road."

"That's good. So tell me—have you found anyone yet?"

"Anyone what?"

"Anyone special, that's what."

"Nothing's changed since last week, Mom. You asked, and I told you I was seeing a woman who's a sportscaster on the news here."

"What is she, a tomboy?"

"She's a very successful journalist, Mom."

"Maybe you should marry her, dear."

"Would you like that?"

"You mention a girl once over the phone and I'm supposed to know if she'll make you a nice wife? What

99

am I, a prophet? Mrs. Bernstein's daughter lives in Providence, Harvey, a nice girl."

"No, thanks, Mom."

"Maybe you're too picky. Norman's married."

"I'm not Norman, Mom. Norman's also an English professor, which I'm not."

"You could have been a history professor."

"I could have been an astrophysicist, too, but I'm a baseball player. Anyway, I make four times as much money as a professor."

"Since when is money everything? Is that how we brought you up? A good thing Big Al's not around to hear you talk like that. In three years, you're not going to be a baseball player. Then what?"

"Seven years ago you said the same thing to me, and I'm still playing."

"That's because you choked up and learned how to hit on the average."

"*For* the average, Mom."

"On, for, it's not easy telling people my son is thirty years old and plays baseball."

"Look at the bright side, Mom. Not everyone has a son who's batting three hundred in the majors."

"Well, excuse me. I didn't realize I could be so lucky. Here I was all these years, thinking how nice it would be to have a son who used his head for a living, who healed the sick, who taught the uneducated, even, God forbid, who could draw up a will or help with the income taxes. All along, I was ashamed he wore a uniform with the name of a city on the front. And a three hundred average! This I didn't know what a thing this was! 'Mrs. Blissberg, so how is Harvey doing these days?' 'Fine, Mrs. Schottsky. My son is now hitting three hundred. And how is your son?' 'Oh, David is all right, I guess. He just found the cure for cancer.' So forgive, Harvey, I didn't know you were such a big deal. I see you're playing in Boston this week. What night are you coming out for dinner?"

"Not dinner, Mom. They're night games. But why don't you drive into the city one day and I'll buy you lunch."

"I'll buy *you* lunch, boychik. I'm still your mother."

"How's Monday?"

"Tuesday."

"Fine, Tuesday it is. Come by the Sheraton around one or so.

"Whatever you say, dear, is fine with me."

There had been a time, when Harvey was younger, when a cunningly timed phone call from his mother almost always caused him to have a hitless game. Now it merely made him queasy. But what caught his eye when he turned to the sports pages in front of him made him particularly ill. He read the paragraph in Lassiter's column twice:

> **Blissberg is one of the few players who'll talk at all about the mysterious death of relief pitcher Rudy Furth. Although he won't elaborate, the Jewels' center fielder has suggested two intriguing possibilities—that the murderer may have been a member of the team or that the killer could have been connected with organized crime. That, to say the least, is more than we've gotten from the Homicide Division of the Providence police Department.**

When he entered the clubhouse before Sunday's doubleheader with Milwaukee, he felt like Menachem Begin walking into an OPEC conference. Les Byers and Happy Smith looked up briefly from their game of Boggle on the table in the middle of the locker room and then quickly bent over the white lettered cubes. Cleavon was just coming out of the trainer's room naked, with fresh tape on his ankles, and he stopped to run his eyes over Harvey. Rodney Salta and Angel

Vedrine were draped over their chairs by their lockers, listening to salsa on a cassette player the size of an American Tourister. The atmosphere was cold enough to skate on.

Harvey went to his locker and undressed. He put on his jock and his shorts and his sweatshirt with the dark green sleeves and then his sanitary hose and his stirrups and taped them around the tops of his calves. When he reached in to yank his jersey off the wire hanger, he saw the rat. It was taped by its spindly tail to the back of his locker at eye level. Its neck was broken, and its head was twisted to the side with the mouth open in a frightened smile of tiny yellow low teeth. It was big even by Rankle Park standards. Its horny little feet stuck out stiffly, like escargot forks.

The salsa played on, and Harvey finished suiting up. He pulled his practice uniform over on the rod so he didn't have to look at the rat. There would be a better time to dispose of it.

No one on the team spoke to him for the entire afternoon. He went 0-for-8 as the Brewers swept the Jewels easily, 9–3 and 6–0. "You guys better start playing some baseball," Chris Lentini, the Milwaukee first baseman, said when Harvey reached base for the only time all day, on a fielder's choice late in the second game. "Else they'll move the franchise to a small island somewhere in the Atlantic next year."

"Try the Bermuda Triangle," Harvey said and watched Cleavon strike out to end the inning.

He drove back to his apartment with the intention of spending Sunday evening with the new Grant biography. Next to Mickey, it was the most congenial company he could think of at the moment. As he climbed the darkened, splayed staircase to his apartment, he smelled a sweet burnt odor. He was still trying to imagine what Mr. Hughes on the third floor could be enduring for dinner as he worked his key into his lock. A voice froze him.

"Oh-for-eight, Professor. That's not like you."

Ronnie Mateo, in a wine-colored leisure suit, was sitting halfway up the flight of steps to the third floor. He was suckling a blunt cigar.

"I'm still not interested in any of your necklaces," Harvey said. His key ring was in the lock, ticking softly as it swung against the plate.

"I'm not selling none, but invite me in anyway," Ronnie said, holding the cigar in front of his face to examine it with exaggerated nonchalance.

"I was thinking of spending the evening reading about General Grant."

Ronnie put two long hands on his knees, pushed himself up, walked down to the landing, and put his face a foot from Harvey's. He smelled of sausage and peppers. "Grant's dead," he said. "And this won't take long."

Harvey took a step back. "What won't take long?"

"Just open the fucking door before I use your head to do it."

"Oh, what the hell," Harvey said gaily. "Come in and have a drink."

Ronnie followed Harvey into the kitchen. Harvey opened two Rolling Rocks and poured them into tumblers with a trembling hand.

"General Grant," Ronnie said, helping himself to a club chair in the living room. "To tell you the truth, Professor, I don't know too much about him. What war was he in?"

"Civil."

Ronnie plunged the cigar in and out of his mouth a few times. "You're an intelligent guy," he said and threw an arm over the back of the chair.

"Not intelligent enough to know why you're here."

"Oh, yes you are. And you're smart enough to know better than to say what you did to Bob Lassiter, and

I'll bet you're just smart enough to keep your nose out of what you don't know nothing about from here on out." He drank half his beer, unaware of the parabola of foam that collected on his upper lip.

"What's my nose been in?" Harvey was still standing. Ronnie just stared at him.

"Okay," Harvey said, "it was a stupid thing to say. I didn't mean anything by it."

"I get it. You just felt like making Lassiter's day."

"I hardly ever talk to those guys."

"You talked loud enough yesterday, Professor."

Harvey managed his first sip of beer. "Look, I don't even know what this has to do with you. I don't even know who you are. I don't know what you do for a living."

"I'm a brain surgeon," Ronnie said. "And if you keep your mouth shut, maybe I won't operate on you."

"What's it to you?"

"You're getting dumber every second, Professor." Ronnie got up from his chair. "I don't know what you think you know, but I want to know about it."

"About what?"

"Your roomie's murder. I want to know what you think you know about it."

"I don't know anything."

"Then why do I see you in the newspaper this morning? I know you talk to Linderman." He relit his cigar and was in no particular hurry to suck it back to life.

"I told you I don't know anything and I don't know who you are, so why don't you get out of here?"

Ronnie picked up his glass from the table. "I don't like this beer," he said and threw the contents in Harvey's face.

Harvey stepped up and shoved him in the chest. Ronnie fell back in the chair. He opened his leisure suit so Harvey could see the small automatic under his arm.

"I don't think you understand, Professor," he said. "We're not in the same league."

It was one of Harvey's failings that he could never quite believe that anyone truly wished him harm. Only when Ronnie Mateo showed him his gun was he totally willing to accept the fact that someone so pathetic could wield the least bit of power over his life. A bitter juice gurgled in his gut as he wiped the beer off his face with a sleeve.

"Who sent you here?" Harvey said.

"Guys who want to know what you think you're doing, so why don't you go ahead and tell me?"

"I don't know anything."

Ronnie got up again and came toward Harvey. "I feel myself getting very angry with you."

Harvey flinched.

"Don't worry. I'm not going to touch you yet. It won't look good if you go on national TV tomorrow night in Boston with something wrong with your face. I'm just using the gentle arts of persuasion." He stood in front of Harvey and squeezed out the words: "Tell me what you know."

Harvey breathed deeply. "All I know is about some typewriters in Rudy's apartment. That's it."

"Typewriters," Ronnie said.

"Yeah, he had some typewriters in his place when he was murdered."

Ronnie's mouth imitated a smile. "So what's a few typewriters?"

"Right, what's a few typewriters?"

"Maybe the guy collected typewriters."

"Sure."

"Maybe he was starting a typewriter repair business."

"Sure."

"What else do you know?"

"That's it."

"You're making a mistake if you don't tell me now. It don't count if you decide to tell me later what you could tell me now. Am I right?"

"That's all I know."

"Just the typewriters?"

"Why, is there something else?"

Ronnie rolled the cigar from one side of his mouth to the other. "How should I know? I'm just the guy asking questions. Look, Professor, I don't know what happened to your roomie, but I would think that what you called the mob, whatever that is, would have a better way to ice somebody than to stuff him in a whirlpool. Would you agree that there're better ways to take someone out? And three thousand bucks—that's not the mob's kind of money, would you agree? Those guys tip more than that in a week."

"Sure."

"And would you agree"—he tucked his shirt in in back to give Harvey another look at his gun—"that whenever you think that what you call the mob has something to do with your roomie's untimely departure, when you have such thoughts, Professor, you will now know that these are not good thoughts to have, and that you will keep your mouth shut about what you don't know nothing about? Am I right?"

"Sure."

"I enjoyed the beer," Ronnie said and cast a glance around the apartment. "I figured a class guy like you for a nicer place."

"Next time I'll bring out the good silver," Harvey said.

"And the crystal." Ronnie picked up his empty tumbler and heaved it against the wall, where it shattered. "Good arm, huh?" he said and left the door open behind him.

Ten minutes later, the phone rang, and Harvey rose from the love seat to pick it up.

"It's Linderman."

"Oh, hello," Harvey said in a voice he didn't quite recognize as his own.

"I'm just calling to say that was a stupid thing you told Bob Lassiter in the papers today."

"I know. Someone was just here expressing similar sentiments.

"Who's that?"

"Ronnie Mateo. I think we acted out a scene from *The Big Heat*."

"Well, I can't say I'm surprised. He didn't get physical, I hope."

"Basically he just threw beer in my face and showed me his gun collection."

"I see," Linderman said. "You want to press charges?"

"What do you think?"

"Yeah, yeah, yeah. Look, Harvey, I know you want to get to the bottom of this thing, but talking to reporters about this and that doesn't help anyone, understand? It just makes my job tougher, and I don't think you're making any friends. You play baseball, and I'll run the investigation. And stay out of Ronnie Mateo's hair, for Christ's sake."

"But, Linderman, if he's got something—"

"But we don't know that, do we? My boss wouldn't like it if I took a guy off the street without evidence."

"What's he doing always hanging around the park?"

"What do I know?" Linderman said. "Maybe he's a baseball nut. Harvey, stop asking questions. Stop talking to reporters. Stop worrying about this thing. Let me handle it over here. Keep your mind on the game. You guys can still make the first division."

"Thanks," Harvey said. "I appreciate the support."

Boston's Fenway Park was like Rankle Park—small, misshapen, a compilation of architectural afterthoughts. It was six-thirty on Monday evening, September 3, two hours before game time, and the bleachers were dotted with a few shirtless worshipers of the sun, which hung above the grandstands along the third base line. Harvey had played five years in this park, knew the contours of its strange outfield, the feel of its infield dirt, and he wished more than ever that he still played in Boston.

Alan Resnick was standing next to him behind home plate with his hand mike cluched between his knees, fidgeting with the knot of his gold tie. An associate producer from ABC had phoned Harvey at the Sheraton Boston earlier that afternoon to arrange the taped interview, to be used later during that night's national telecast. Harvey recognized an opportunity to redeem himself after his indiscretion with Bob Lassiter over the weekend; he would show viewers across the country how little he knew about the murder of Rudy Furth.

"I'm delighted to see you batting three hundred," Resnick said, wrestling with his tie. "I'd always assessed you as having that potential. Andersen was telling me today that he can't figure out how to pitch to you anymore. When he was with the Angels, he owned you. Now you're batting something like four hundred against him. What's the difference this year?"

"I guess he's just not aging as well as I am." Harvey smiled.

"Heh, heh. But seriously, has Strulowitz changed your stance?"

"No, except we've been trying to get rid of a little hitch in my swing."

"Well, you know what Strulowitz says about hitches."

"Yeah, that bad hitters have them, but good hitters have rhythm."

"Don't step on my lines, Harvey." The crew signaled to Resnick that they were ready. "Why don't you use that line about aging better than Andersen? I'll set you up."

The cameraman, dressed head-to-cuff in prewashed denim, flipped the switch on the Ikegami, and Resnick slithered a long arm around Harvey's shoulder.

"You're hitting over three hundred this season, a dramatic improvement over your career average," Resnick began, assuming his public cadence, "and you've suddenly become one of the batters whom American League pitchers are averse to seeing up there in critical situations. Frank Andersen, whom you'll be facing here tonight, and who has overpowered you in games past, confided in me earlier that he's baffled by you this summer. What's the difference?" He squeezed Harvey's shoulder lightly.

"Frank's not aging as well as I am," Harvey said.

Resnick chortled dutifully. "In fact, despite its recent tailspin the entire Providence squad has performed with a continuity of excellence beyond most people's expectations. Are you surprised?"

"Not really, Alan. The team drafted wisely, and any time you've got as many veterans on a club as we do, you're going to win a few ball games." Just relax, Harvey thought to himself and cleared his throat. "I'm pleased, Alan, but not surprised. Of course, we haven't exactly been tearing up the league lately."

"And no wonder. Last week, your team experienced

a tragic, tragic incident. A relief pitcher on your team, a superb athlete with many good years of baseball ahead of him, a genius with men on base, was found senselessly slaughtered in the team clubhouse in Providence. I'm speaking, of course, of Rudy Furth, who was liked and admired by all who had the pleasure of playing with or against him. Over the years, baseball has had its share of tragedies—the fatal beaning of Cleveland shortstop Ray Chapman in nineteen twenty, the shootings of Eddie Waitkus and Lyman Bostock, the deaths of the great Roberto Clemente and Thurman Munson in plane crashes—but it's hard to say whether the game has ever witnessed anything like this.

"Harvey," he went on, "you knew him well; you knew him perhaps better than most, being, as you were in this, the first season for both of you with the Jewels, his roommate. Not only that, but tragically, you were the one to find his body. I know how you must feel, how difficult it is for you to talk about it."

Had he asked a question? Another squeeze on the shoulder notified Harvey.

"I guess I don't have to say what a great loss and a horrible thing Rudy's death was," Harvey said. "There seems to be no explanation."

Resnick shook his head solemnly. "Harvey, there's one last thing I want to ask you. The Jewels' manager, Felix Shalhoub, a gentleman I've admired for years, not least for the way he handled that much publicized drug problem on his San Diego club a few years ago, is married to a fine woman and a knowledgeable baseball fan, Frances Shalhoub, who, in an arrangement unique in baseball history, has been sitting in the Providence dugout during many games this season. It is some reporters' opinion that she is not only sitting in the dugout, but is in fact contributing managerial decisions, in effect acting in the capacity of baseball's first female coach. Is there some truth in this, as you see it?"

"Not really, Alan. Frances takes a great interest in the team and apparently feels she can get to know it better by being in the dugout. But this is Felix's ball club."

"Do you think baseball will someday see its first female coach?"

"I don't know, Alan," Harvey said and could think of nothing else. "I love this game."

"I'm sure you do," Resnick said. He thanked him and handed the mike to his sound man. "Well, that was discreet," he said, leading Harvey toward the Providence dugout.

"What do you mean?"

"Number one, I mean that Frances Shalhoub is helping to run the club, and you know it. Maybe it's because Felix has a bad case of the shakes, but I'm not sure. When she had her public relations outfit in New York, she'd do anything to get clients. Now that she doesn't have the business anymore, I wouldn't be suprised if she wants to get her hands all over the club. Number two," he said, lighting a cigarette, "someone on your team has got to know something about Rudy's murder because people don't simply walk in off the street into a major league clubhouse and kill players. But nobody's talking. Are you?"

"No," Harvey said.

"All right, champ," he said, squeezing the back of Harvey's neck. "Have a good game."

He had a bad one, and so did the rest of the team. Bobby Wagner was wild in the first, filling the bases on walks before Tony Jallardio fouled out to Randy Eppich to end the inning. In the second, Boston jumped on Wagner for three straight singles and a 1–0 lead. Keith followed by parking one in the left field net for a 4–0 lead. In the fourth, Randy unloaded on an An-

dersen curve with Cleavon on base to cut it to 4–2, but
Jallardio returned the favor with Sammons on in the
bottom of the inning. Boston was up 6-2, and Felix
trudged to the mound faster than usual, as though
embarrassed to be seen on national television, and
pulled Wagner out of the game. He brought in Eddie
Storella, a lean kid who had just joined the Jewels
from their Wheeling, West Virginia, farm team. Storella
walked two batters before finding the strike zone; the
Red Sox were only too glad when he did find it, and
the score after four was 9–2. When it was over, the
score was 13–4, Harvey had gone 0-for-5, the team had
lost six in a row, had been outscored 51 to 10, and was
only half a game ahead of the seventh-place Tigers.

Harvey ducked the press and stood under the stiff
hot spray of the shower, his head tilted back. He
soaped up, going easy on the outside upper part of his
left thigh, where years of sliding burns had branded a
dull ache. His body bore witness to the game he played,
but he had been lucky so far. They were mostly little
things: a perpetually tender heel, a minor ligament
tear in the right knee, a broken middle finger on his
throwing hand that throbbed when the humidity rose.
Happy Smith came into the shower carrying a bottle
of prescription shampoo, looked in Harvey's direction,
then moved to the farthest shower away.

When he was dressed, Harvey passed Bobby Wagner
standing at a long mirror by the clubhouse door. Bobby
was wearing a double-vented sky blue sports jacket
and beige slacks, and he was trying to manipulate his
cowlick. Harvey inspected his own face in the mirror
and said to Bobby's reflection, "Shake it off, Wags."

"I'll do that," Bobby said.

"I had a bad year once when I couldn't hit the
fastball. I felt I was waving at bullets up there. It's
funny. The next year, I could hit the fastball all right,
but I couldn't hit the curve.

Bobby looked at Harvey in the mirror. "The boys are giving you a hard time, aren't they?" he said.

Harvey thought for a second. "If you mean about talking to Lassiter, I guess I deserve it."

"Well"—Bobby patted his cowlick down; he wore a fat World Series Championship ring on his left hand—"you should watch it. But you know baseball players, Professor. If we were any smarter, we wouldn't be playing major league baseball, and if we were any dumber, we'd still be in the minors."

Harvey lowered his voice. "But Wags, don't you think it's all a little fishy?"

Bobby slid his comb into his inside coat pocket. "I don't smell any fish. With the security they got at Rankle Park, hell, anybody could walk in and pick a fight."

Harvey hopped a cab back to the Sheraton, creeping through the thick ball game traffic along the Fens. Through the window, he saw two teenagers in Red Sox caps chasing each other through a river of fans on the sidewalk. The cab driver, a middle-aged man in an unseasonable knit cap, eyed Harvey in the rearview mirror.

"Can't win 'em all," he said. "Isn't that how it goes?"

"I just don't want to lose them by nine," Harvey said.

"I used to come out and watch you when you was with the team, you know. Personally, I didn't think they shoulda let you go like that."

"They're doing all right without me."

"Sure," the cabbie said, accelerating out of traffic onto Boylston Street. "But wait till they find out the kid they got in center now couldn't throw nobody out if he had a howitzer. Then they're gonna wake up and wish they had Ha'vey Blissberg back. Then they're gonna wake up and wish they hadn't thrown you away like that. You was always my kind of ball player. Never read about you fighting with the owners, holding out, getting some fancy agent to stick up the team for more dough. Some of these guys today oughta drive my cab for a while and see what real work is like. But I'm not complaining. What do you make now, just for instance?"

"Oh, I don't talk about that stuff," Harvey said.

"Naw, you can say. Look, I make a good dollar. I got a little summer place on the Cape. I'm putting a daughter through Emerson College. It's not like you're gonna say what you make and then I'm gonna say, hey, you don't deserve that kind of dough. You're not gonna be making it forever, are you? Go ahead, you can say. How's this?" He pulled under the portico of the Sheraton. "Go ahead, what kind of dough do you make?"

"I make six figures," Harvey said, counting out some bills.

"You got kids?"

"No kids."

"You pay alimony, something like that?"

"No."

"So what do you do with that kind of dough? You got a fetish? You blow it on dames? Drugs? What?"

"I salt it away," Harvey said, opening the door.

The cabbie blew some air. "Six figures is good dough. I remember a catch you made last year in some game, you ran about two miles and crashed into the wall. I guess if you can do that, you deserve that kind of dough. That kid who got murdered last week—Furth? He probably made that kind of dough, too, huh? That's a good dollar, but a lot of good it's gonna do him now, a lot of good."

Harvey went straight to the hotel bar, a dark lounge with a Hawaiian motif. A black-haired woman with platform shoes and enough makeup for the lead in a Kabuki play intercepted him at the door and trilled, "You must be a ball player."

"And you must be about a hundred bucks a night,"

he said and brushed past her into the lounge. It had straw mats all over the ceiling. Seated at the bar in front of a margarita was a woman less burdened by cosmetics. He circled around to get a better look at her profile. It was not her first margarita, and she was not happy.

"Aloha," he said. "Do they make those things with real egg whites in this place, or what?"

"I was just thinking about you," said Frances Shalhoub.

 She was wearing a gray shirtwaist dress and a matching jacket with pewter buttons. On the bar next to her drink was a straw hat with a band of guinea hen feathers around the crown. The outfit looked better in the bar than it had in the dugout earlier in the evening.

"How are you, Harvey?" she said.

"Fine. I won't ask you how you are. It didn't work too well last time."

"That's all right," she said. "I'll tell you anyway. I'm reasonably drunk." Her green eyes shone out at him from under tweezed eyebrows. "In fact, I may be unreasonably drunk."

Drunkenness violated her; her beauty should have been impervious to alcohol. Harvey suddenly saw in her drunkenness a basis for compatibility with Felix that hadn't occurred to him. "What's the occasion?" Harvey said after he had ordered a Bass ale.

"I wish to hell we would get some pitching."

"Where's Felix?"

"He's at the park, where else? He needs his shot of postgame camaraderie."

"What do you need?"

"Another margarita, a tummy tuck, and a new life."

"Is it Rudy?" Harvey said.

Frances said nothing. She found a long chocolate-colored Sherman's cigarette in her purse and had it lit before Harvey could reach for the bar matches. She burned half an inch of it in one drag and said, "I see that you and Bob Lassiter had a nice little chat the other day."

"You're the fourth or fifth person to remind me, although I'm happy to say you put it more gently than the others."

"I guess people feel it's the cops' business, not yours." She drew smoke up her two delicate nostrils and spat it out in a cirrus cloud. "You don't owe it to him, Harvey."

"It's not him I owe it to. Don't you care what happened?"

"I care about what happens to all the players. I make it my business to care. But I think I'll leave the investigation to the guys who get paid for it." She smiled without parting her lips. Her left hand fished for his knee and found it. "I've always liked you, Harvey."

"Part of the nucleus, right?"

"I also like a man who drinks Bass ale."

Harvey took her hand and returned it to her own knee.

"Forget it," she said. "I told you I was unreasonably drunk."

"Can I buy the manager's wife another margarita?"

"No, thanks. But unless you're waiting for someone, why don't you walk me upstairs to my room? I don't think I could find the elevator in my present state. In fact, in my present state, I couldn't tell you if this place *has* an elevator."

She signed for the drinks, and they rode up to the fifth floor like strangers, staring at the illuminated numbers. Harvey held her lightly by the elbow in the carpeted corridor. She turned to face him in front of her door.

"Come in for a second. I've got something to show you," she said.

Frances disappeared into the bedroom of the suite while Harvey sat down in a brocaded French provincial chair. He was pulling some stray threads off his jacket when Frances came back into the room. She was wearing a white cotton nightgown with a low-cut lace yoke. Her feet were bare, and her toenails were painted pink.

"What did you want to show me?" Harvey said with a nervous smile.

"I'm showing it to you." The lace yoke of the nightgown barely covered her nipples.

"That's not what I expected," he said.

"I thought this was pretty good for a forty-year-old woman."

"I meant, I thought you said you were going to—I thought it might have something to do with—"

"How else was I going to get a shy boy like you into my room?" She stood so that the light from the bedroom backlit her body through the nightgown.

"Now don't you think Felix—" Harvey began.

"No, I don't think Felix. Felix goes out drinking after the game. You know that. Even if he walked in, he'd be too loaded to notice you. I like you, Harvey."

"You said that before." He got to his feet.

"But now I'm sober," she said and stepped toward him. She let her arms fall lightly around Harvey's neck and bent her head to one side to look at him, like someone peering around a corner. Harvey watched her face, breathing slowly through his nose. She had no scent.

"Older women don't scare you, do they?" she said.

Harvey said nothing, and Frances locked her arms around his neck and pulled his face to hers. Her lips on his were as soft and warm as a cheek. She moaned and tried to force Harvey's mouth open. "That's the way," she murmured.

Harvey felt as if he were being instructed about a lifesaving maneuver. She tried to push her tongue into his mouth and it wouldn't go, but she kept her lips against his, and finally Harvey, despite himself, felt her tongue winding around his.

"That's good," Frances whispered. "You taste good, Harvey." Her hand clawed the back of his shirt. "That's good," she said.

Harvey ran his hand up her back and played with the top of her nightgown.

"Everything's good," she was saying.

He kissed her on the side of the neck, brushed her hair aside, then moved his fingers along the border of the nightgown and toyed with the label. With a circular motion, she rubbed her breasts against his chest. Suddenly, he pushed away from her.

"I want to talk about Rudy, Frances," he said.

"Let's talk about you," she breathed. "Let's talk about you and what you like to do."

"I like to talk about Rudy." He dropped down into the chair. "I guess you knew him pretty well."

"What are you talking about?" She stood over him, threading her hand through her hair and then tucking it behind her ears. "I thought we were busy with something else here."

"I said you knew him pretty well."

"I try to know as much as I can about all the ball players." She sighed.

"You knew more about him than most."

"Why don't you tell me what you're getting at?" Two voices in the hall passed the door and faded.

"I'm not kidding, Frances. I want you to talk about Rudy."

She went over and sat in the companion French provincial chair and drew her knees up under her chin and pulled her nightgown down over her ankles. "You're a funny fellow," she said.

"Tell me about it."

The expression on Harvey's face, or rather the lack of one, must have meant something to her. She exhaled, rolling her head down and then upward, as though coming up for air. "You tell me what you think you know. Then I'll tell you the truth about it."

"You two were seeing each other."

"Don't be ridiculous."

"Look, Frances. He told me about it. It didn't matter then because that was between you and him. But he's dead now, and I want to know about it."

"What did Rudy tell you?"

"You and he had a thing. That's what he told me."

"You're wrong." She picked up the imitation marble ashtray on the table between the chairs and held it in her lap. "Yes, I saw him a couple of times outside the ball park, but not socially. I suppose it's just like Rudy to have hinted that there was something between us."

"He didn't hint, Frances. He told me about it."

"He did think of himself as a latter-day Bo Belinsky. Or would Joe Namath be more like it?"

"I said he didn't hint."

She went on working the ashtray around in her hands. "Actually, he was worried about his status on the team. That was it. As you know, he wasn't having the season we expected from him, and he was worried we might send him down to Wheeling."

"What do you mean,'we'?"

"The team. The team might send him down. Felix and Marshall. He was losing games in the late innings. It was getting to him, and he wanted to talk."

"Well, that's funny," Harvey said. "Rudy and I talked a lot about baseball. Sometimes, it was all we talked about. But he never said he was worried about being sent down. But Frances, why would he talk to you about it? Why not Felix?"

She had examined the ashtray from every possible angle, and she now started over again. "Felix is a distracted man. Not good with personnel matters. I guess Rudy found me more accessible, so he came to me."

"You went to Rudy's town house to talk about how he didn't have to worry about being sent down to the minors?"

"I never went to his house. We went out and had a drink."

"I thought you said you saw him a couple of times outside the park."

"All right, we had drinks a couple of times. What's the big deal? He was worried. You know he was a lonely guy. He had no real parents. I think it helped to talk to an older woman."

"You're nice that way, Frances."

"Look, Harvey," she said, clapping the ashtray down on the table. "If Rudy told you he was having an affair with me, he was lying to you. Men do that. You can believe what you want, but I won't sit here and be grilled by you. Am I getting through? I don't know anything about Rudy, and I don't know anything about what happened to him, and I don't appreciate you bringing it up in the middle of what I thought was a very promising kiss." Her eyes filled with tears, and she made a strange sound at the base of her throat.

"Save it for your shrink," Harvey said. "You're a liar."

She jumped to her feet, walked to the door, and leveled a finger at him. "Get out of here. Right now."

Harvey rose and went toward her, feeling a twinge in his right leg from the dive he had taken in the outfield during the game. He stopped in front of her with his hand on the doorknob. "By the way," he said, "I like your nightgown. I noticed it comes from one of my favorite stores—The Bare Essentials."

"You're not funny. You're queer."

"You have something else from that store, Frances. A teddy the color of cream that snaps under the crotch. You're probably wondering how in hell it ended up in Rudy's closet."

Frances's eyes had grown large and now narrowed again.

"Anyway, I was wondering about it myself," Harvey said, opening the door.

"Wait." She put her hand over Harvey's on the doorknob and closed the door.

"What is it, Frances?"

"Wait, I, uh—Look, okay, I won't lie to you anymore. There was something. Not much, but something. You can understand—with Felix—it wouldn't be good. You can't let this get out. You've got to promise me."

"I'm not interested in telling Felix, or anybody else, for that matter. You can hump whoever you want, Frances. I just want to know who killed Rudy."

"I wish I knew, too," she said and paused a long time. Then she asked, "How do you think I felt when he was murdered? There was no one to talk about it with. So now there's you, but you don't want to hear about it."

"Not the lurid details, anyway. I want to hear about who could've killed him."

"I'm not very happy," she suddenly announced, squeezing the bridge of her nose.

"Save that for your shrink, too. You can't spend time in bed with a guy like Rudy and not have some idea about what's going on in his life. About what danger he's in."

"Yes, you can. Just as you could sleep in the

same hotel room with Rudy for four months on the road and not know what you'd like to know. Or do you know?"

"If I did, Frances, I wouldn't have come to your room in the first place. And I still think you're holding out on me."

"If I find anything out," she said, touching Harvey's nose with her finger, "you'll be the first to know."

"You're still a liar," Harvey said.

When he reached his room, the phone was ringing. It was his brother Norm, who knew the name and telephone number of every hotel where the team stayed. "Where you been?" he said.

"Out."

"I hope she was Jewish," Norm said.

"That's great, Norm. What's up?"

"Speaking of great, Harv, you guys sure looked sharp out there tonight. I'm glad you all saved your best game for national TV."

"Well, look, we're not exactly—"

I didn't know whether I was watching a game or a game show. You know, like *What's My Line?* The panel would've had a hard time guessing you guys are baseball players."

"Good, Norm—"

"I mean, I thought they were going to call it on account of ineptitude."

"Norm, why don't you try standing in there against Andersen when his curve's working?"

"I tell you, I wouldn't mind batting against Bobby Wagner. Jesus, what's wrong with the guy? It's hard to believe he almost won the Cy Young twice. He looks like he ought to win the Cy *Old* award."

"Let me know when the routine's over, Norm."

"Take it easy, Harv. It's just the coke kicking in."

"You? Coke? My own flesh and blood?"

124

"C'mon. You guys know all about coke."

"But English professors?"

"Sure. Harv, I got another statistic for you."

"The league ought to hire you, Norm. There's no reason why you shouldn't get paid for all the time you waste. What is it?"

"Did you know that in night games this season you've hit three-forty-three, but you've only hit two-thirty-nine in day games? You'd win the batting title if you only played at night."

"I'll see if I can get the commissioner to reschedule the rest of our games."

"All right, I won't keep you. Let's get together when you guys play Chicago."

"When's that?"

"C'mon, Harv, it's *your* schedule. Night games on the twenty-fifth and twenty-seventh and a twi-night doubleheader on Wednesday the twenty-sixth. But watch out: the White Sox haven't dropped both ends of a doubleheader all season. Now, if they only played twin bills, they'd be in first place in the Western Division. I'll buy you dinner at Berghoff's."

"You're on. How are Linda and the kid?"

"Fine. Linda sends her love and wants to know when you're going to get married. Nicky's favorite Jewel is Cleavon Battle. He's got six of his cards. I tried to get him to collect yours, but the kid won't listen to reason."

When he hung up, Harvey studied Boston's dark skyline out the window, then ordered up some shrimp cocktail from room service and called Mickey.

"I hate to admit it," she said to him, "but I miss you."

"That's the best thing anyone's said to me in two days."

"I should hope so. What's the worst?"

"At the moment, it's a four-way tie between Ronnie Mateo, Linderman, Bobby Wagner, and Frances Shalhoub. They've all told me with varying degrees of menace to stop sticking my head in the Rudy business. Somebody put a dead rat in my locker yesterday. Having great time. Wish you were here."

"You might've been a tad more circumspect with Lassiter."

"Okay, okay, I learned my lesson. Anyway, Mick, I know something new. I think I know who Rudy was in love with, but I don't know what it means. Ready?"

"Set."

"Frances Shalhoub."

Harvey listened to Mickey's breathing for five seconds. "How do you know?" she said.

"You know the nightgown in Rudy's place? The label said it came from a place called The Bare Essentials in White Plains, New York. Tonight I discovered that Frances has a nightgown from said boutique." Harvey had failed to foresee the implications of that remark, and stopped.

"I'm only a little more interested in this information than I am in how you came by it," Mickey said.

"Right," Harvey said. "Well, it's like this," he began and finished at the point where Frances emerged from the bedroom in her lingerie.

"I see. And you got close enough to read the label?" Mickey said. "Or did you simply tell Frances that you're a connoisseur of nightgown labels and would she mind if you had a little peek?"

"Let's just say that I was the victim of a vicious assault that momentarily left me in a position to read it. I ran screaming from her chamber almost immediately thereafter."

"I see," she said. "Well, she does have a good body for a woman her age. But, of course, you didn't notice her body."

"How could I? The nightgown was a floor-length flannel job with a hood. Now look, it took me a while to get it out of her, but she finally admitted to having had a short fling with Rudy. She said she didn't want to say so because of Felix, but I don't know whether to believe her. She said she didn't know anything about Rudy—that is, about what kind of trouble he was in. Maybe she's hiding something, maybe she's protecting somebody; but on the other hand, her behavior was perfectly logical for a manager's wife who was cheating with a relief pitcher. In the same way, if Frances is the one Rudy was in love with—if theirs was the relationship he said was doomed—then maybe all he meant by that was that Frances was already married. To his boss, no less. Then again, Rudy wasn't the sort of guy to let a detail like a husband get in the way of an affair. Unless he really loved her, of course."

"But Frances is in a different class than Rudy, in every sense."

"She knew that, but I doubt if Rudy did. He wasn't exactly into class consciousness. Anyway, maybe she did love him. Rudy had his charms, which even you'll admit. After all those years with Felix, Rudy might've been just the stud an aging beauty like Frances was looking for. Or there might've been something else going on. But if so, Frances isn't saying, and if she isn't saying, maybe it does have to do with Rudy's death. Am I going in circles or what?"

"Rhomboids," Mickey said.

"Okay, we've got Frances plus Ronnie Mateo plus three typewriters plus Cleavon's bat plus—plus, wait, the shrimp cocktail."

"What's that have to do with it?"

"Hold on a sec. My shrimp cocktail's at the door." Harvey got up, signed for the shrimp, and tipped the waiter three singles. "Can you believe this?" he said when he picked up the phone. "Eight bucks for four Gulf shrimp. And they're mealy."

"Do me a favor, Bliss. Don't get wrapped up in this thing."

Harvey finished chewing. "First you tell me I don't

care enough. Now I'm not supposed to get involved.
It's one thing for Ronnie Mateo to twist my arm, but
it's something else for you to—Mick, something very
weird was going on in Rudy's life."

"I'm not telling you to forget it, but you could get
hurt."

"We're talking about Rudy, Mick. Two weekends
ago, the three of us were eating johnnycakes in
Newport."

"I know. But I don't want you to get into trouble.
Remember, you're not a free agent anymore."

"What's that supposed to mean?"

"I own part of your contract now, Bliss."

"Oh, yeah?" He ate the second shrimp and fell back
on the bed. "As long as I get to renegotiate it after the
season."

"And what does that mean?" she said.

"It means we could always make the terms more
binding."

"Now you hold on a second, Blissberg. You know
I'm just a rookie in the game of love."

"You're a bonus baby where I'm concerned."

There was a pause. "I've run out of metaphors,"
Mickey said.

"Have a shrimp."

"I got a call from New York today."

"ABC?"

"They want me down there for a second interview."

"You think they might offer you something soon?"

"That's between God and Roone Arledge."


On Tuesday morning, Harvey walked through Back
Bay to the Ritz for French toast and coffee and learned
from the *Boston Globe* sports section that he was now
batting .302 and had dropped to the tenth spot in the
American League batting race. He skipped the account of last night's loss and skimmed a short feature
on Bobby Wagner headlined,"Will the Real Bobby

Wagner Please Stand Up?" It was another in a flurry of articles that seemed to appear in every city on the road, all of them provoked by Wagner's indifferent record. He was now 8 and 16, pitching in the shadow of lesser men like Van Auken and Crop. The *Globe* article was largely a review of his often brilliant career in Baltimore, plus a few standard paragraphs about the current season, buttressed by familiar comments from players and coaches around the league. One quote came from an unnamed source on the Jewels: "His arm's shot. He's been pitching on sheer guts."

Harvey studied the box scores over more coffee and had an idea. He turned the page to see where Minnesota, Rudy's old team, was playing that day. When he got back to his room at noon, he picked up the phone and called Jimmy Skeete, the Minnesota Twins' catcher, at the team's hotel in Oakland.

"I wake you?" Harvey asked.

"No, it's all right," Jimmy said. "I've been up for hours. I got hit with a pitch last night in my forearm, and the bugger woke me up at seven."

"Speaking of which, sorry about that collision in Providence." In July, he had run Skeete over, scoring from third on a sacrifice fly, and Skeete had sat out a few games with a bruised shoulder. "You know, I didn't get off so light, either. I couldn't turn my head to the left for a week."

"It wouldn't have hurt so much if you'd been out. But I'm warning you, Harvey, next time you come down the line I'm going to be carrying a switchblade."

"I wouldn't worry about a next time, Jimmy, the way we're playing. I don't think I've been as far as third base in a week."

"Yeah, I read the sports pages. I guess a murder in the clubhouse'll do it to you every time. God, it sounded gruesome. Have the cops figured it out yet? The papers aren't saying much."

"Neither is anyone else. It's a goddamn mystery. Look, you roomed with him last year, didn't you?"

"I still haven't caught up on my sleep. What a wild man."

"Yeah, but did he have any real enemies?"

"None I can think of. Unless you count Davis in Detroit. There was one season when Rudy must have plunked him in the ribs three times. The third time it cleared the benches. Of course, John does love to crowd that plate."

"For what it's worth," Harvey said, "Davis was nowhere near Providence the night Rudy was killed. Can you think of anything else?"

"I wish I could help you, Harvey. But for all his faults, the guy did not strike me as a murder victim."

"Did Rudy throw a lot of money around?"

"Throw it around? Naw. Just the usual, I guess. He sprang for dinner once in a while after a game."

"That's it?"

"Why're you asking? Was he throwing a lot of money around before he was killed?"

"That's the thing. As far as I can tell, he was generous only with his friends. Nothing more. But he had three thousand bucks on him when he was murdered. In very large bills."

"How large?"

"The kind that only banks'll make change for you. Listen, do you think Rudy was the kind of guy, you know, who'd want to make some easy money on the side?"

"No. I mean, he wasn't the greedy kind. I think it got to him that he was only making fifty, sixty grand here. No one likes playing alongside guys making three, four times that, but the guy wasn't a criminal. Anyway, he was making good money with you guys, wasn't he? I always thought of him as just a sort of lonely guy waiting to grow up."

"Yeah," Harvey said. "Listen, thanks. Go put some heat on your arm."

"Let me know if I can help, Harvey."

Harvey hung up, then dialed directory assistance in New York and got the number of an old schoolmate from the University of Massachusetts who worked in public relations in Manhattan. "Of course," the old classmate said, "of course I know Frances Shalhoub. Everyone in the business knows her. She was doing so well, we couldn't figure out why she just packed up and sold the firm." He gave Harvey what he wanted: the name and number of a former associate of Frances, one Sharon Meadows, who now worked for another public relations company in Manhattan.

"Ms. Meadows," he said after introducing himself on the phone, "I have a request of some, uh, sensitivity. I'm going to be in New York with the team on Thursday, and I'd like to take you out for a drink and ask you about Frances Shalhoub. Just general questions. And I've got to trust you not to tell anyone I've called you. Now, I know that's asking a lot, but—"

"But nothing," she broke in. "I'd love to talk about her. Really, she's one of my *most* favorite topics in the world."

The Providence Jewels filed into the plane late Wednesday night with the air of weary package-deal tourists wondering what city they were leaving and which one they were going to.

The Jewels were in fact leaving Boston, where they had lost 3–2 to the Red Sox on Tuesday night and 5–1 on Wednesday night, and heading for New York and a four-game series with the first-place Yankees. An eight-game losing streak had depleted the team's already small reserve of goodwill, and the players spread themselves out as far apart as they could among the seats. Even the flight attendants shared the prevailing mood. Roaming the aisles looking for unbuckled passengers, they smiled wanly, as if they had been hustled by one too many manufacturer's rep with an idea about how they would like to be entertained in the next city. Not even Rudy, Harvey thought, could have made any headway with them tonight.

Harvey found a seat by himself in first class. He hadn't been there long and was still trying to find his place in the Grant biography when Frances Shalhoub, wearing a white silk blouse and putty-colored blazer, dropped into the seat next to him. When he looked up from his book, she was busying herself with the in-flight magazine. She didn't say anything until they were somewhere over Connecticut. She was halfway through her martini and on her second bag of smoked almonds, and Harvey was nursing an after-shave sized bottle of California burgundy.

"I hope you didn't think I was asking anything of you the other night," she said.

"Why would I think that?"

"Forty-year-old women sometimes do crazy things when they're drunk."

"Really?" Harvey said, closing his book and putting it in the seat pocket. "I thought by the time they reached forty they lost all interest in sex."

"You must be thinking of fifty-three-year-old men," she said, creasing her empty foil smoked almond bag into a fan. "What're you doing in New York?"

Across the aisle in the row ahead of them, Felix was asleep with his head on his chest and his chin bunched up in grayish folds. "As far as I know, I'm playing four against the Yankees," Harvey said.

"You can be a creep, Harvey."

"Yeah, I know. But I try to hide it behind a devil-may-care demeanor."

"What're you doing in New York when you're not playing the Yankees?" She was now smoothing out the cocktail napkin on her tray table.

"I plan to stuff myself with culture. Museums, galleries, foreign films, Nathan's hot dogs with a lot of sauerkraut."

"Would you like to do something together?"

"If it doesn't involve sex, I might consider it."

Frances placed the olive from her martini on the tip of her tongue, and then both olive and tongue disappeared between her lips. "Why?" she said. "Is there something wrong with sex"

"No, there's nothing wrong with it. It's just that I'm spoken for at the moment."

"Oh, how quaint," she said. "You mean Mickey Slavin?"

"Is there something wrong with Mickey Slavin?"

"Nothing a little seasoning wouldn't improve," she

said. "Forty-year-old women have experience on their side."

Harvey emptied the rest of the wine into his plastic cup. "Except when it comes to the subject of Rudy, you're an extremely blunt person, Frances."

"When you get to my age, it's the only way to be. I could always be coy, but I'd be fifty by the time I got you in the sack, and neither of us would enjoy it as much."

"You really want me in the worst way, don't you?"

"No, Harvey, what I really want is an autographed baseball."

"Why so interested, Frances?"

"Let's see," she said, clapping her hands. "You're tall. You're single. You're reasonably good-looking. You have a trace of sophistication. You're one of the few people on this plane who doesn't think that mussels *marinière* has something to do with bodybuilding at the Coast Guard Academy. And it doesn't hurt that you're batting three hundred." She laughed.

Harvey didn't. "Is there a chance you might also be interested because you know something about Rudy's death that you're not saying and you don't like it that I'm so curious and you'd like to buy me off by getting me to fall in love with you?"

Frances picked up the foil bag and squeezed it into a ball. "I'm glad this is only a thirty-minute flight," she said.

"The way I look at it, Frances, is that you were sleeping with Rudy and you also sit in the dugout, and those are two pretty good positions in which to learn something. Maybe you don't know anything, but I'm not convinced. You act as if you want to hide something from me, and what I can't figure out is why you would."

"I told the police what I know, and that's all you need to know." Her voice had iced over. "Don't forget whom you're talking to, Harvey. If you keep it up, you could find yourself sitting on the bench for the rest of the season."

"Oh, that's great," Harvey said, forcing a laugh. "One minute you're propositioning me, and the next you're benching me. I thought Felix managed this ball club."

She tried to drink out of her martini glass, but there was nothing left in it. "Felix listens to—" She stopped and broke into a smile as genuine as one of Pro-Gem's three-dollar charm bracelets. "You do have a way of yanking my chain, don't you? Look, I don't blame you for being upset. I am, too. I can't tell you how sad it was to pick up Rudy's foster parents at the airport. It was heartbreaking. They were such a lovely couple, and they acted as if they had lost a real son." Frances patted her skirt. "And I don't blame you for being put out with my, uh—advances, but I do like you. I was afraid it was"—her voice was girlish now—"because you don't find me attractive. I should've thought of that."

"You're right. You should've thought of that, Frances. But it's not the reason."

"It's really Mickey?"

"Just call me old-fashioned." Harvey reached forward to retrieve his book. "By the way, Frances, do you happen to know anybody who has a thing about rats?"

"Rats?"

"You know, who likes to break their little necks and hang them up by the tail to dry."

She made a disgusted face. "Harvey," she said, "have you ever considered getting professional help?"

It was the last thing they said to each other for some time.


On Thursday afternoon, September 6, at four-thirty, Harvey walked into the visitors' dugout at Yankee Stadium in his street clothes and looked out at the

cavernous park with a childlike awe that six years in
the majors had failed to diminish. He considered himself a connoisseur of old ball parks. He appreciated
them in the way that a carpenter admires the beauty
of a well-crafted—but now rotting—piece of furniture.
Cincinnati's Crosley Field, Pittsburgh's Forbes Field,
the Polo Grounds, Brooklyn's Ebbets Field, Philly's
Connie Mack Stadium, St. Louis's Sportsman's Park,
D.C.'s Griffith Stadium, Kansas City's Municipal
Stadium—he had never played in those great historic
structures. There were only a few of that generation
left. The rest had made way for too many symmetrical
suburban parks with candy-colored seats and parking
lots you could land a DC-10 in. Harvey couldn't understand why people enjoyed watching the game in
places that looked like they had popped out of a giant
injection-molding machine. Baseball itself was an asym-
metrical game, full of randomness and decisive acci-
dents. Line drives were caught while apologetic short
flies fell for extra-base hits. One weak ground ball
found its way through the infield and brought in the
winning run while another, harder hit, became the
game-ending double-play. The new ball parks—big,
perfect concrete chafing dishes—looked as if they
wanted to deny that the game was unfair.

Yankee Stadium had escaped, more or less. The
renovations it had undergone in the 1970s had marred
its original grandeur, but it was still strange and
lop-sided and full of echoes. However, Harvey had
another reason to stand in the dugout watching the
nearly empty field. It was where Rudy Furth had
pitched his best game of the season, maybe the best of
his career. In late May, he had come in for starting
pitcher Stan Crop in the third, and for seven innings
Rudy had pitched one-hit baseball and picked up a 4–1
victory.

"Just think, Professor," he had said to Harvey on
the bench before the team went out for the bottom of

the ninth. "Only fifty or sixty more games like this one and you can reserve a seat for me in the Hall of Fame."

Harvey knew what it was like to play so far over your head you could look down and see yourself in action. Three or four times in his career he had enjoyed a string of games when he actually believed he could will his bat to hit the ball anywhere he pleased. For three days in Texas in July, he had gone 11-for-13 at the plate, and the two outs had been the result of sparkling catches of line drives in the outfield. He felt he was drawing on such remarkable, neglected powers that he had had to ask Campy Strulowitz to verify that his whole style and batting stance had not been inexplicably altered by something beyond his control. When the team left Texas, he had turned back into just another ball player.

"This park gives me the chills." Harvey started at the voice next to him.

"Well, well. Detective Linderman. What brings you to New York, business or pleasure?"

"I'm mixing them," he said. His crew cut was shorter than before, and his crusty scalp showed through the bristles. Under his seersucker jacket he was wearing a navy blue polo shirt with little white sailboats all over it and a lilac collar. Where his stomach was, the boats sailed farther apart.

"What's the business part?" Harvey said.

"Tell me about this Steve Wilton."

"Keep the ball up and in, and if you get ahead on the count, play chin music. He scares easily at the plate." Harvey smiled.

Linderman matched the smile in size but not spirit. "He didn't scare too easy a few years ago in the minors. He was booked for malicious assault when he punched out the lights of a guy on the other team. The guy's jaw was wired for six months. Wilton wriggled off with a fine, a public apology, and a dozen roses.

He's the only guy on your team with any kind of criminal record."

Harvey hawked. "That doesn't surprise me. Steve'll never make the diplomatic corps."

"That's all?"

"That's all what?"

"All you have to say about him?"

"You're running the investigation, Linderman. I'm just trying to finish the season at three hundred."

"I'm wondering if there isn't something you're not telling me, Harvey. I know ball players have loyalties, not that I think the jerk who crammed Furth in that whirlpool is a teammate of yours."

"Rudy was my best friend on the club. *That's* my loyalty right there. As for Wilton, if you want me to suggest a motive, you're out of luck."

Linderman petted the top of his crew cut with a palm. "Yeah, yeah, yeah, the market in motives is very depressed these days."

"Where do typewriters fit in?" The two of them stood side by side watching a member of Yankee Stadium's grounds crew water the yellowing path of grass between home plate and the mound.

"Typewriters?" Linderman said. "Oh, the boys are tracing them back in Providence. What's the talk in the clubhouse about all this?"

"No talk in the clubhouse. At least not where I'm concerned. Someone put a dead rat in my locker in Providence last weekend."

Linderman's eyes brightened. "You could've told me about it."

"I'm a big boy now," Harvey said.

"Only one of your teammates would do something like that, right?"

"I guess. I wonder who the naughty boy was."

"Well, I don't think it's funny, Harvey."

"I don't think you have to worry about my thinking

anything's funny at this point," Harvey said, too sharply.

Linderman worked his mouth; he didn't appear to be listening. "What a way to make a living," he finally muttered.

"Yours or mine?"

"You ever feel silly out there, wearing knickers at your age?"

Harvey unwrapped a stick of gum and chewed it around before answering. "How I look at it, Linderman, is that there're some guys who know how to fix car engines. It may be all they know how to do, but they do it better than anyone else. It may not take any great genius, but they took the time to learn how to do it well, and you could offer them a big job in an office and they wouldn't take it because they're happy fixing cars. I'm a guy who knows how to catch baseballs better than almost anyone else. It's what I do, and I'm lucky they pay guys more for being good at catching baseballs in the twentieth century than they do for fixing cars. But I'd do it anyway, knickers and all." It was only half true, but he wasn't going to ruin the effect by telling Linderman he could actually think of several jobs he would gladly take now, jobs where he'd be able to wear pants that went all the way down to his shoes. "It's good to be good at what you do."

"That's touching, Harvey. Very touching."

"How good are you at what you do, Linderman?"

The detective's expression split the difference between a grin and a sneer. "I'm like these Bic pens," he said, touching his breast pocket. "They're not fancy, but they always work."

Harvey hawked on the dugout floor. "If they always work, how come you have so many of them?"

"What's that supposed to mean?"

"Nothing. Just a bad joke."

"No, I'm serious, Harvey. Why the slap at me?" His eyes got small and dark.

"It's nothing," he said, but he knew he was going to say it anyway. "1 heard you had some trouble in the sixties, that's all."

Linderman looked around, then poked a square finger in Harvey's chest. "I want to know something, good buddy. Are you one of those guys that's got to run the whole show? Is that what I'm dealing with here?"

"No," Harvey said blandly.

Linderman hiked up his pants. "Good. Because if you are, you may have some trouble right here in the eighties." His pants fell back down around his hips, and he left them there. "What a smart-ass," he muttered and walked back toward the clubhouse.

At seven-thirty, the Jewels were all standing in the Yankee Stadium visitors' dugout listening to a man with three chins and legs like duffel bags sing the national anthem at home plate. By seven-thirty, they had gone down one-two-three in the top of the first. Manomaitis popped up to third for the first out. Harvey stepped in, looked at a slider low and away, and lined the next pitch, another slider from Bruce Taunton, to that vast terrain that is left center in Yankee Stadium. Hazelwood was an eight-dollar cab ride from the ball, and Harvey was already thinking triple on his way to second when he looked up and saw Hazelwood flag the ball down, taking the last ten feet in a horizontal position. Hazelwood sat cross-legged way out there on the outfield grass, holding up his gloved hand with the ball in it for the second base umpire to see. Forty-five thousand fans got to their feet cheering. Harvey loped back, head down, to the dugout.

He had barely shoved his batting helmet back into its cubby hole when Cleavon bounded Taunton's first pitch to Rumpling, who threw him out by two steps.

Harvey found Cleavon's first baseman's glove and infield ball and carried them out to him at first base, then ran out to center. Something didn't feel right

about his own glove when he slipped it on. He knew it
so well—it was a MacGregor with an open web he had
been using for five years—that he would have noticed
if the thumb strap had been tightened a sixteenth of
an inch. But it wasn't the thumb strap. There was
something wedged deep into the glove's middle finger.
When he got to center, he reached into the finger and
pulled out a small piece of paper folded into quarters.
When he opened it, he saw that it was a corner that
had been ripped off a larger piece of wrapping paper,
and there was a message on it, printed in childlike
block letters:

PLAY BALL NOT PRIVATE EYE
OR YOU MAY BE THE NEXT TO DIE

 He knew who hadn't written it. Ronnie Mateo's style of intimidation was less poetic, and he probably wasn't even in New York. Someone could have been acting as Ronnie's messenger, but that someone had to be connected with the club. His glove hadn't been lying unattended in the dugout for more than twenty minutes before the game while he took batting practice; it was unlikely that anyone not with the club would have walked casually into the dugout and sifted through the various gloves until he found the one with BLISS written along the thumb in black marker. Whether or not Ronnie Mateo had had anything to do with it, the note was the work of somebody on the Jewels, somebody who would look perfectly natural picking up a glove, somebody, perhaps, who also liked to handle rats. It couldn't have been Frances; if she wanted to send messages, she would find more civil ways. Had somebody seen him talking with Linderman and, putting that together with what Harvey had said to Bob Lassiter, figured that Harvey knew more than was good for him? If so, somebody was giving him too much credit.

Harvey juggled Huddleston's easy fly ball before catching it to retire the Yankees in the bottom of the first, and jogged in on heavy legs. He was playing one game against New York in front of forty-five thousand people. He was playing another, but he didn't know against whom.

The Providence dugout was quiet in the way dug-
outs are quiet when they're occupied in September by
teams with nowhere to go. Harvey tossed his glove on
the bench near the end where Felix and Frances were
sitting and sat down next to it. Felix clapped his
hands slowly, like a man doing it underwater. Frances had a clipboard on her crossed legs and was doo-
dling in the margin of a pitching chart. Harvey looked
the other way, down a frieze of profiles: Salta, Rapp,
Penzenik, Wilton, Van Auken, Wagner, Crop, Stiles,
Manomaitis, Byers, Vedrine, Smith, Bayman, Bentz,
Battle, Potter-Lawn. He looked across the field to the
distant Jewels bull pen at Marlette, Other, O'Donnell,
Weatherhead, Storella, Charness. One of them was a
good enough poet to rhyme "eye" and "die."

Harvey turned to Felix on his right. "How's it going,
skipper?"

Felix closed a fist over his big nose and milked it a
few times. His eyes were rheumy. "Going good," he
said, "going good. I think we're about to move into a
winning posture, but we've got to get mad to win. Mad
as the snake who married the garden hose. We've got
to get mad and play like there's no tomorrow. This
guy Taunton can be taken to the cleaners."

Frances lifted her eyes from her clipboard, and they
met Harvey's for an instant. He turned away and
clapped once loudly.

"Let's jump on Taunton!" he shouted. "Let's jump on
this guy and eat him up!"

Harvey didn't want to leap to conclusions, but the
Jewels seemed to be staging a rally. A Randy Eppich
double, a Steve Wilton single, a John Rapp sacrifice
fly, a Charlie Penzenik double, an intentional pass to
Les Byers, and a Rodney Salta bloop single gave Providence a 3–0 lead and runners at the corners. Taunton
bore down and fanned Chuck Manomaitis for the second out, bringing Harvey to the plate.

"Some powerhouse ball club you guys got tonight,"

said DiFazio, the Yankee catcher, as Harvey pawed at
the batter's box with his left spike.

"I think somebody forgot to tell us we were playing
a first-place team. We really hate to embarrass you
guys like this."

"How 'bout a curve to start you out?" DiFazio said.

"As long as you put it right about here." Harvey
waved a horizontal hand at his waist.

"Would that be the usual, sir, or an off-speed curve?"

"Surprise me," Harvey said and guessed, correctly,
a slider. He put the fat part of the bat on the fat part
of the ball and drove it to the same spot as in the first
inning. This time Hazelwood didn't have the proper
cab fare, and the ball rolled past him, a white pea on a
shiny green cloth under a black Bronx sky. Center
fielder Bob Corley ran it down quickly in the gap with
a backhanded stab, and as Harvey touched the inside
corner of second he suddenly had doubts about reaching third. But he wanted a triple. Doubles were banal;
there were too many ways to get them. Home runs
were too sudden, and the excitement was only in where
the ball went, not in what was happening on the field.
But triples were aberrations, the rare product of location, circumstances, and speed. The game was not
built for triples. Rudy had understood about triples. "I
never mind giving up a triple," he had said once.

Carlos Bonesoro at third was trying to decoy Harvey. He was standing casually with his feet straddling
the bag, watching Harvey, who was not fooled and
knew a good relay from Rumpling would beat him. He
put his head down and drove for the bag. Tony
Cantalupa was on his knees in the coach's box, signal-
ing him to slide toward the home plate side of the
base. Harvey faded with a hook slide and caught the
base with his right toe as the slide carried his body
into foul territory. Bonesoro gave him a sweep tag and
fell on top of him. Through the dust, Harvey looked
for the ump. Toby Kline pointed at Harvey, as if

denouncing him at a political rally, and then jerked his arm back and shrieked, "The man is out! Oh, yeah," he repeated, "the man is out! C'mon, Harvey, pick yourself up."

It was a close play, and Harvey would have bitched about the call, except for two things. On a close play with a sweep tag, the baserunner rarely feels the tag at all; he had no idea whether Bonesoro had gotten him or not. The second thing was that he had turned his left ankle when his spike caught the dirt on the slide, and the pain had temporarily taken his breath away. He lay where he was, on his back, while Tony screamed at Toby Kline.

"Toby! His toe was there! The man just executed a perfect hook slide! Bonesoro missed him! Carlos, you tell him," the third base coach yelled after the Yankee third baseman. "Carlos, come back here and tell the man you tagged air!"

"No, no, no, Tony," Kline was saying. "He got him on the shoulder before he hit the bag."

"Toby! Listen to me! The man was on the bag for a week before Bonesoro was anywhere near him!"

"Now look, Tony. Let's be reasonable. You already got five runs out of the deal. What do you want?"

Arky Bentz, the Jewels' trainer, was kneeling over Harvey now, manipulating his ankle. He took an aerosol container of ethyl chloride out of his pocket and sprayed it over Harvey's sock. Arky helped him hobble back to the dugout on his frozen ankle. "I think that's it for tonight, Professor," he said and took him down the runway to the clubhouse.

Duncan Frye was sitting on a folding chair next to a table with a transistor radio on it. "The radio said it was a nice slide, Professor," he said.

Arky removed Harvey's shoe and sock, looked at the ankle again, tied on an ice pack with an Ace bandage, and went back to the dugout. Harvey sat with his left leg up on a chair and listened to the radio with Dunc.

Rick Stiles, who had gone in to play center for Harvey, made a nice running catch on a Hazelwood drive. But Stan Crop got into trouble, and New York got a couple back in the inning. Dunc wandered into the trainer's room and returned with a pint of apricot brandy, two Dixie cups, and a paper bag.

"Let's you and me have a nip, Professor," he said. "Purely for medicinal purposes." He poured two fingers in each cup and handed one to Harvey.

"Whyn't you go out and look at the game?" Harvey said. "You don't have to keep me company."

"I've seen nine hundred thousand baseball games in my life. Nothing new in it for me." He reached for a dirty towel in the bottom of a locker and folded it and dropped it to the right of his chair. He shot about three ounces of tobacco juice on it.

"Dunc, what's it like drinking brandy with chewing tobacco in your mouth?"

"What's it like without it?" he said and fired into the towel again. He nodded at Harvey's ankle. "Bad?"

"Nah. Two-day sprain if I coddle it. What's in the bag?"

Dunc picked it up off the floor. "Some stuff of Rudy's."

"Stuff of Rudy's?"

"Here, take it. There's not much in there, just some stuff I found on top of his locker after the cops had gone through and taken everything else. You two being friends, I thought you'd want it. I got to carrying it around for some reason, but I'm not the sentimental type."

There were only a few things in the bag. One of the pocket combs Ronnie Mateo had given Angel Vedrine, a half-finished pack of Camel Lights, a pair of Polaroid wraparound sunglasses, an errant pair of dirty sanitary hose, and a hardcover book about real estate investment. Harvey remembered that Rudy and his foster father had invested some money in a town house complex somewhere in Wisconsin.

"I don't know what you want to do with it," Dunc said, pouring himself another finger of brandy. "You could just give it to the cops if you want."

"Sure, I could do that," Harvey said. "Why were you carrying the stuff around with you?"

"I don't know. Like I say, I'm not the sentimental type." A glob of fresh tobacco juice landed audibly on top of the others. "But he was an all right kid, and I miss him, Professor. I don't guess there was many guys here who liked him much, except maybe you and me and maybe one or two others who could stand his ratchet-jawing. So I don't know why I held on to the stuff, except maybe that, and you and me being the ones to find him and all."

"What do you make of it, Dunc?"

"Damnedest thing."

"You hear anybody talking?"

"More like the guys are making a point out of not talking."

Harvey wanted to show him the death threat, but didn't. "Rudy never gave you a clue?"

"Uh-uh."

"And the night you left him in the whirlpool, he didn't say anything unusual?"

"Nope."

"Did it seem like he might be waiting for someone?"

"Nope. He was just like I'd seen him on other nights when he stayed late to soak."

"And you're sure he was the only one left in the clubhouse?"

"Far as I know, Professor. 'Course I didn't look every—I guess there're a few places you could hide. Sometimes I get this thought about Rudy's killer waiting down in the catacombs, just waiting for everybody to clear out. Seems to me whoever killed him would've had to know he was already in the whirlpool and was fixing to be there awhile."

"So you're thinking what I'm thinking?" Harvey asked.

"That it was one of the guys?"

"Or somebody who knew one of the guys who knew that Rudy liked to soak. But I guess that doesn't get us too far."

"Here you go," Dunc said and poured more brandy into Harvey's cup. They listened to the game, which the Yankees now led 6–5 in the fifth. In the sixth, Dunc got up to putter around the clubhouse and lay out fresh towels. They had worked their way down through most of the pint, and Harvey's ankle felt pretty good. He undressed, showered, and eased into his street clothes—a pair of lightweight gray slacks, a white shirt, and an old pair of penny loafers. Dunc helped him wrap his ankle up again with more ice, and by the time Harvey made it down the runway to the dugout, it was the bottom of the eighth and the Jewels were down 8–6. The noise of the Yankee Stadium crowd, an endless liquid tittering, surprised him after the silence of the clubhouse.

In the top of the ninth, Chuck Manomaitis walked to lead off, but was erased when Rick Stiles hit into a tailor-made 6–4–3 double play, and the Jewels were one out away from their ninth straight loss. Cleavon blooped a single to left, but when Randy bounced one down to Rumpling at short, the dugout began to pack up. However, the ball hit the lip where the infield grass meets the dirt and skidded under Rumpling's glove and out into short left center. Two men on and Steve Wilton was up.

Steve soaked a 3–2 count for all it was worth, fouling off five straight fastballs from reliever Jerry Flacke. Some of the players stood in the dugout and told Steve to have an eye and be a hitter and bear down up there. The next Flacke fastball was in Wilton's wheelhouse, and Flacke turned away in disgust. The ball swam up into the night and reached the apex of its arc tiny and white against the sky. Hazelwood huddled in a crouch against the left field wall, waiting to leap, but as the ball descended, his body relaxed and straightened, and he turned back toward the infield, slapping his glove against his leg. The ball fell in the fifth row, and the Jewels were leading 9–8.

When Steve crossed the plate in his high-waisted, self-satisfied trot, a few of the players went out to greet him and clap him on the back and rub his head. In the dugout, Felix got up and tousled Wilton's hair. "How to be, big kid, way to hack it," Campy hollered, "you're the stick up there." To show there were no hard feelings, Harvey yelled, "Nice job, Steve." It would have been just like the old days, if there had been any old days for the Providence Jewels.

Marcus Marlette mopped up in the bottom of the ninth, and the Jewels had broken the string. They were 64 and 74, still five games ahead of Toronto, and Harvey, with his 1-for-2 showing, was batting .302.

Back at the Warwick Hotel, just before eleven, Harvey asked at the front desk if there were any messages for him.

"Sir, may I inquire how you fared tonight?" the desk clerk said. The British inflection covered his Queens accent about as thoroughly as *The New York Times* covered professional wrestling.

"Sir"—Harvey winked—"the awesome Yankee juggernaut was repelled by the lowly Providence armada by a tally of nine to eight."

"My felicitations," the clerk said and gave him a note scrawled on hotel paper in a large looping hand. It said, "You'll find me in the bar. Sharon Meadows."

Sharon Meadows waved energetically to Harvey from a table in the middle of the bar, and he hobbled over. She was a small woman in her late thirties with short black hair cut to look like a helmet. She had on a peach-colored blouse and over it a magenta Chinese tunic with embroidered parrots and pagodas and over that some kind of fuzzy shawl. She was wearing too many clothes, too much makeup, and too much jewelry. Her smile revealed a lot of gum, and she spoke with the adjectival incontinence of a press release.

"Please don't apologize," she said after Harvey excused himself for being late. "Apologies are so useless most of the time, don't you think? I mean, they're *squandered* on such small occasions when we really ought to save them up for those *larger* moments when we really need them. I'm so *happy* you won tonight. The Yankees deserve a periodic lesson in humility. Winning must be such an *exhilarating* experience."

Harvey asked her to move to a more obscure table at the back of the bar, in case Frances Shalhoub made a practice of drinking in hotel lounges. As they threaded their way among the tables, he said, "Well, you sound like a baseball fan."

"Oh, I *am*. It's such a tranquil, yet somehow passionate game. It's somehow larger than life. I knew who you were the moment you came in because you have that marvelous, sturdy, athletic, *tall* look about you."

"I'm only five-one. It must be the lighting."

"You know—here, let me get the waitress—you know, it was Frances who first exposed me to baseball. We were doing some public relations for the Mets—special events and such—and I went to some of the games and met some of the players. I mean, they were such *driven* individuals, yet so relaxed at the same time. I don't suppose that football players are quite like that. Their sport isn't so . . . so what—so leisurely, so pastoral. Baseball absolutely fascinates me, it really does. I must confess"—she blushed into her drink—"I must confess that I'm somewhat awed just meeting you. I mean, baseball is something of a religion in this country, isn't it, and that makes you what—that makes you, it gives you an aura, a kind of *glow*. I'm so pleased to meet you."

Harvey ordered a bourbon on the rocks and tried to grab a piece of the conversation. "Well, I'm pleased to meet you, too. I always wondered what Frances's former associate was like."

"Oh, Frances, of course. You know, I almost forgot why we—you know, it's a mystifyingly funny thing how the mind works, how it—of course, you wanted to ask me something about Frances. The Wicked Witch of the East herself."

"Wicked Witch? Why's that?"

She nibbled from a bowl of dry-roasted cashews. "Oh, I guess I felt like poor Dorothy compared to her, I really did. The PR business, you know, has its share of kooks and crazies. It's such an *intense* way to make a living. And there's so much hype, so much exaggeration of what people really are. PR people tend to start believing all those marvelous things and simply lose their perspective."

"I can well imagine."

"And so, to make a long story short, it's so highly competitive, and so many people will do just *anything* to get ahead, but, what I mean is—"

"But what, Sharon?"

"What I mean is that Frances was, well, at least as far as *my* moral ethics and value systems were concerned, Frances did get—get what? Out of bounds, you might say. Well, I suppose that's why she got ahead. I mean, other people I know in this business actually used to envy my working for a successful firm like Frances's. If only they knew. Well, she did one thing, I remember—well, but usually she would just treat clients in a kibbitzing but underneath, I guess the word for it is *mean* way."

"For instance?"

"Well, for instance, we represented several restaurants in New York, and there was one very fancy, very *visible* restaurant whose account we were trying to get—I mean, it's like you couldn't check your coat for less than ten dollars—and, well, I remember Frances on the phone with the owner, and she was simply *merciless* with him, but I guess in a funny sort of way."

"A funny sort of way."

"You know, Frances has got what—a certain patina of charm, and so she'd say things like, 'Alan, if you don't give me your business, I swear to God I'll never talk to you again, I mean it, you know what a great job we did with that French place on Fifty-third, and they're absolutely in your league, Alan.' Stuff like that. Oh, and, 'Not only that, Alan, if you don't come with me, I'll make sure that no one I know—and I do know a lot of people in this city—ever sets foot in your place again. Alan'—this is just how she sounded—'Alan, you know I have a way with restaurants, and I'll hate you for the rest of my life if you don't come with me. But worst of all, Alan, believe me, you'll hate yourself. You wouldn't want all that hanging over your head, would you?' Honestly, it was so *New York*. She would say, 'Alan, it just so happens that a couple of big clients of mine are looking for a place to hold their

Christmas parties, and I don't mean finger sandwiches and crudités, either, Alan. We're talking sixty, seventy dollars a head, and it would be a shame if you weren't in a position to get that business, because I know you would do a perfectly splendid job.' "

"You mean she'd threaten them?"

"Well, exactly. You know, she'd plead and threaten and just keep at it to the point where I would be sitting there at my desk listening to her on the phone with this look of *utter* disbelief on my face, to the point where—well, but she did treat the people who worked for her extremely well, you understand. I'm not complaining; it's just that she would do *anything* to get clients."

"Anything to get clients" was the phrase Resnick of ABC had used to describe Frances on Monday night in Boston.

"I mean, she wouldn't resort to kidnapping," Sharon Meadows went on. "She wouldn't lie down on Fifth Avenue and threaten to take her own *life* just to get an account, I mean, but she would cheat and she would lie. Well, of course, I don't have to tell you that she didn't have any clients who were interested in having Christmas parties at this restaurant." She finally touched her Pernod and Perrier. "That wasn't the worst of it, of course."

"It wasn't?"

"Oh, no. You know, there was this computer dating service a couple of years ago that was trying to decide between us and another PR firm. Frances got wind of which other firm it was, and she wanted this account in the worst possible way, so she called the head of the dating service and told him to come to the office so we could really sell him on what we could offer them. So this macho type—I mean, the guy looked like he was wearing a pair of rolled-up sweat socks in his crotch—this macho man comes by and Frances and I take him into the conference room and we lay out our wares and Frances is pounding the table, telling him absolutely *everything* we'd do to give them the *deepest* possible market penetration, the *highest* recognition factor. And then suddenly—and I mean I was not prepared for this one—suddenly she tells him she knows that they're talking with another firm—which happens to be run by two *wonderful* gals I know personally—and Frances suddenly tells this macho man, 'You can't possibly go with this other firm, and I'll tell you why. It's because the women who run it are lesbians, and the last thing a dating service needs is to be represented by two goddamn *lesbians*.' And, of course, they're *not* lesbians. They're not lesbians at *all*. But Frances got the account."

Harvey drained his bourbon.

"And you know what I can't figure out?"

"What's that, Sharon?"

"I can't fathom for an instant how a sweet man like Felix ended up with a woman like Frances."

"That utterly *fascinates* me, too," Harvey said. He swiveled and scanned the bar to make sure that neither of the Shalhoubs had sneaked in for a nightcap. "On the basis of what you know about her, what do you think her interest in baseball really is?"

"Oh, I think it's *intense*, which is the way she does everything. I read somewhere, I think, that she sits in the dugout with Felix. Just like her, you know, close to the action."

"What do you make of that?"

"Well, if you owned a piece of something, wouldn't you *absolutely* want to have a say in how it's run?"

Harvey blanched. "Frances doesn't own a piece of the Jewels."

Sharon shook some bracelets down her forearm. "Of course, I can't be absolutely sure, but I'm almost positive that's why Frances sold the firm. She bought into the team. I mean, she wasn't going to sell an *immensely* successful business and move to that dumpy city just to be with poor Felix."

"How much of the team do you think she owns?" Harvey had begun to gobble cashews.

"That I simply couldn't say. The firm was sold for nearly a million and a half, and then, of course, there's the family money. Her father made a mint in scrap metal or some dreary thing like that. Frances is *very* restless, you know, can't stay put, and she's always looking for the opening, always looking."

Harvey fiddled with the table lamp. "You're sure she invested in the team?"

"Like I say, I can't be *absolutely* sure, but I do remember early last fall when she said to me, she said, 'Sharon, I don't know what owning part of a major league baseball team is like, but I've never failed at anything in my life.'"

Harvey's ankle had begun reminding him that it was sprained. He winced, more noticeably than he might have had he not been stricken with the need to take leave of Sharon Meadows. "Excuse me," he said, "but as you probably saw, I did something to my ankle tonight, and it's acting up."

"Oh, my goodness," she gasped, as if he had just revealed a terminal condition. "Oh, it must be so painful, and here I am, going on and on about Frances and probably boring you to tears. Does it hurt badly? Let me buy you another drink, and we'll talk about something else. We'll talk about baseball. I'd *love* to know what it's really like."

Harvey made a particularly good wince. "I think all this ankle needs is a little ice and a little rest."

Sharon's face fell, then rose hopefully. "You're sure?"

"I'm sure. But thanks." He reached for his wallet.

She put her hand on his arm. "I'll get this one. But look, I'm in the book. I mean, that is, if you're in New York again and—Well, look, anyway, it's been *awfully* nice, and just between you and me, you will let the Yankees win one or two from you guys, won't you?"

There were two things he liked about her. The first was that she had given him information that sounded extremely useful. The second was that he had not even had to ask for it. In his room, lying on his back on the floral bedspread, he dialed Mickey's number in Providence. After Sharon Meadows's torrent of words, Mickey's voice was soothing.

"How's the ankle?"

"Word travels fast," he said.

"So does the electronic transmission of light waves into radio waves and then into light rays. We had the game on television in the newsroom tonight. Nice win. And you looked safe to me, by the way. Your sprain also came over the sports wire. It must be nice to twist your ankle and have the whole world know about it within minutes. So how is it?"

"I wish you were here to kiss it."

"I don't do ankles."

"How are you?"

"A little depressed. They've been on my case at the station. I don't think they like the fact that I'm talking with ABC, so they've got me doing a lot of soft features as punishment. They had me fill in for Gail today and do a story on the biggest cauliflower at a farmer's market in Rehoboth."

"I always thought the station's coverage of the cabbage family was pretty weak."

"Yuk, yuk," she said. "And Providence depresses me."

"How could you say such a thing? It's the heartbeat of the nation."

"Sorry, Bliss. I'm too tired to laugh tonight." She demonstrated by yawning into the mouthpiece. "I mean, where *is* Providence? I have this fantasy that I'm going to look at a map of New England one day and it's not going to be there. And no one will miss it. How come you're in such a good mood?"

"Hardly. I saw Linderman at Yankee Stadium before the game, and there're still no leads except for Ronnie Mateo. It's unbelievable."

"Did you hear that the baseball commissioner's announced a twenty-five-thousand-dollar reward for information leading to the arrest and conviction?"

"Certainly can't hurt. But what I really wanted to tell you, Mick, is that someone stuffed a death threat in my glove tonight. I found it when I went out to center in the bottom of the first."

"No."

"Yes. Wait a second, here it is: 'Play ball, not private eye, or you may be the next to die.' "

"My God, what's going on? Bliss, maybe it's time to let Linderman take over."

"No one's stopping him."

"If you got killed, it would put a real damper on our relationship. Sounds like someone on the team's getting pretty nervous."

"Mick, after the game I had drinks with a woman who used to work for Frances at her PR firm in New York."

"Harvey!" She hadn't used his first name since they'd met.

"Mick, according to Sharon Meadows, Frances is baseball's answer to Muammar el-Qaddafi. Guess what?"

"What?"

"This woman is almost certain Frances owns part of the team."

"Can you be sure?"

"I can find out for sure."

"And if she does, where does that fit in?"

"Damned if I know," Harvey said.

After a pause, Mickey said, "I don't know if nice Jewish boys should be getting mixed up in things like this." Another pause. "What else did this woman say?"

"Now you're interested, aren't you?" Harvey told her more about Sharon Meadows.

"So much for sisterhood," she said when he was through. "Frances sounds perfectly charming. But do me a favor, Bliss, and just lie low, okay? Don't stick your neck out. Someone out there is getting pretty serious about you. Frances probably isn't even involved in this thing."

"That would be nice."

"Nice?"

"The less I have to do with that woman, the better. But if she *is* involved. . . ." Harvey ran out of words.

"Can't you leave it alone?"

Harvey said nothing.

"You feel guilty about Rudy, don't you?"

Harvey said more nothing.

"Are you there?" she said.

"There're some pieces missing, Mick," he said.

"I'll say" She blended a sigh and a groan. "I'm coming down to New York on Monday to see ABC. I'll miss you."

"We'll be in Baltimore," Harvey said.

"So I guess I'll see you in Providence, then. In a week."

"Yeah. Be good, Mick," he said and hung up, visualizing himself and Mickey as two little dots moving randomly across a map.

He went to the desk in his room and found some creamy Warwick Hotel stationery and made three lists.

## RUDY

slept with Frances
presents for Mick and me
typewriters
$3,000
Wisconsin real estate
seemed depressed on night of murder

## FRANCES

gets her own way
slept with Rudy
owns stock in team?
helps Felix in dugout: how?
wants to sleep with me

## HARVEY

doesn't want to sleep with her
rat
death threat
nice guy
now batting .302
would really like some Japanese food

Harvey looked it over a few times, but the only item that caught his attention was the last one under his name. He threw on a sports jacket, hobbled down to the street, and took a cab to a place on Columbus Avenue that served sushi all night.

"I hurt about your hankle," Mr. Molikoff said in a crusty Eastern European accent, sitting in the wingback chair in Harvey's hotel room on Friday morning. He was a gaunt man with a small, mottled face and a blizzard of white hair that formed a high drift on one side of his head. He was wearing a brown suit that probably was not the best one he owned, and there was room for another neck in his yellowing shirt collar. Mr. Molikoff had phoned an hour earlier from the offices of a Yiddish daily newspaper in New York to ask for an interview. Now he held an incongruous reporter's notebook in his large hands, ribbed with veins. "I hope it's not in too bat shape," he said.

Harvey was reclining on the bed with a hotel heating pad wrapped around his ankle. "With heat on it," he answered, "I should be back in the lineup in a day or two."

"That's goot," Molikoff said, finding an empty pipe and sucking airily on it. "I thought I might ask you about the relationship between baseball and a Jew."

Harvey had other things on his mind, but he had agreed to the interview, and he forced himself to pay attention. At least it did not promise to be an ordinary clubhouse give-and-take. "I guess I don't think about it much," he said, stuffing another pillow behind him. "You know, there're only three of us in the majors now, and I don't think anybody notices anymore, except a reporter now and then. It's not the most obvious career for a Jew, but"—he unclasped his hands behind his head and held them out—"here I am."

"There is no, let us say, anti-Semitism?" Molikoff was writing with birdlike movements as he talked.

"I remember when I was with Boston, once one of my black teammates said to me in the clubhouse, 'Your people are the ones who own all the slums in the ghetto, aren't they?' And I told him, 'Yeah, that's right. And your people are the ones who're shiftless and eat watermelons all the time.' After that, we became fast friends."

Molikoff removed his pipe in order to smile appreciatively. "Let me tell you, bink a Jew in baseball used to be sometink," he said, suddenly shaking a fist proudly at Harvey. "I've studied this. In nineteen forty-one, the New York Giants opened the season with four Jews. Let us see, Harry Feldman was pitchink, Harry Dannink was catchink, and in the outfield, you hat Sid Gordon and Morrie Arnovich. Hah! You remember Wally Moses? When the managers found out he *wasn't* Jewish, they kept him out of the majors for many years!" He tilted his head back and regarded Harvey professorially. "Now I will tell you sometink else you don't know. There was a player named Moses Solomon. He only played a few games for the Giants in nineteen twenty-tree. For his whole career, he was only tree hits in eight at-bats, and he did not hit any home runs. No home runs, but you know what they called him? They called him the Rabbi of Swat! The goyim hat their Sultan of Swat, and we hat our Rabbi!"

Harvey was smiling at this unlikely fount of baseball lore. "You were here during those years?"

"No. After the war. The second one. But I like baseball. A peaceful game. Maybe not so peaceful now. That was certainly terrible what happened to that

pitcher on your team." He shook his fragile head.
"How does this happen?"

"I wish I knew," Harvey said. "He was my roommate, you know."

"No one knows? It is somebody's responsibility to
know what happened."

"They'll find out who killed him. Eventually."

"They? Who's they?" Molikoff was on the edge of his
chair, pointing at Harvey. "Let me tell you an old
Hasidic story. Do you mind? There was going to be a
big weddink celebration in a small village, and all the
guests were to brink a bottle of vodka to pour into a
big barrel for everyone to drink. So there was one
man who had the thought—with all this vodka, who
will know if I put water in my bottle? So the weddink
came, and hundreds of people came and poured their
bottles into the barrel, and then the first man drew a
glass. He brought it to his lips and he drank it. It was
water. The whole barrel was water."

Harvey found himself nodding. "I know," he said.
"Somebody has to bring the vodka. Speaking of which,
can I order up something to drink for you?"

Molikoff clucked his tongue. "No, no, I am fine." He
took off his suit jacket and turned over a new page in
his notebook. "So," he said, "what about your family?
They are baseball fans?"

Molikoff was wearing a short-sleeved shirt, and
Harvey saw the pale blue numbers tattooed on his
forearm.

"This?" Molikoff said, raising his forearm.

"You know," Harvey said, "when I look at that, it
makes me feel slightly ridiculous being a baseball
player."

Molikoff regarded his tattoo impassively. "Not to
worry. My bat luck. But you see"—it was his turn to
spread his hands and shrug—"my luck was not so bat.
Here I am."

*     *     *

On Friday night, the Yankees beat the Jewels and Bobby Wagner 7–2, dropping his record to 8 and 17. On Saturday, Harvey's ankle was strong enough for Felix to insert him in the lineup as the designated hitter while Dan Van Auken scattered nine New York singles for a 5–3 victory, the Jewels' second in their last nine games. On Sunday, Andy Potter-Lawn was cruising along with a four-hitter for six innings before three Providence errors in the seventh cost him his composure and the lead. New York won 6–4. Harvey went 4-for-9 in the four-game series and was batting .304.

Baltimore was next, and the Orioles were as hot as the wilting weather. On Tuesday night, Baltimore's Henry Ludell held the Jewels to two runs and four hits, but twenty-two-year-old Eddie Storella, after vomiting twice in the clubhouse before the game, proved better, and Providence won 2–1. Stan Crop took the loss on Wednesday, 8–2, and Bobby Wagner could barely get anyone out in the first inning on Thursday on the Jewels' way to a 5–1 defeat. The Toronto Blue Jays had somehow managed to win five of six in the past week, and Providence was only two games out of the Eastern Division cellar, with a record of 66 wins and 78 losses. They were 3–11 since the night Rudy was murdered; the team batting average had dropped from .256 to .246. Harvey kept his average afloat at .306. It was September 13, and there were seventeen days left in the season.

On his way down to the Baltimore Hilton coffee shop on the morning of the team's last day in Baltimore, Harvey ran into Les Byers in the elevator. Byers was dressed in a purple acetate shirt and ivory pants, and he was complaining about a bad investment in a friend's soybean curd dairy in upstate New York. "I underestimated the future of tofu, my man," he said. "Join me for some eggs over easy?"

Les spotted Steve Wilton alone in a booth in the coffee shop and dragged Harvey over. Steve was absorbed in the Jumble word puzzle in the *Baltimore Sun* and mumbled an unintelligible greeting when they sat down. He was running the eraser of his pencil back and forth over his lip.

The menu was written on the placemats, and a waitress in a stiff red uniform, her lacquered hair set in swirls like the icing on a chocolate cake, took down their orders for two Number Threes and a Number Four. Steve pushed his newspaper under Harvey's nose.

"I can't unscramble this one," he said. "Take a crack at it, will you, Professor? The letters spell 'nigame.'"

"Enigma," Harvey said.

"What?"

"I said 'enigma.' As in who killed Rudy."

"Yeah, that's right," Steve said.

Les jumped in. "Man, this club is bad news. I don't know who killed him, but just about every mother on the team thinks some other mother on the team did it. So nobody want to bring it up with anybody 'cause they afraid they might be talking to the dude hisself."

"You're not afraid to bring it up," Steve grumbled without raising his eyes from the newspaper.

"And, man, nobody want to bring it up 'cause they afraid the people'll think they the murderer. You know, like just by talking about it the people'll think they covering up." Les took a few sugar packets out of the wire holder and began dealing them out on the table in front of him. "You'd think that if anyone of us the one," he went on, "we be acting weird. At least he be screwing up on the field, and then the people'd know. Man, there no way you kill some dude and then go out and play good baseball. The problem is"—he shuffled some sugar packets—"everybody on the team be acting weird, so how do you know? Now, all I know, man, is that there no way it be somebody in the infield. See, infielders social. We all nice dudes in the infield, get along with everybody else. Infielders just don't be the killing kind. But outfielders, they something else." He panned from Harvey's face to Steve's. "You guys loners. You stand out there all alone having evil thoughts, man. Your basic antisocial type of dude. What you think of that, Steve?"

Steve looked up, then slid his newspaper under Harvey's nose again. "I'm having trouble with this one, too, Professor." He pointed to a scramble of letters that read "davip." "Take a crack at it for me, will you?"

Compared with Baltimore, where the weather still thought it was summertime, Providence had autumn written all over it. The air was cool and thinned out, and the trees up on College Hill were blotchy with red, gold, and orange. The fall semesters at Brown and the Rhode Island School of Design were a week old, and the sidewalks were filled with students in their baggy corduroys and knee socks. At the bottom of the hill, the sun struck the planes of the buildings at a sharp angle. On the north side of town, the white Georgian marble dome of the State House glistened like a varnished egg. The city almost looked like a place you would want to live.

The Jewels were glad to get to Providence, but so were the Toronto Blue Jays. Before two more healthy Rankle Park crowds, the Blue Jays embarrassed the Jewels 4–0 on Friday evening and 7–5 on Saturday afternoon. The two teams were now tied for the honor of last place in the American League East. A winning percentage of .452 was among the highest in years for a last-place team this late in the season, but it was little consolation for the Jewels, who only two and a half weeks before had been on speaking terms with .500.

Harvey was having bad dreams. On Saturday night, he dreamed he came up to bat at Rankle Park and the scoreboard flashed his average as .044. Rudy Furth was pitching to him, and he was throwing the ball underhand.

**20**

Frances was wearing a shrimp-colored knit dress and sunglasses with huge circular lenses. Linderman was in his polo shirt with the sailboats again. It was eleven o'clock on Sunday morning, September 16, and they sat together in the fourth row of the boxes behind the Jewels' dugout at Rankle Park. They both had their feet hooked over the seats in front of them, and they seemed to be enjoying themselves.

Harvey was on his way to the batting machine under the left field stands, carrying two new bats that were a couple of ounces lighter than his usual. His arms had been tired at the plate for the last few games, he hadn't been getting around well on the fastball, and he wanted to see if a lighter bat made any difference. The field was empty and peaceful except for two members of the grounds crew motoring around the outfield on their Lawn Boys. Then he heard Frances's light laugh, and he turned to see her in the boxes, her head thrown back so that the rich fall sun burned whitely on her arched neck. Linderman was leaning toward her with his arm resting casually on the back of her seat, and he was explaining something to her with the aid of his left hand. He was animated, like a man who thinks he may be getting somewhere with a beautiful woman, and Frances was laughing with a forced gaiety that showed he wasn't.

That afternoon, Harvey carried one of his new bats

to the plate in the ninth inning of a 4–4 with Toronto, singled to left center, stole second and third, and came home with the winning run on Randy Eppich's sacrifice fly. Providence was a game ahead of Toronto, and Harvey was back at .309.

"Hi, Norm," Harvey said Sunday night when he picked up the phone in his living room.

"How'd you know it was me?"

"The ring of the phone has a certain insistent quality when you call. What's up?"

"How could you guys let the Blue Jays take two out of three?"

"I'm tired, Norm."

"And how could Felix pull Van Auken out of the game on Friday night in the fifth, when he's only one run down and he's throwing smoke?"

"What makes you so sure it was Felix? Maybe it was Frances Shalhoub."

"Are you telling me those rumors are true—that she's actually calling the shots in the dugout? What kind of shitshack ball club are you?" Norm's voice was careening.

"Look, Norm, I don't know what she does or doesn't do in the dugout. Half the time I'm standing out in center field. But even if she is making decisions, she'd be no worse than Felix."

"Listen, Harv, if you'd study the statistics, you'd know that Van Auken gets stronger the longer he's in the game. If he makes it to the fifth, he's usually good for a full nine. Now look"—Harvey heard him rustle some papers—"Van Auken's taken a lead into the sixth inning nine times this season, and he's won seven of those games. In none of those seven wins did he give up more than a run after the sixth. How could they take him out?"

"He had a blister, Norm. On his index finger. And he broke it open in the sixth. And you can't pitch if you have an open wound on the index finger of your throwing hand."

"Oh," Norm said, finally. "Listen, I didn't call about that, anyway. I called because I've been looking over some Jewels statistics—"

"You don't say."

"—and look what I found. This is fascinating. Stan Crop has started twenty-five games for you this season. In all but two of those starts, Harv, he's given up at least one run in the second inning. In twenty-three out of twenty-five second innings, he's scored on. You know what that tells me, Harv? The guy ought to come into the game in the third inning, that's what. You ought to throw a reliever in there to pitch the first two, then bring in Crop because, I'm telling you, the guy's a wizard after the second inning."

"That's fascinating, Norm."

"C'mon, Harv, this is me, your brother. We grew up together. We used to spend hours over the box scores, quizzing each other about starting lineups. Right?"

"Right."

"I'll bet you can't remember the starting nine for the 'sixty-two Washington Senators anymore."

"You win."

"Okay," Norm said. "Harry Bright at first, Chuck Cottier at second, Bob Johnson and Johnny Schaive split the job at third, Ken Hamlin at short, an outfield of Jim King, Jimmy Piersall, and Chuck Hinton, and Bob Schmidt behind the plate."

"Norm?"

"I know, Harv. You're going to tell me how crazy I am."

"Ken Retzer, Norm."

"Ken Retzer?"

"Yeah, Norm, Ken Retzer. I think you'll discover that Ken Retzer started more games behind the plate in 'sixty-two than Schmidt."

"Ken Retzer?"

"That's what I said, Norm. Ken Retzer."

There was silence for ten seconds. "You're right," Norm said at last. "Damn you, Harv, you're absolutely right. Okay, I owe you one. Remember, dinner's on me in Chicago next week."

Monday morning's paper contained a squib on page three saying that the police investigation into Rudy's murder was continuing, but had not turned up any convincing leads. "We're not giving up by any means," Linderman was quoted as saying, "but this is one of the more baffling murder cases we've seen in a while." The sluggishness of the investigation was indirectly explained on page one. A few days earlier, two school-children had been found strangled to death in a play-ground on the city's affluent East Side. Rudy's death had taken a back seat.

Harvey fried an egg, melted some grated Parmesan over it, slapped it between two slices of toasted rye, and dialed the phone number of Pro-Gem, Inc., in Pawtucket. Marshall Levy's secretary, who sounded as if her larynx had ascended into her sinuses, put him right through.

"Well, how nice to hear from you, Harvey," Levy said with executive cheerfulness. "It's not contract time yet, is it? I thought you guys only spoke through your agents."

"Actually, Mr. Levy, this call has nothing to do with me. It's about someone else."

"Well, I've got a few minutes. Go ahead."

"It's something I'd rather see you about in person. As soon as possible."

Levy hmmmed. "Let me look at the old calendar. Hmmm. I've got lunch at one, and it looks here like I'll be tied up all afternoon. But I'll tell you what. If you can get over here this morning, I don't see why we can't chat for a minute or two."

Lost in thought, Harvey sped through a red light on the way to Pawtucket. If Frances did own a piece of the team, how could it possibly profit her to put Rudy in a position to be killed, or to have him killed, or—the likelihood of this was so remote that he flicked it off his thoughts like a crumb—kill him herself? He tried to draw lines from Frances through Ronnie Mateo to Rudy, then from Ronnie through Frances to Rudy. If the thread passed through someone else entirely—a player on the team, perhaps—he was still at a loss there. He had ceased trying to read significance into his contact with his teammates—into Les Byers's nervous chatter, Steve Wilton's sullenness, Cleavon Battle's protestations. If he ever learned what he didn't know now, it would probably come in an unguarded moment, like a fastball up under the chin when you were expecting a curve.

Harvey drove up to the low white brick plant in a Pawtucket industrial park and slipped his Citation in among the Buick Regals, Chrysler Cordobas, and Ford Grenadas. Next to the path leading to the smoked-glass entrance, a rectangular sign in the grass read: Pro-Gem: Distinctive Jewelry for America.

The Rhode Island costume jewelry industry was in its worst downturn since World War II and a constant target for the local media. It thrived on a huge illegal underground of Portuguese and Southeast Asian immigrants, who did piecework in sweatshops and at home. The small costume jewelry operations around the state were characterized by unsanitary work conditions, metal dust and chemical fumes, unvented vats of hot acid, violations of minimum wage and overtime laws, and the threats of epoxy poisoning, chronic trachial bronchitis, asbestosis, and severe skin diseases. Only the few big firms, of which Pro-Gem was the largest, were aboveboard, and there were rumors that even the big firms could no longer survive in the market without the help of poor people making cheap earrings in shabby back rooms without toilets.

Harvey walked down the side of the plant to an

open doorway next to the loading docks. He stepped inside to an area as large as an airplane hangar. Women in hair nets sat at rows of long tables gluing rhinestones to rings, and carding and linking jewelry pieces. The air was powdery with blue smoke pouring from two enormous casting machines off to the right. Men in T-shirts and goggles ladled molten metal into machines that pumped out tiny angel figurines into twenty-gallon tubs. Solderers in overalls pushed huge wheeled racks in and out of the chemical plating room in one corner. The floor at Harvey's feet was covered with metal shards and glittering colored dust.

A powerfully built short man in a Hawaiian shirt walked quickly past, looked at him, and said, "You are the one waiting for the bill of lading?"

"No."

"Who are you?" the man asked.

"I work for Mr. Levy."

"What is it, then?"

Harvey pulled a necklace out of his pocket, the one Ronnie Mateo had given him. "Is this one of the items we make?"

The man barely looked at it. "We make about half a million of 'em a year. How come you work here and you don't know we do about half a million of those a year?"

"I'm new," Harvey said.

Marshall Levy's office was decorated with silver Levolor blinds, a charcoal carpet, cushioned teak armchairs, George Kovacs lamps, and a marble-top desk on which you could play half-court basketball. Levy rose from behind it in a chalk-stripe gray suit, a light gray spread-collar shirt, and a red silk tie. There was nothing cheap about him, and he had enough oil in his voice to deep-fry a seafood platter.

"Gosh, Harvey, it's good to see you," he said, shaking hands over the desk. "Sit down. Gee, you've been playing great baseball for us this season. Frances keeps saying you're the only offense we've got left. I wish your hitting was contagious." He laughed without moving his lips.

"It's about Rudy," Harvey said.

"Gee, that was a terrible, terrible thing." Levy lowered his eyes solemnly and pressed his palms together in front of his mouth. "You know about the scholarship fund we set up in his name, don't you? And his pension money is going to his foster parents out in Wisconsin."

"That's good."

"The authorities don't seem to be getting anywhere with it." He moved three paper clips from one side of his blotter to the other. "But you know this town, Harvey. You can never tell which side of the law anybody's on."

Harvey ran his finger along the edge of Levy's desk. "Rudy was a good friend of mine."

"Sure, sure. You two were roommates, after all."

"I've got this vague feeling that Rudy may have been mixed up with some unpleasant types."

"What do you mean?"

"There's a guy who hangs out at the park a lot before games. I've even seen him at practice once. Now, the night Rudy was murdered, this guy called me over and wanted to sell me a bunch of costume jewelry. Just like that. This same guy once tried to sell Rudy some color television sets, and I don't know if you know, but the cops found some IBM typewriters in Rudy's town house after he was killed."

"That's interesting, Harvey. But why'd you come to me with this?"

"As I say, he tried to sell me some of these." Harvey laid the necklace on Levy's desk. "It's one of yours."

"Now, that's strange, isn't it?" Levy said evenly. "But gee, Harvey, there're hundreds of jewelry manufacturers in this state, and a lot of them—"

"No, it's one of yours. I checked already."

"I see." Levy reached over to pick up the necklace and played with it in his fingers. "Why don't you describe this man to me?"

"Thin build, sort of a pale guy, wears colorful suits. Smokes cheap cigars."

Levy rocked back in his chair.

"Maybe his name'll help you. Ronnie Mateo."

Levy repeated the name and moved the three paper clips back to the other side of the blotter. "Doesn't ring a bell."

Harvey drummed his fingers on the desk. "What about that?" he said, pointing at the necklace in Levy's hands.

"This?" He tossed it across the desk to Harvey. "Gee, I don't know where he got hold of it."

"He wanted to sell me a gross, Mr. Levy."

"Well, I'll be frank with you, Harvey. We have had a little problem with shrinkage lately. Every once in a while a carton disappears off the loading docks. I'll look into it, I certainly will. Thanks for bringing it to my attention." He got up, went to the windows, and closed the blinds by turning a thin Lucite rod. "Too much sun," he said distractedly. "I understand your concern, Harvey. I wish I could tell you more."

"You can tell me how much interest Frances owns in the ball club."

The weather changed slightly in Levy's face, and he turned toward the blinds briefly, twirling the rod in his fingers. "I'm sorry," he said. "What did you say?"

"I'm just curious," Harvey said pleasantly.

"I'm curious, too—why you think she owns any."

"I don't know. I guess these things get around."

"Well," he said, giving up. "As you know, it's not a matter of public record—"

"Oh, don't worry about that," Harvey said eagerly. "I just wanted to get the facts straight. I hear various figures."

"You do?"

"Yes. Why don't you just tell me the correct one?"

"I see. Well, Frances owns twenty percent. Can I ask if this has some significance for you?"

"Should it?"

"No, of course not." Levy walked over and stood behind his desk chair. "After all, she's not involved in running the team."

"Not formally, you mean."

"Not formally? I don't get you."

"Well," Harvey said, smiling, "you know how some people interpret her being in the dugout."

"Oh, that." Levy shrugged. "I look at it as her just keeping Felix company. You know, Frances and I go way back. When she was getting her M.B.A. at Columbia, I was there taking a semester of courses; you know, a kind of brush-up for middle-aged executives." His hand jumped to his tie. "You don't want to hear about that." He laughed.

As if on cue, Harvey got to his feet.

"It's been great seeing you, Harvey."

"Thanks for your time."

At the door, Levy put his hand firmly on Harvey's shoulder, as if he could keep Harvey permanently in his place by doing so. "My pleasure. And I want to tell you how pleased I am with your performance this year. Gosh, we were smart to grab you in the expansion draft."

Harvey smiled again. "Well, I hope you don't regret having complimented me like that when it comes time to renegotiate my contract.

Levy's left eyelid fluttered. "Here at Pro-Gem, we always aim to please."

Harvey offered Levy's secretary his best smile on his way out. When he turned onto the path to the parking lot, he looked over his right shoulder at the window of Levy's office. The blinds were open again, and Marshall Levy was looking through them.

Harvey pulled into the players' parking lot at Rankle Park that afternoon for the opener of four against Detroit and backed in next to Rodney Salta's Jaguar. Linderman was seated on the Jaguar's fender in a glen plaid suit, smoking a cigarette.

"Got a minute?" he said.

John Rapp and Charlie Penzenik passed on their way in.

"Hi, John. Charlie," Harvey said.

"Professor," they nodded.

Harvey stood over Linderman and said, "I've got a minute, but not here."

"What's wrong with here?" With enough force to grind glass, Linderman flattened his cigarette butt under a black Corfam shoe.

"The last time I talked to you at a ball park, someone left me a death threat. Let's take a walk."

They turned left onto Roger Williams Avenue, which ran between one looming gray side of Rankle Park and a block-long warehouse with bricked-over windows. At the curb, a man and a woman unloaded cardboard boxes of souvenirs—pennants, batting helmets, Providence Jewels pen and pencil sets—on the back of their station wagon.

"A death threat," Linderman said. "You don't tell me anything, do you?"

Harvey was trying to decide whether it merited an

answer when Linderman continued: "For chrissakes, Harvey. When you get a death threat, that's when you're supposed to go to the cops. Maybe you're too dumb to be scared. What did it say?"

Harvey worked his wallet out of his pants pocket and handed Linderman the note. "I suppose you're going to tell me who wrote it."

Linderman held it in his hands. "It so happens I know a thing or two about graphology, but this is written in block letters by somebody's off hand. Cursive writing is what tells you something." He gave Harvey the note. "Now, you could go get writing samples from everyone you think might want to write you a note like that, and we could have our handwriting man spend a few days looking them over and comparing them to those block letters, but the odds are pretty slim, and then you'd probably need a handwritten term paper from all the suspects to even have a shot at it." He gave a rueful laugh. "I wish I liked you more," he said.

"It would ruin the symmetry of the relationship."

"You're right. Let's keep it the way it is. Now look, I wanted to tell you something about your friend Rudy."

They turned the corner and headed up another side of Rankle Park. On their left, the stadium light towers rose freakishly over them. On their right, a shadow passed in the window of a leather supply company.

"After reading the paper this morning," he said to Linderman, "I figured the trail was cold. Now you've got those two strangled kids on the East Side."

"Don't worry, there's still movement on it. But I hit a brick wall today and thought you'd want to know about it."

"What happened?"

"Let me put it this way. After finding those three typewriters in Rudy's place, I thought I had a pretty good idea where that money came from. The three thousand bucks."

"Ronnie Mateo," Harvey said.

"Yeah, yeah, yeah. You're making the same mistake I did. Only natural. When you've got a bunch of typewriters lying around where they shouldn't be, some big bills, a guy who's been soaking in the bottom of a whirlpool overnight, and Ronnie Mateo, it's easy to jump to conclusions. I mean, the mob's just not that interested in typewriters, but a guy like Ronnie might be. And the way Rudy was put away was not a professional job, and Ronnie is not a professional-type guy. But when we finally traced the serial numbers on the machines, we ended up with a much different picture."

They walked around a stickball game three kids were playing against the back of Rankle Park's left field stands.

"Get this, Harvey. There's an orphanage in Woonsocket. Rudy went there to give talks a couple of times this summer, and he got pretty fond of the kids there and the nuns who run it. Makes sense, right? So one day he tells the mother superior that he wants to buy something for the kids. She tells him the kids have everything they need, but the orphanage staff is banging away on Royal manuals from about 1915 and they're working on a shoestring, and you guessed it. We traced the machines to an office supply outfit in Cranston, where Rudy went and paid cash for three new IBMs three days before he was murdered. He was just holding them in his apartment until he could get out to the orphanage. Our luck that Rudy told the guy who sold him the machines that he was buying them for an orphanage and he wanted the best they had. Cost about eleven hundred bucks a pop. So we tracked down the orphanage, and it all checked out." Linderman brought both hands up to his crew cut and massaged it. "I thought being nice to orphans died with Babe Ruth. Now who the hell would want to kill a guy like that?"

Harvey didn't say anything for twenty yards. Then: "Where does that leave Ronnie? There's still that money."

"He says he's clean, and maybe now I believe him."

"Okay, then, why'd I get a visit from him?"

"I didn't say he had nothing to hide."

"Then what is it?"

"I'll tell you, but I don't want this thrown around, I don't want it in the papers, I don't even want you to repeat it back to me. Because this city needs this ball club, and this is the kind of thing that could get the team in hot water with the league. All right?"

"All right."

Linderman lit another Marlboro. "All right, it's pretty simple. When Rankle Park was a minor league park all those years, a company called Vendorama ran the concessions. Everything, from the beer to the paper napkins, came from Vendorama. When Levy brought you guys to town this season, Vendorama went to him and said they expected to keep running the concessions at the park, everything as usual. Now Levy may've had his own ideas, but when he asked around and found out what kind of muscle Vendorama had, he's a smart businessman, so he said, 'Sure, why not?' And Vendorama dictated terms. So Levy doesn't see a penny from the concessions."

"Bunny Mateo," Harvey said.

"You catch on fast. When you do business with that crowd, the deal has nothing to do with the price of doing business with them. It only has to do with the price of *not* doing business with them."

"And Ronnie?"

"A *putz* who happens to be related to a guy who definitely isn't. So he gets to roam around the ball park and try to sell some crap he picks up off the back of a truck somewhere. So he came to see you because he didn't want to see his name in the papers and lose his special status and get his brother angry and also because he likes to think he's a legbreaker. There's more inside a cannoli than there is in his head."

"There's still that money."

"I thought *you* might have some bright ideas," Linder-man said.

"What about Frances? Doesn't she have any?"

Linderman shoved his hands in his pants pockets. "Yeah, yeah, yeah, Frances Shalhoub and I are keeping in touch."

They had walked all the way around the park. Linderman went one way, and Harvey went into the clubhouse. Most of the team had already suited up and gone out to the field. He could forget Ronnie Mateo and the typewriters. He could forget Ronnie Mateo and the necklaces. Maybe he could forget Ronnie Mateo, period. He could forget Valerie Carty. He couldn't forget Frances and the three thousand dollars and a lot of bits and pieces, but the only way he could still get Frances and the money into the same thought was if Frances had been paying Rudy to keep his mouth shut about their affair.

But extramarital affairs were as common as 6-4-3 double plays, and why would Rudy threaten to talk? Anyway, Frances was the sort of woman who would tell Felix, if she had to, that it just wasn't true about her and Rudy, and Felix would believe her. And if by some chance Felix didn't believe her, what would he do about it? The guy barely had the energy anymore to leave the dugout and beef to an ump about a bad call. Still, Harvey thought as he tied his spikes and folded the tongues back over the bows, he hadn't really spoken to Felix at any length since the day after Rudy's murder. He didn't really have any bright ideas, but when he passed Felix's office and saw him sitting alone at his desk playing with a pile of the wooden tongue depressors that the players used to scrape the mud from their spikes on rainy days, he walked in.

Felix had cleared a space on a desk cluttered with sports pages, lineup cards, mementos, and the vinyl-covered loose-leaf notebook containing the team statistics. He was gluing the tongue depressors into what looked like picket fences.

"What's doing, Felix?"

"Why aren't you out on the field?" He made a brief attempt to conceal his construction project.

"I'm a little late getting started today."

"Listen, Professor, I'm batting you third tonight. I like the way Stiles has been getting on base lately, and I want to bat him second so you'll have somebody to chase home. Okay?"

"Fine, Felix, fine. Don't worry, we'll get you some runs tonight. Nice guys shouldn't have to finish last."

Felix looked up at him with sad eyes. His nose had a red, rubbery look.

"Felix I'm not going to tell you you look like the picture of health these days."

"Good. I hate liars." He put the cap back on the Elmer's glue. "Why do I have to have an unsolved murder on my ball club? Isn't it enough we've lost fourteen of our last eighteen? Why couldn't it have been the Yankees? They're always fighting among themselves anyway. Why couldn't it have happened to whoever's managing them these days?" He chuckled morosely at his own joke.

"He's got Morrissey to deal with. You don't."

Felix grimaced at the mention of the Yankee's principal owner. "At least Morrissey's got the money to buy himself a winner. This organization's not in a healthy financial posture. I'll probably lose half the team to free agency in the next two years. Assuming I'm still here." He braced his temples with his palms. "Harvey, are you sleeping with my wife?"

"Excuse me?" Harvey said.

"I've got a right to know, I think."

"No, of course not. For God's sake, Felix, why would it even occur to you to ask?"

"Don't you think I know when my wife's off on one of her romantic expeditions? Just tell me and I won't ask any more questions."

"Felix, I swear I'm not. I mean, not even close."

"Good," he said. "That's more than I could say for someone else, may he rest in peace."

"Rudy?" Harvey felt he was shaking his head in disbelief too obviously.

"It may come as a surprise to you, although God knows why it should. Perhaps you've noticed she takes a fancy to younger men. Sometimes I don't know why she even married me."

"You put up with it?" he said, when he couldn't think of anything else.

"The marriage?"

"The younger men."

"What can I do? I just about owe this job to her."

Harvey pretended to be occupied by something on the floor. "Yeah, I know she owns part of this ball club."

"It's not a matter of public record, Professor, but my wife owns twenty percent. Her own money. That gives her just enough leverage to get her husband the manager's job. Who else was going to touch me, with my record?"

"Felix," Harvey implored, but Felix was on a confessional binge.

"Sometimes I don't even feel like the job's mine. Levy drools all over Frances, and between the two of them they run most of the show."

"Can't you talk to Levy about it? You're a baseball man, Felix; you're a good manager. You've just had lousy teams."

Felix ignored Harvey's effort at praise. "I've gone to Levy. He says, 'Well, certainly, Felix, you're the manager, but it's good for the team to have Frances around, and it's good for Frances.' The guy's telling me what's good for my wife! Truth is he gets a hard-on just looking at her, and she owns a piece of the property. Money talks. Felix just sits here and spills his guts to his goddamn center fielder."

"Does Linderman know about Frances and Rudy?" Harvey asked.

"If he does, I sure as hell wasn't the one to tell him. What's the point, anyway? What's there to know? If Linderman knew, it'd be all over the place. What's it got to do with Rudy's murder?"

Felix had phrased it as a question, as if he too felt the matter was still open. "You know about the money in Rudy's sports jacket," Harvey said.

"Sure, Linderman told me about it."

"And you know he feels there's no way that money was a gambling bribe? There was no unusual betting action on Jewels games."

"And no gambler'd be dumb enough to work through a relief pitcher. Starting pitchers and big hitters throw games, not relievers."

"And you know the typewriters are out, right?"

"Yeah, Linderman just told me about that, too," Felix said. "Now how in hell am I supposed to hate a man who's slept with my wife when he's buying typewriters for a goddamn orphanage and then gets murdered in my goddamn clubhouse?"

"You got any ideas, Felix?"

"No, and Linderman doesn't seem to have any, either. Between you and me, Professor, Linderman never seemed too sharp to me."

Harvey let the comment pass. "Whoever killed Rudy was extremely smart or extremely lucky, or both." He stood up. "I know this is crazy, Felix, but you don't think—"

"Forget it. And if she *was* the murdering sort, love's the last thing she'd kill for, if that's what you're thinking."

"Sorry, Felix. I must be getting pretty desperate." Harvey started to leave, then stopped. "What'd they talk about, Frances and Rudy?"

"Beats me. Only time I overheard them, they were talking about real estate. I gather Rudy was investing in some."

Harvey stood in front of Felix. The Jewels' schedule

was taped to the tiles on the wall behind Felix's chair. Providence had these four against the Tigers, three over the weekend with second-place Boston, a quick road trip to Chicago for four, and back to close out the season with three against first-place New York.

"Why don't you go out there and put your mind on the game," Felix finally said. "At least you can try to salvage a three hundred season for yourself."

Harvey waved a hand at him. "I'd just like to see the team finish up on a winning note."

"You can save the bullshit for the press. Just go out there and get a few hits tonight."

After the 6-3 loss to the Tigers, Harvey went back to his apartment and took out the paper bag that Dunc had given him four days ago in New York and spread the contents on his kitchen table. He threw the half-finished pack of cigarettes, the sunglasses, and the sanitary hose back in the bag and began leafing through the book about real estate investment. He was searching his memory for anything Rudy had ever said to him about real estate when an envelope with a cellophane window fell out from between the pages.

In it was a July checking account statement in Rudy's name from the Industrial National Bank. It couldn't have been his regular account because the balance was only a bit over four hundred dollars. Rudy had made a few relatively modest withdrawals on the account in July and only one deposit—on July 19, for the sum of three thousand dollars.

 On Tuesday morning, September 18, Harvey picked up his phone and started dialing. Through his living room window, he glanced at the Industrial National Bank building down-town in sunlight so hard and bright it looked as if it would chip. It was a stout art deco building rising in ever-smaller rectangles that were quilted with windows. On the top was a huge yellow beacon framed by a quartet of stone eagles standing guard over the city. In 1928, it had been considered the greatest thing before sliced bread, but now its elegance was oppressive. With its Stalinist sobriety, the building could have been something in downtown Moscow.

Somewhere in the bank someone was about to answer his phone call. When a woman did, Harvey asked for Central Records and devoutly hoped that whoever picked up the phone next was not a fan of the Providence Jewels or of baseball in general. If a male voice answered, he would play it safe and hang up.

"Records," a young female voice said. "Miss Galizio."

Harvey took a breath. "I wonder if you could help me. I've managed to lose a few of my monthly statements for my checking account at the bank and my accountant is hounding me for them. Any chance you could have the computer spit them out again? Would that be a lot of trouble?"

"No, just a modest amount," she said sweetly. "Why don't you give me your name and account number?"

185

"The name is Furth. Rudolph Furth. F-u-r-t-h."

"Yes, Mr. Furth," she said without hesitation. "And your account number?"

Harvey read it to her from Rudy's July statement.

"One second, please." There was silence for ten. "Here we go. Oh, I see you only opened your account with us in June. Would you like all the statements?"

"Yes, that would be fine."

"Would you like them sent to this address, on South Main?"

"No," Harvey said quickly. "I'll come pick them up."

"All right, then. They'll be ready for you here tomorrow morning. How's that?"

"That's great. Thank you."

"And thank you, sir."

Harvey strolled down Planet Street to South Main and had cappuccino and two croissants at a new place with pyramids of Menucci pasta boxes and hanging prosciuttos in the window. As he sipped, he peered across the street at Rudy's town house. It didn't look as if it had yet been rented. In front of the town house next to it, a woman in furry slippers was trimming the hedge in her minuscule front yard. Rudy wouldn't have known her very well; she was not his type. But then, Harvey never would have guessed that Frances was his type, either. He was pursuing the murderer of a man he seemed to know less and less about. Rudy had made a mistake, and he had paid for it, and it was none of Harvey's business. What did he owe Rudy? What was he trying to prove, and who was watching him prove it? Now that he had decided Rudy was guilty, he should simply look the other way and forget it. But Harvey felt his purpose sharpened; he was like a spurned lover who was now willing to risk everything to find out exactly how he'd been wronged. He brushed the last flakes of croissant from his mouth, paid up, and went home.

Once again, Bobby Wagner didn't have it that night. By the fifth inning, he was taking an early shower. By the sixth, with Detroit ahead 7–2, so were the fans. The clouds that had been pulling into position over the park during the game finally broke and shed a warm autumn rain. The grounds crew swarmed onto the field in their green and black windbreakers to drag the tarpaulin over the infield. The box seat customers joined the drier fans under the grandstand roof to watch Mel Allen narrate last week's baseball highlights on the screen of the electronic scoreboard. The rain outlasted Mel Allen, and Rankle Park's organist burst into a show tune medley. When the umps called the game after a seventy-minute delay, the Jewels were in the clubhouse and only too glad to be able to undress. Another team might have been sorry not to have the chance to come back and win the game. Harvey showered, dressed, and drove downtown to Leo's, a roomy bar beneath the 1-95 overpass.

Over the bar at Leo's were windows cut into the wall so you could look out and watch the cars up on the overpass. For a long time, Harvey sat there looking at them wetly slide by, their headlights fanning out and then disappearing. He was on his second ale when he lowered his eyes and saw Mickey on the screen of the television set suspended above the tiers of liquor bottles. She was saying that Toronto had beaten Cleveland and that the Jewels were once again tied for last place. She looked smooth, elegant, and untouchable in her emerald blouse and tweed jacket. Sitting in a row of solitary drinkers at the bar, Harvey felt as if he couldn't possibly know the woman.

"Best looking cunt on television," the man on the stool next to him said. He was in his thirties, heavyset, with the doughy face of a former college football lineman. Three empty Narragansett bottles were lined up in front of him, and he was drinking from a fourth.

Mickey gazed down at them as she editorialized about Brown University's chances in the approaching Ivy League football season. "I'll bet you anything she loves to ball," he said.

Harvey tapped his glass lightly against the mahogany bar.

"Yes, sir, I'd like to have those legs wrapped around my neck one of these nights," the man said. "Wouldn't you, pal? Hey, pal, I'm talking to you."

"How'd you like to have your own legs wrapped around your neck?" Harvey said.

"What's that, pal?" He was wearing a plaid flannel shirt with a down vest over it. "What's that?"

"Just have a little respect for the woman," Harvey said, not meeting the man's eyes. "I'm sure if she likes to ball, you're the last person she'd want to do it with."

The man swiveled on his stool to face Harvey. "How would you know, pal? You don't look like you've had any in a while."

"I don't want any trouble, but I think the point is that you're a little out of line." Harvey's heart was pounding halfway up his esophagus and, with a long pull on his bottle of ale, he tried to wash it back down where it belonged.

"Or maybe the point is that *you're* a little out of line, jocko. If I happen to think that Mickey Slavin is the biggest piece of tail in Providence, I don't see where that's any of your business."

"It so happens it is."

Nick the bartender had come down the bar and stood in front of them, cleaning an imaginary spill with his towel. "Harvey, What's the trouble?" He looked at the other man. "C'mon, Ken. Don't you know who he is?"

"Yeah," Ken said. "He's some asshole who—"

"Easy, Ken," Nick said. "Not in my place. Anyway, you're talking to—"

"I don't care who I'm talking to. This asshole was telling me I can't say what I want about Mickey Slavin." He turned to Harvey. "What's it to you?"

"She's my girlfriend," Harvey said.

Ken gave a nasal laugh. "Yeah, and I'm married to Barbara Walters."

"Easy, you guys," Nick was saying. "Whyn't you just drink your beer, and we'll all sit here peacefully and watch Johnny Carson together?"

"Your girlfriend's probably a boy," Ken said to Harvey.

Harvey exhaled. "You know, you're turning out to be even dumber than you look." He felt as if Mickey was watching.

"Pal, how'd you like me to rearrange your face?" He jabbed a finger in Harvey's shoulder.

"Not if it'll look like yours." Harvey took Ken's right arm by the wrist and pushed it away. Ken shoved it at his shoulder again. Harvey took a deep breath, rotated his body away from Ken, set his left hand against the edge of the bar, and with his right hit someone in the face for the first time since he was eleven. His punch glanced off Ken's chin, but knocked him partly off his stool so Ken stood now with his left leg draped over it.

"Damn it, Harvey," Nick was pleading.

"My turn," Ken said and came at Harvey with a flurry of hands and elbows, dropping him to the floor. Harvey got up, tasting blood in his mouth, and threw his right fist at Ken's face as Ken's right struck his shoulder. Almost immediately, Ken's left hand found Harvey's forehead, and Harvey staggered back among the tables, tripped over an empty chair, and skidded to a stop on his back. He wiped two streaks of blood from his nose with his shirtsleeve and clambered to his feet. His right hand felt numb, his forehead unusually large.

Ken was threading his way uncertainly between the tables, as their occupants got up from their seats and backed off. "Let me at that fucker," Ken was saying over and over. Harvey thought of Carlos Bonesoro decoying him at third in New York two weeks ago, and straightened up with his hands at his sides, looking less than eager to continue. It was not difficult to summon the expression.

Ken stopped a few feet in front of him and dropped his guard long enough to inquire, "Had enough, jocko?"

Harvey suddenly slammed his right fist cleanly into Ken's nose, feeling something cartilaginous give under the impact of his knuckles. Ken danced backwards in a clumsy cha-cha, his arms swimming pathetically at his sides.

"Jesus, Harvey, this isn't like you." It was Nick's voice at his side. "I'll get you a towel. Your nose is leaking."

"Not yet," Harvey said. Ken was coming at him again. Harvey tried to land the first blow, but Ken blocked it with a forearm, and Harvey turned his head away from Ken's flying right. It caught him over the ear, and he stumbled back, bouncing off the Space Invaders game near the door. He steadied himself against it. Ken was getting ready to make another run at him from ten feet away. He was dimly aware of Leo's patrons circled about him. His legs felt thick and heavy. Ken started to rush, but had only taken a step when two arms came up under Harvey's armpits from behind and wrenched him aside.

Ken stopped in his tracks. "Let him go," he yelled. "I want at him."

"No, that's it," a voice said easily in Harvey's ear. "Party's over." The hands slipped out from Harvey's armpits and slowly spun him around.

"You're a little tougher than I thought you were, Professor."

Harvey tried to focus on the face. "I didn't know you drank here," he said, each word costing him a breath.

"I didn't know you boxed here," said Bobby Wagner.

Bobby helped Harvey over to the bar, Nick wrung out a wet towel, and Bobby cleaned up his face for him. In the background, people were putting the furniture back in order. At one of the tables, Ken was pressing a paper napkin to his nose.

"Did I look like I had anything left," Harvey asked Bobby, "or were you just rescuing me?"

"You didn't need to be rescued," Bobby said. "You were doing all right. Just get lower down when you want to hit somebody. That way you come up and put your whole body into the punch. You can't fight with just your arms."

Harvey tested his jaw. "You won't tell Felix about this?"

"Naw. What started it, anyway?"

"We were watching Mickey on the news, and he had a few too many opinions about her."

Bobby asked Nick for some ice to put in the towel. "She's a sweet kid," Bobby said.

While they were at the bar, several of the customers came up, most of them to talk to Bobby. They called him Bobby, as though he was part of the old gang. That was the difference between being a pretty good outfielder and being a great right-hander who almost won the Cy Young and sold deodorant on national television.

Ken approached the bar with his right hand extended. "I apologize," he said to Harvey. "Friends?" Ken glanced at Bobby, as if he needed permission.

"No. Not friends," Harvey said.

"Go on, Professor," Bobby said. "Shake the man's hand." Harvey shook it sullenly.

"Those guys told me who you were," Ken said. "Hey, I'm real sorry. I feel like a jerk."

"You are a jerk," Harvey said.

"Hey, look, I said I'm sorry. I deserved to get punched."

"I didn't."

"You're not hurt bad, are you?"

Harvey didn't say anything, and Ken stood there with a contrite, expectant look. Harvey was afraid that he was suddenly going to ask for his autograph.

"Whyn't you leave now, buddy?" Bobby said. "The Professor forgives you." Ken shrank from the bar in small steps.

"Just another asshole," Bobby said to Harvey.

Nick placed a brandy in front of Harvey and he drank it. It took the edge off the pain in his right hand, his shoulder, his forehead, his left ear.

"So long, Wags," he said, finally sliding off the stool.

"Take care, Professor," Bobby said.

The next morning, Wednesday, Harvey spread Rudy's June, July, and August statements from the Industrial National Bank on his kitchen table.

The only transaction on the June statement was a deposit on the twenty-fifth for $3,000. In July, there was the $3,000 deposit on the nineteenth, which he already knew about, and $4,843 in withdrawals. Harvey put his head in his hand as he read over the August statement. On both the second and the eleventh, Rudy had deposited $3,000.

From June through August, Rudy had deposited the sum of $3,000 four times in this separate checking account. The crumpled thousand dollar bill in the whirlpool and the two just like it found in his sports jacket made five. Fifteen thousand dollars: for someone who made more than that for a month of bull pen work, it was not the kind of money to risk your life over, but there it was.

Linderman was sitting behind a gray metal desk at Homicide at police headquarters wearing his red Chemise Lacoste and brown pants. In one hand, he held half of a diagonally sliced tuna salad sandwich and with the other he was fingering Rudy's checking account statements. He took a sip of chocolate milk from a half-pint carton and with a mouthful of tuna salad and milk said, "Yeah, yeah, yeah, this is very interesting, Harvey. Very interesting." He sounded like a wash cycle.

It had crossed Harvey's mind not to show Linderman the statements at all, but he was more interested in finding out who murdered Rudy than in mistrusting Linderman. Anyway, he had kept a set of photocopies. "Does that change your mind about Ronnie Mateo?" Harvey said.

Linderman gazed at the August statement. "I don't know what it does. So Rudy had himself a separate little account. How'd you get hold of these?"

Harvey told him.

"That's not kosher, Harvey." He sucked the rest of his chocolate milk through a straw and dropped the carton into a gray metal wastebasket.

"It's okay. I come from a reform Jewish family," Harvey said. "Are you going to thank me for those?"

"Yeah, yeah, yeah, thanks."

"So I guess I'll be going." Harvey got up.

"By the way, where'd you get the Technicolor on your forehead and the funny knuckles? You in a scrape?"

"It's nothing." Harvey waved it away.

"You don't seem like the type of guy who gets into fights."

"No, it was just some guy and me throwing hands last night in a bar."

"My, my, you live dangerously." The detective smirked and lit a Marlboro.

Harvey felt like someone who had won the lottery and was still waiting for his check to come in the mail. Not only had the documented bank deposits not immediately produced a solution to Rudy's murder, as Harvey in his frustrated, exhausted state imagined they should, but in fact he did not hear from Linderman at all.

While the Detroit Tigers crushed the Jewels and Dan Van Auken 10–0 on Wednesday night and beat Andy Potter-Lawn 4–1 on Thursday night, Harvey sat anxiously in the dugout. Arky Bentz had checked out Harvey's right hand before Wednesday's game and told him nothing was broken, but it hurt too much to hold a bat. The bench was quiet except for Campy's exhortations and Felix's sad clapping. Everyone wanted the season to end as soon as possible, and the Jewels seemed to be doing everything in their power to shorten the games. They flapped their bats at bad pitches. They dogged it down the line. On Thursday night, Randy ran through Tony's signal at third and was thrown out at the plate by twenty feet.

Harvey spent a lot of time at the water cooler at the end of the dugout, just to have something to do. While he was drinking from it late in the game on Thursday night, a voice said over his shoulder, "How's your investigation coming?" It was Frances, in a white turtleneck sweater, sitting in the corner of the bench with a clipboard on her lap.

Harvey straightened up from the water cooler. "What investigation?"

Frances made a notation on her clipboard as Potter-

Lawn threw a curve in the dirt to Davis. She looked up, simple gold loop earrings sparkling in her streaked hair, and smiled thinly. "I must have made some mistake. I thought you were conducting an investigation."

"You thought wrong," Harvey said, slipping his hands into the pockets of his warm-up jacket and smiling back. "Chilly night," he added.

"Ice cold team," Frances said.

"Yeah," he said, "this is one ball club I'd hate to own any part of." He felt her penetrating gaze all the way back to his spot on the far end of the bench.

The season ticked away to its last seven games, and the clock was running out on Harvey. His friendship with Rudy had been bounded by baseball, and so his search for the murderer was somehow bounded by it, too. In a little over a week, Harvey would crate the few things in General Burnside's mansion, and he and everyone else on the club would withdraw to unfamiliar lives and wait for spring training. On Friday, September 21, the Red Sox came to town on a roll. They were closing fast on the first-place Yankees and were only two games out at the start of the three-game weekend series. During their infield practice before the opener, Boston had a lot of chatter and good hop on their throws, and Harvey watched his former team from the dugout with the regret of someone viewing home movies of more prosperous times. It was a cool evening, and the setting sun seeped through the arches in the concrete wall of the grandstands and glinted off the vinyl-covered padding on the outfield fences. For Boston, it was a pennant race; for the Providence Jewels, baseball only seemed to be intruding on weather meant for other things. The Jewels had lost seven of eight, and eighteen of the twenty-two games they had played since Rudy's death. The Rankle Park crowds had been dwindling, and on Friday night the chill quieted those few who came out, so that only the vendors' lonely cries rose from the stands.

Boston took all three games and left town on Sunday only one game out of first. Toronto had dropped three to Chicago, so Providence stayed a game behind them. Harvey had a bad series at the plate, going 2-for-13, and his batting average now stood exactly at .300.

An hour after the game on Sunday, Harvey and Mickey were heading down Route 1 to have some steamers at a clam shack near Narragansett, overlooking Rhode Island Sound.

"Do you think I'm a good reporter, Bliss?" she said, turning off the car radio.

"Sure you are."

"But am I really good?"

"You're really good."

"Really, really good?"

Harvey adjusted the rearview mirror. "I get it," he said. "You heard."

"Yes."

"From a certain organization whose call letters are the first three letters of the alphabet. In their proper sequence."

"Yes."

"When?"

"Yesterday." She smiled.

"You got the job!" Harvey shouted.

"Yes."

"Mick, that's great."

"I'm scared."

"You're going to be terrific."

"They offered me a lot of money."

"You deserve it." He leaned over and kissed her.

"No, I don't."

"Then give it to me and I'll support you."

"You'll hate me if I go to New York. I'll start calling everyone 'honey' and drinking expensive mineral water at lunch."

"I'll hate you if you don't go. This is the proverbial big break."

"I'll blow it."

"The hell you will, Mick. You're hot, you're a comer."

"Stop it. You sound like Campy Strulowitz."

"You're the kid, babe, you're the one, hum-a-now, have an idea."

"Oh, stop it!" Mickey laughed.

"You're the looker, be a kid, hum babe, you the babe."

"Stop it! I'm going to wet my pants."

"When do they want you?"

"Sometime in November. Bliss, I don't want to leave you."

"You're not leaving me. You're just heading down the road a piece."

"Maybe I can get a clause in my contract that says the Yankees have to trade for you so we can be together."

"I'd even settle for the Mets. Hell, maybe I'll just get Marshall Levy to transfer the franchise to New Rochelle or something."

"I'd like that."

"Better yet, Mick, I'll retire and come to New York, and you can support me in the style to which neither of us is accustomed. I'm tired of baseball."

"Retire? You've never played better."

"It's a fluke. Three seasons ago, I was hitting the ball better and I ended up with a two-seventy-two average. This year they're just falling in. It's a difference of about fifteen hits falling in for you, that's all."

"Don't be silly. You're just a late developer. You'll see. Next season, you'll be up there again."

"It's wearing off, Mick."

"You're just in one of your famous moods." She stuck her head out the window, and he stole a glance at her profile. When she brought her head back in, she said, "Are you upset about my new job?"

"Of course not. I couldn't be happier. Why would I be upset?"

She picked at a fingernail. "You know. Athletes use themselves up at such a young age. You're not through yet, believe me, but here I am, just really getting started in my career." Harvey didn't say anything. "I didn't mean to depress you, Bliss."

"No, it's not you. Obviously. It's me. You know, the worst part about being an average ball player having a good year at my age is that it makes you think there's still time to become a great ball player." He switched lanes. "Just two careers passing in the night."

"Don't get maudlin on me."

"I don't want to be one of those guys who sit around on the weekend reading their scrapbooks."

They were at a rotary. Mickey clapped her hands together and pointed at a miniature golf course set behind a Dairy Freeze.

"Please," he said sourly. "Anything but miniature golf. The only sport I hate more is actual-size golf."

"Not the golf, dummy. Next to it. The batting cages."

"Batting cages? Where?"

"Look. Next to it. Those machines."

Harvey saw the cages. "No, Mick. I've had enough baseball for one day. I've had enough for one lifetime."

"Please. You get to hit all the time. I never get to. I want to show you I can hit."

"I already think of you as one of the guys. I'm hungry."

"Don't be selfish, Bliss."

They waited in line behind some teenagers who were hitting against the two machines, one fast and one slow, positioned at the far end of the netted cage. An old man in a T-shirt emblazoned with the name of a rock group sat on a stool behind the machines and periodically loaded the rubber-coated baseballs into bins that fed them one at a time down a chute and between two rapidly spinning discs that propelled them across the plates. After every pitch, no matter how well his customers hit the ball, he announced loudly, "You're out!" and spat copiously on the ground.

"You could be in the league another five years," Mickey said as they watched the teenagers. "Your legs are good."

"Not as good as yours."

"I wish you wouldn't feel this way."

"Maybe it's Providence. I haven't played for a loser since high school."

"Maybe it's Rudy," she said, as if she'd been wanting to say it all along.

Harvey watched a towheaded kid hit line drive after line drive off the slow machine. "Yeah," he said, "it's like I lost him twice."

"Twice?"

"Rudy wasn't Rudy."

She took his hand. "You haven't heard from Linderman since you gave him the bank statements, have you?" she said, as the towheaded kid came out of the cage.

"No."

"Give me a quarter, will you?" Mickey kicked off her sandals, selected a batting helmet and bat from the management's aging collection, and fed the quarter into the coin box behind home plate. She dug her bare feet expertly into the dusty batter's box and rotated the bat in frantic circles over her head. The towheaded kid and his friend, intrigued by the sight of a woman in a sundress preparing to do battle against the machine, hung along the netting and shouted encouragement.

"Let's go, lady, step into one!"

"Break the machine, lady!"

Mickey stroked the first arching pitch high into the net behind the machine.

"You're out!" the old man bellowed and spit.

"Looking good, Mick," Harvey called out.

She pushed her hair behind her ear with an index finger and waited for the machine's next looping delivery. "Why do you think you haven't heard from him?" she called.

"Who?" Harvey said.

"Linderman," she said. She bounced the second pitch solidly up the middle.

"You're out," the old man bellowed.

"Pretty good stick up there, huh, Bliss?" Mickey said. "Do you think Linderman knows anything?"

"Way to hit, lady," the towheaded kid's friend said.

"I know he thinks Ronnie Mateo's out of the picture," Harvey said.

Mickey powdered the next pitch, adjusted her helmet, and to the delight of her audience, sent a small stream of saliva behind her into the dust. "And Frances?" she said. "What could Rudy do that'd be worth fifteen grand to her? Keep their love a secret?"

"I doubt it was love on Frances's part. Anyway, Felix already knew about the two of them. No, it's something else, Mick. If it was Frances, she was paying him for something else. But what? What can a relief pitcher do?"

Mickey lined the next pitch into the net, a solid base hit. "This is fun, Bliss," she said. "But even if Frances *was* paying Rudy for something, you don't think she's the one who killed him, do you? That's too crazy." She spit in her left hand. "I need a batting glove."

"Tough it out, Mick." She popped up the next pitch. "Keep your back shoulder up, Mick," he said. "No, I can't believe she'd ever kill anybody, but I swear to God she's in there somewhere. She's too interested in making me and in making Linderman not to be. She's hiding something, Mick, but I don't know what she's hiding. There's one piece missing. I need one piece, Mick."

Mickey bounced the next one, and it hit the machine.

"Break it, lady!" one of the teenagers yelled.

"You're out!" the old man bellowed again.

"Well, look," she said, waiting for the seventh and final offering. "You said Ronnie Mateo works for the guys who run the concessions at the park where the team that Frances owns twenty percent of plays, and therefore"—she fouled off the last pitch—"Damn!" She flung the helmet aside and strutted out.

"You're out!" said the old man.

"And therefore what?" Harvey said.

"Oh, I don't know," she said, stooping to put on her sandals. "What was that woman's name?"

"Which woman?"

"The one in New York. Who used to work for Frances."

"Oh, you mean Sharon Meadows," Harvey said. "What do you want with her?"

Mickey brushed dust off her dress. "It may come in handy."

"One piece, Mick. That's all I need."

"Mister, let's see you in there," the towhead said. "C'mon, I bet the lady's better'n you."

They got on Route 1A above Saunderstown and drove south to a shingled clam shack with a gravel apron and a string of red and blue bulbs running from one corner of its roof to a telephone pole beside the highway. After dinner, they threw their shoes in the car and walked over the scrubby dunes to a slender band of cold beach. Low over the water, the darkening sky was striped with purple, copper, and rose. Their only company was a gathering of quizzical fat gulls at the water's edge scavenging among the remnants of a picnic. They kicked along the damp sand for a hundred yards and came to a clearing in the dunes. Harvey took Mickey by the hand and walked over to it before he realized what it was.

The clearing was an abandoned Little League field set between the highway and the beach. The infield had grown over with weeds, and the rest was a ragged pasture of tall grass. The chicken wire on the primitive backstop had pulled away from its wood frame and curled back like a page. At center field, behind the rusty chain-link fence that described the tiny outfield, was a scoreboard, a splitting sheet of painted plywood nailed to two two-by-four posts. According to the numbered plywood squares still hanging by small hooks, HOME was leading VISITORS 3–1 in the top of the fourth inning. Mickey and Harvey stood at home plate, a piece of wrinkled rubber, with the light fading fast over the Sound and the wind picking up, and it seemed as if the world had ended long ago, in the middle of a Little League game.

 The White Sox treated Providence poorly in Chicago, winning Tuesday night in Comiskey Park and sweeping the Wednesday twi-night doubleheader. The Jewels broke their new seven-game losing streak on Thursday night when Dan Van Auken, on only three days' rest, pitched a five-hit shutout. Harvey accounted for all the runs with a long fly ball in the fourth that crept up a westerly breeze and landed in the first row of the right field seats, scoring Manomaitis and Stiles ahead of him.

He was sitting in front of his locker with a can of Pabst Blue Ribbon when two hands grabbed him from behind around the neck.

"Goddamn it!" Harvey yelled and turned around. "Oh, it's you. How'd you get in here? I said I'd meet you outside."

"The clubhouse guard took one look at me and knew I wasn't lying when I said I was your brother," Norm said, slapping Harvey on the back. He looked like an inflated version of his younger brother, slightly taller, heavier, puffier, and paler. At thirty-four, Norm wore a few more creases around his eyes and mouth that implied what would become of his face. In his fist, there was a scorecard filled in with a professorially florid hand. "So this is it," he said, glancing around the clubhouse at the half-naked ball players and fully attired reporters. "The madcap, zany guys who make up what is, at the moment, the worst team in professional baseball."

"Good to see you too, Norm. Want a beer?"

"No, thanks. But, hey, thanks for hitting a home run for me out there. Looked like a tough pitch."

"It was a lousy hanging slider, and I should've parked it in the upper deck." Harvey wrapped a towel around his waist.

"Okay, okay, excuse me." Norm reached into his brother's locker and picked up his baseball glove. He tried it on.

"Nice piece of leather, Harv. You know, when you were round the bases, I kept thinking about the Wiffleball games we used to play in the backyard and how every time you hit one off me into the Milners' yard you'd prance around the imaginary bases, taunting me. Remember?"

"I'm going to take a shower, Norm. Can you keep out of trouble?"

"Gee, you're in a great mood, slugger. Can't a guy reminisce?"

In Norm's Saab, they headed north to the Loop along Lake Shore Drive. Norm talked about his family as if he were its manager: "Nicky's really coming along, we're looking for him to have a great year in sixth grade, and Linda's new job's a real bonus for everybody. . . ." Harvey stared out the window at the city's huge sparkling skyline. Providence was small; it could hardly even be called a city. Boston was prissy and didn't have the look of a place where important things got done. New York was a real city, but a claustrophobic one with nowhere to stand and take its measure. But Chicago, especially if you saw it from Lake Shore Drive on a clear night, looked like what you would imagine if you had never seen a city, only had one described to you.

They went for broiled Lake Superior whitefish at Berghoff's in the Loop, where the waiters embodied the efficiency and kindness of a family doctor, even though the hour was late. Norm wanted to talk about their childhood—about Big Al Blissberg's old restaurant, summers on the Cape, endless games invented to pass the time growing up. By the time Harvey had laid two beers on top of the one he had drunk in the clubhouse, he, too, was in a nostalgic mood.

"Remember the summer we played stickball against the grammar school every day and kept records for each game?" Norm was saying. "Don't think I've forgotten that I struck you out four hundred twenty-three times in one summer."

Harvey piled fragments of a parsley potato on the back of his fork. "You were crazy about statistics even then."

"Speaking of which, Harv, I've got another one for you."

"You promised."

"All right, forget it," Norm said.

"Well, one more can't hurt. Let me have it."

"No, no, I don't want to . . ."

"Damn it, Norm, what is it?" The restaurant was almost empty, and a white-haired waiter a few tables away looked up in their direction, then resumed collecting silverware.

"Okay, I was looking over the pitching statistics for the entire season—"

"What do you do, anyway? Cut out every Jewels box score?"

"And mount them in a scrapbook. Now listen. This is interesting." Norm swabbed his plate with a piece of seeded roll. "You guys have used four pitchers in the starting rotation most of the year: Stan Crop, Bobby Wagner, Dan Van Auken, and Andy Potter-Lawn. I was going over the season, and I began to notice how many times they had actually carried a lead into the late innings, only to be taken out of the game with men on base." He dabbed his mouth with a napkin.

"It happens all the time, Norm."

"I'm not through. Seventeen times, Harv, seventeen times your starting pitchers have been taken out of the game with a lead in the seventh, eighth, or ninth inning, and then you guys have gone on to lose the game. Is that bad managing or what?"

"I know we've lost a lot of games in the late innings," Harvey said between sips of de-caf, "but that's what happens when you've got a mediocre team. The starting pitcher gets tired, and Felix isn't going to leave him in the game in the late innings, even if he's got a small lead. We're not a high-scoring team, and we're not going to pad that lead and make the pitcher's job any easier for him, so Felix wants a fresh arm in the game. You've got to use your relievers even if you've got a weak bull pen. Anyway, Norm, a bull pen that loses seventeen games in the late innings sounds about average to me for any second division team."

Norm was finishing his last few string beans with his fingers. "Okay, but you can't fault me for trying. It beats preparing for my lecture tomorrow on Flaubert's letters to Louise Colet."

"There's a limit to what you can squeeze out of statistics."

"I still think I ought to be managing a major league ball club." Norm wiped his fingers along the tablecloth, leaving parallel smudges.

It was two days before Harvey understood the meaning of what Norm had told him.

It had been raining for two solid days in Providence. When the team returned to town on Friday, the city looked like something that had been left out in the yard overnight. On Friday afternoon, in his damp apartment, Harvey opened the sports pages of the *Journal-Bulletin;* he and his exactly .300 batting average clung to the bottom of the American League's top ten batters list. Next to it were the standings.

## AMERICAN LEAGUE
### East

|            | W  | L  | Pct. | Games Out |
|------------|----|----|------|-----------|
| New York   | 95 | 63 | .601 | —         |
| Boston     | 94 | 64 | .595 | 1         |
| Baltimore  | 90 | 67 | .573 | 4½        |
| Milwaukee  | 87 | 71 | .551 | 8         |
| Cleveland  | 78 | 71 | .494 | 17        |
| Detroit    | 72 | 85 | .459 | 22½       |
| Toronto    | 69 | 89 | .437 | 26        |
| Providence | 68 | 90 | .430 | 27        |

Harvey counted the satisfactions left to him in the season: spoiling the Yankees' pennant hopes on this final weekend; helping the Jewels creep out of last place; getting an average of at least three hits in ten at-bats against New York pitching; and finding Rudy's killer.

He finally put in a call to Linderman. "Tell me something," he said.

"Well, let's see. We got a guy down here at headquarters right now who might've killed those two kids on the East Side. A Brown University senior, no less. I know the Ivy League has had to lower its admission standards to fill its dorms during economically hard times, but child-murderers is really stooping. That is, if this guy's our man."

"Congratulations. Tell me something else."

"We had Ronnie Mateo down here the other day, and I showed him the bank statements. Is that what you want to know? He said to show him what he was paying Rudy off to do and he'd consider making a confession. Otherwise, he said, quote quote, leave me the hell alone. We had a couple of men in Wisconsin asking some questions, but anyone who knew Rudy there seems to think he was a gentleman and a scholar. I'm sorry, Harvey. We're still looking for threads. I've

got two commissioners on my back about this thing,
the police one and the American League one."

The clouds broke by game time Friday evening. The
Rankle Park crowd, inspired perhaps by Lassiter's column in the morning paper suggesting that the finan-
cially troubled Jewels might be moved to another city
before next season, swelled into the low twenties. The
weather was balmy. Behind Andy Potter-Lawn, the
Jewels rewarded the fans with a 6–0 shutout victory.
Boston had already won in Baltimore, pulling the Red
Sox into a first-place tie with New York. Toronto beat
Seattle at home and remained a game ahead of Providence.

At eleven-thirty that night, Harvey watched Mickey
do the sports wrap-up in his apartment. She narrated
a minute of tape showing the Jewels' fourth inning
rally. Harvey saw himself leg out a double, executing a
perfect hook slide to the right field side of second base.
Then he heard his name again. "During the last month,
when the Jewels have been anything but a good baseball team," Mickey was saying, "one of the few bright
spots has been Harvey Blissberg's race to finish with a
three hundred batting average. Tonight's action left
him batting just that. If he finishes the season this
Sunday with nothing less, it will be his first three
hundred season in six years of major league play. From
all of us here at 'Eleven O'Clock Edition,' Harvey, we
wish you good luck." Mickey had finally mentioned
him on the air. Harvey toasted her image with a bottle
of Rolling Rock.

On Saturday, Providence beat New York for the second day in a row, on Les Byers's home run leading off
the bottom of the tenth. That night, after Mickey made
salad and spaghetti carbonara for Harvey at her place,
they made slow, anxious love. When Mickey fell asleep,
the white bedroom was so quiet that Harvey heard the
little numbered metal leaves of her digital clock radio
fall into place every sixty seconds. He watched her roll

over on her back, clutch a pillow to her breast, sputter dryly, and melt back into a dream. He got up and went to the living room, where he pressed his forehead against the cool window and gazed down at the throbbing sign of the Play Den Disco on the other side of I-95. When he returned to bed, the clock read 3:57 A.M. Behind the clock, propped up against the lamp, was the baseball card that Mickey had taken from him after he found it at Rudy's place. He stared at it, saw himself smiling back, and closed his eyes, afraid that the mere tension in his body might wake her up.

Suddenly, a small opening appeared in his thinking, and through it he saw his brother and him eating dinner in Chicago. "Seventeen times," Norm had said, "your starting pitchers have been taken out of the game with a lead in the seventh, eighth, or ninth inning, and then you guys have gone on to lose the game." It hadn't seemed an especially interesting statistic at the time; Norm's obsession had yielded far better. Seventeen was not an ungodly number of times for relievers to lose a lead in the late innings.

But Norm hadn't said which relief pitchers had squandered how many leads held by which starting pitchers. "What can a relief pitcher *do?*" he had asked Mickey at the batting cage. It was simple: a relief pitcher could prevent a starting pitcher from winning games. But why would he do it?

The figures on the digital clock changed from 3:59 to 4:00. With what seemed like a series of mental clicks, the leaves of the crime's logic fell into place. Harvey sat up in bed, sweating profusely, and wondered if it could all possibly be true. It had taken him less than two minutes to finish the work begun almost five weeks ago. Whoever had written the death threat—and he now knew who had—had been afraid of just these two minutes. The whole thing was too incredible, but what little doubt he had could be removed by some quick statistical research of his own.

He was buttoning his shirt when Mickey stirred, subsided, stirred again, and said hoarsely, "What? What is it? Bliss? What're you doing?"

He bent over her. "I've got to go to the ball park. Go back to sleep."

"What? What ball park?"

"I've got to go to Rankle Park, Mick. I've got to see about Rudy."

She rose to one elbow and shook red hair out of her face. "What're you talking about? It's four o'clock. See what about Rudy?"

"I think I know now."

"Know *what?*"

"Know what happened to him. But I've got to check on something, and then I'll know for sure. Go back to sleep, Mick. I won't be long."

"It can't wait?"

"No, it can't wait, Mick," Harvey whispered as he zipped up his pants. "For nearly five weeks, everyone and his uncle has been trying to get me to forget about this thing. But I just figured it out, and if I wait till morning to do what I have to do, I won't be able to do it at all, Mick."

"Then let me go with you."

"No, Mick. Go back to sleep. I'll call you later."

She fell back on the bed. "Then be careful, Bliss. I've got to protect my investment."

"Sweet dreams, Mick."

"Oh, Bliss," she called as he was leaving the room. "Yeah?"

"It *was* Frances, wasn't it, who was paying Rudy off?"

Harvey nodded. "It was Frances. Why?"

"I just remembered something I have to do."

"All you have to do is go back to sleep."

"Will do, Bliss," she said.

Harvey rode the too-bright elevator down to the little glazed-brick lobby and walked out to the dark parking lot. It was cool and misty; he heard a diesel truck whine into gear two blocks away on the expressway. Somewhere in the Beaumont West lot, a car started up.

He drove through downtown and up the hill to his apartment. He found the photocopies of Rudy's bank statements in his sock drawer, got back in his car, and headed for Rankle Park. Norm, he thought, your statistics finally came in handy. Statistics—without them, the game of baseball would float away, a vapor of dimly remembered clutch hits, hot dogs, and traffic jams outside the stadium. If baseball was a religion, as Sharon Meadows had said, then statistics were its bible. They fastened the game to history, made it a science, made its fans technicians, its managers and players probabilists. With numbers, lists, percentages, averages, the game was played constantly, over morning coffee, in bars, in the dead of winter. Statistics everywhere—for Most Times Hit into Double Plays in Single Season, Most Passed Balls in a Career, Ratio of Strikeouts to Walks among National League Relief Pitchers, for, as far as anyone knew, Most Stand-Up Triples when the Moon is in Virgo.

But there was one they didn't keep track of—for Number of Games Lost by a Relief Pitcher in Relief of a Particular Starting Pitcher in a Single Season.

The streets in the warehouse district around Rankle Park were empty except for a few parked cars and the welter of discarded programs and Pepsi cups from Saturday's game. The park's monstrous black silhouette, relieved here and there by security lights, rose ominously over the warehouses. A dog stood under a streetlight near the players' parking lot, eating popcorn out of a paper cone on the curb.

The gate in the chain-link fence around the lot was secured by a heavy chain and padlock. Harvey considered scaling the ten-foot fence, but the padlocked chain was long enough so that, by forcing the two swinging sides of the gate as far apart as he could, he made enough room to slip through. The only car in the lot was Steve Wilton's Honda, and Harvey wondered if his battery had died on him again.

Harvey found the clubhouse key on his key chain. Inside, the locker room was filled with dark bluish light. The ice chest hummed. A uniform hung sadly in each cubicle. A scratching sound stopped him; one of Rankle Park's rats. Harvey walked slowly across the room to Felix's office. The door was unlocked. Everything was going his way. He reached in through the doorway and turned on the light. Felix's office sprang to fluorescent life.

From the top of the metal filing cabinet in the corner behind Felix's desk, he took down a heavy three-ring notebook with a piece of adhesive tape across the cover that said, SEASON STATS. He sat down at Felix's desk and opened it. The old General Electric Telechron clock over the door read 4:32.

Each page of the notebook contained a detailed box score of a Jewels' game, beginning with the season opener at home on April 9. All of them had been neatly typed and Xeroxed by Ray Spanner, the team statistician.

Bobby Wagner had pitched the opener, a complete game victory over Toronto, 4–2. Harvey flipped the pages until he found the next game Bobby had pitched, on April 16 in Cleveland. Rudy had relieved him in the eighth, with one out, one man on base, and Providence leading 3–1. Rudy had retired five straight batters to pick up his first save of the year. Final score: Providence 3, Cleveland 1. Winning pitcher: Wagner (2 wins, no losses). Bobby was off to a good start.

Harvey turned pages furiously. Rudy did not pitch again in relief of Bobby until May 6, against the Angels in Anaheim. When Bobby was removed in the seventh with one out and two men on, the Jewels led 6–4. Rudy gave up a double to the first Angel batter, and both baserunners scored. The two runs, of course, were charged to Bobby. With the score 6–6 in the eighth, the Jewels scored twice and went on to win 8–6. Winning pitcher: Furth (1–0).

On May 23, Bobby was losing badly to Minnesota in the fourth, 7–1, when Rudy went in to pitch two innings and gave up one run. Rudy was in turn replaced by Marcus Marlette in the sixth. Final score: Minnesota 11, Providence 4. Losing pitcher: Wagner (4–2).

No, that wasn't what Harvey was looking for. He leafed through the pages of the notebook. He finally found what he wanted, on June 18 in Boston.

It was the same night that Harvey had found Mickey in his bed at the Sheraton, the night he thought that Rudy slept with her. At Fenway Park, Bobby Wagner had been hanging on to a 3–2 lead over the Red Sox in the eighth. He had two men on base and two outs when Rudy was called in. He gave up a three-run homer to the first batter he faced, Tony Jallardio. Two of the runs were charged to Bobby, hanging him with the eventual 5–3 loss.

Harvey took the folded photocopies out of his pocket and laid them next to the notebook. On June 25, a week after the Boston game, Rudy had made his first deposit in the Industrial National Bank checking account. Harvey found a loose cigarette in one of Felix's desk drawers and lit it. In another drawer, he found a fifth of Smirnoff vodka and helped himself to a long swallow.

The next time it happened was on July 14, against Kansas City. With the Jewels ahead 2–1 in the seventh, Rudy came in to relieve Bobby with one out and the bases loaded. By the time the inning was over, Rudy had allowed all three baserunners to score. All three runs were charged to Bobby. Final score: Kansas City 4, Providence 3. Losing pitcher: Wagner (7–9).

Harvey checked Rudy's bank statements. On July 19, five days after the game, he had deposited another three thousand dollars in the account.

All a relief pitcher had to do was get his fastball up a little or hang a curve or telegraph a change-up or take too much off the slider so that it just sat there over the plate like a plump curve that forgot to break. Maybe in the minors a pitcher could get away with a bad pitch, or two, or three. But the majors were filled with ball players who had gotten there precisely because they knew how to make pitchers pay for mistakes. And if the pitches weren't really mistakes—if you knew, as any major league pitcher had to, the batters' strengths and weaknesses—then you could almost always manage to make a fatal error.

Harvey kept going. In a game with Texas on July 26, Rudy relieved Bobby in the ninth inning with two men on and nobody out. Providence was clinging to a 2–1 lead. Rudy gave up a run-scoring single to Neal Atlas, then another runscoring single to Mason Meyer. Final score: Texas 3, Providence 2. Losing pitcher: Wagner (7–11). On August 2, a week later, there was another three thousand dollar deposit in Rudy's account.

On August 9, Rudy relieved Wagner in the seventh inning with two men on and two outs. Providence led Baltimore 5–4. Rudy gave up a three-run homer to Rob Dorsey. Final score: Baltimore 8, Providence 5. Losing pitcher: Wagner (8–12). Two days later, on August 11, Rudy deposited, for the fourth time, three thousand dollars.

On August 28, Rudy relieved Wagner in the eighth with two men on and nobody out. Providence led Chicago 2–1. Rudy gave up a single to load the bases, then a triple to Mac Bodish that scored all three baserunners. Final score: Chicago 4, Providence 2. Losing pitcher: Wagner (8–15). Rudy didn't live to deposit that three thousand.

Between June 18 and August 28, on five occasions Rudy had come into the game to replace Bobby, blown his lead, and hung him with the loss. Only an extreme optimist would attribute the pattern to coincidence—an optimist who did not have photocopies of Rudy's bank statements in front of him and who did not know how badly Frances Shalhoub wanted to win—and how badly she wanted Bobby Wagner to lose. It all made such horrifying sense that for a moment Harvey regretted having insisted on finding out the truth. He found another cigarette and smoked it with a trembling hand in the greasy fluorescent glare. He took another gulp of Felix's vodka.

There was a crinkle of nylon in the doorway, and a soft, deliberate voice said, "And he would've kept doing it if I hadn't figured it out. He wasn't a smart pitcher, Professor, but I knew he could throw better than that."

Harvey's back was to the door. He swiveled around with the bottle of vodka in his hand.

Bobby Wagner's six-foot-four frame filled the doorway. He was wearing jeans, running shoes, and an unzipped navy windbreaker. One hand was in a windbreaker pocket, the other concealed behind him. He was chewing gum with a leisurely, lateral motion, glowering at Harvey from under his single black eyebrow with a kind of dull satisfaction. Behind him, the row of louvered windows high on the clubhouse wall strained the dawn light into the locker room.

"So now you've figured it out, too," Wagner said quietly, as if afraid he might wake somebody up at so early an hour. "Congratulations."

"You've been following me," Harvey said in a whisper.

"I have," Wagner agreed, not moving from the doorway.

So the car he had heard starting up in the parking lot of Mickey's building had been Bobby's. Harvey ran his eyes over Felix's office to confirm the obvious: there was only one way out and Wagner was standing in it.

"You didn't just happen to be at Leo's the other night, did you?" Harvey felt strangely serene; it was as though they were both on their best behavior. Maybe it was Wagner's faint drawl, Harvey's exhaustion, the hour, the inevitability. . . .

"I sure didn't," Wagner said. "And I also didn't just happen to see you go in and pay Linderman a little visit the other day. I've watched you do a lot of little things."

Harvey's throat tightened. "So why'd—why'd you save my ass at Leo's?"

Wagner brought his hand out of the windbreaker

and picked briefly at his nose with it. He gave the odd impression of simply passing the time of day. "Maybe I was hoping you would turn out to be dumber than I knew you were. Maybe I wanted you all to myself," he said.

"What do we do now, Wags?"

Wagner brought his other hand from behind his back, and Harvey's whole body seemed to make a fist.

Wagner was holding a baseball bat, one of Harvey's. He leaned forward on it, like a vaudevillian resting on his cane. "I'm in kind of a spot, Professor," he said.

Harvey realized he was still holding the bottle of vodka; overmatched, he put it down carefully on the desk behind him. He pictured himself dead in the whirlpool and Dunc finding him in a few hours. Linderman was standing over him, shaking his head, saying, "You had to be the hero, didn't you, Harvey?"

"Don't be a fool, Wags."

"You know the whole story," Wagner said.

Harvey closed the statistics book on the desk. It was true—and he was the only one who did. Bobby could only know that someone had put Rudy up to it, but not who it was; and Frances could deduce who it was that waited for Rudy somewhere in the dark tunnels beneath the stands. But only Harvey knew now for sure.

"Maybe I know the whole story, but you don't," he told Wagner.

Wagner stepped forward out of the shadows in the doorway. There was a slick of sweat over his handsome face, and he held the bat with both hands on the handle in front of him, low near the floor.

"I don't care who it was anymore," he said. "I don't care if it was Ronnie Mateo or one of those other wops or—"

"It was Frances, Wags."

"That so?" Wagner said without interest.

"She was the one who worked it out with Rudy."

"That's what you figure?"

"It's what I know. She owns a fifth of the team, Wags. She has a real stake in it. That's why—"

"I know all I want to know," Wagner said, but he didn't come any closer, and Harvey started talking.

"You can do what you want with me, but you ought to know why you're doing it." He was facing Wagner in the chair, his hands braced on the arms. "She sold her company in New York because she wanted to make a career out of this club. She wanted a winner, Wags, but unless your team plays in a big city with a baseball tradition and all that media money, there's only one way, and that's by being good. And you know, the only way to be good is to buy, beg, or steal the best ball players you can find. And then—then you got to hold on to them."

"Keep talking, Professor. This is good."

"You were the one she wanted to hold on to most of all, the one bona fide star we've got, the cover boy. You're the guy who can put people in the seats, even in Providence. Only one problem, Wags: you were going to be a free agent after this season." Harvey thought of Frances's "nucleus": Bobby Wagner was the only one in it she was going to lose. "To the Jewels," he went on, wondering for how long Bobby planned to let him talk, "you could be the franchise, but you were at the end of your old Baltimore contract, and then your price was going up. If you had a good year this year, and even if you had just a fair year, you were going to be good for more money than this club could afford to pay you. See, Wags, the team's done badly at the gate, and on top of that, Levy's paying through the nose to the mob on the concession money. They might stretch their budget some to keep you, but no way were they going to be able to outbid Morrissey and the other high-rollers in the free agent market."

Bobby stood ten feet away, grinding the bat handle

in his hands. "Go on, Professor," he said, as if extending a final courtesy. "We got a little more time."

"So Frances needed you to build a winner, Wags. She always got her way before, and she was going to get it this time, too. She had to hold on to you, and to do that she had to make sure you had a bad year. She realized it was her only real chance. You've got to understand the way Frances looks at things, Wags. She believed that if you looked as if you were losing it, maybe the other owners would begin to smell a loser. Your value would go down, Wags, and the team would have a shot at you. She didn't care about this season; we weren't really going anywhere anyway. It was next year, and the years after that, she was building for. She just had to make sure that Bobby Wagner would be around to build with."

Harvey's own voice calmed him. As long as he talked, he could look Bobby in the eye. "So the first thing she did—those stories wherever we played this season, the ones about how your arm was hanging by a shred? Your arm's fine. Your old manager didn't trade you because of calcium deposits; he got rid of you because, number one, he never liked you much in the first place and, number two, he was going to lose you anyway to free agency, and this way at least he could trade you and get something for it. Ten-to-one, Frances was behind most of those stories in the papers. As an old public relations pro, she had the contacts and the know-how. It was just a way to get you some bad advertising. But the real bad advertising was that you were going to lose a lot more games than you should've. And Rudy was going to help you do it."

"What'd she have on him?" Bobby said, his jaw working on the gum.

"Nothing, except they were sleeping together. He'd fallen in love, and Rudy wasn't the smartest guy in the world to begin with."

"I thought his taste ran to stewardesses."

"Which is why he'd do anything for someone with Frances's class," Harvey said. "And she cared little enough about him to ask him to do anything. She threw in the cash, just to keep it business, which is how she likes to work. And she found a way into the dugout, where she could make sure the plan worked, where she could make absolutely sure Felix kept bringing Rudy in to relieve you.

"And she's smart, Wags. She knows you're a streak pitcher. Most of those streaks have been winning ones, but she knew that—when was it, Wags, three years ago?—she knew that even when you went something like twenty and thirteen that season, eight of those losses were in a row. She realized that you only knew how to win, not how to lose. She knew that if she got Rudy to throw a few games, you might do the rest of the damage yourself. That was one of the reasons your old manager didn't like you, wasn't it? You didn't bounce back when you lost.

"And Rudy was only a decent relief pitcher, so he could come in and throw a few pitches just fast enough to cost you the game, and no one would ever think he was in the tank. But Frances didn't know when to stop. She gave you a chance to prove you were a little smarter than she gave you credit for. She threw Rudy in the tank once too often, and you smelled it."

Harvey watched the minute hand on the clock over Bobby's shoulder twitch from 5:29 to 5:30.

"What do you care about any of it?" Bobby said evenly. "He was a punk, Professor. He was trash. Why didn't you leave it alone? What did it matter to you?"

"It mattered."

"I never did anything to him."

"That's not how it works."

"He screwed with my career. He screwed with the biggest thing I've got."

"Frances did, not Rudy. Frances did it to you."

"And you were about to screw me even more, Professor." Bobby came two steps closer and stopped, six feet away.

Harvey pushed away from the desk in his chair."I didn't know what I was going to find. I was just looking."

"I wish I could help you, Professor."

"Don't be a fool. Put that bat down."

"He hit me first." Bobby's voice was unnervingly soft. "He wouldn't tell me. Then I found the money, and I couldn't believe it. It was sitting in his pocket, and he still wouldn't admit anything. He just sat in the whirlpool with that shit-eating grin and said he always carried a lot of cash. You get that, Professor? He always carried around a few big bills like that. That's when it got serious." He tapped the head of Harvey's bat against the indoor-outdoor carpeting. "He got out of the whirlpool and shoved me."

"Put the bat down, Wags."

"I didn't have the bat with me then." Bobby appeared almost hypnotized. "Just wanted to talk it out. Then he came at me, and we mixed it up, and he shoved me against the bat rack and—"

"It's going to be all right, Wags." Harvey felt his heart pounding in his neck.

Bobby came forward another step. "It's too late," he said. "It's much too late. I thought you'd understand about the rat. That was strike one." He now held the bat in front of him horizontally, one hand on each end. "Then I left you a message in Yankee Stadium. Why didn't you pay attention? Strike two, Professor."

He slid the hand that was on the head of the bat down to join the other on the handle."Now this." He looked down at the thick book of statistics on Felix's desk. "Now you know too much. And you know what they say. Strike three you're dead."

"Goddamn it, you—"

Bobby swung the bat back over his head like an ax and brought it down.

Harvey grabbed the statistics book just in time and held it up with both hands in front of his face, twisting his head as far to the side as he could. The force of the bat flattened the book against his shoulder and carried Bobby's body forward on top of Harvey.

Before Bobby could recover his balance, Harvey speared him in the groin with an outstretched leg, leaped from the chair, and dashed for Felix's door. He ran across the locker room toward the runway that led to the dugout.

The metal door swung outward, and Harvey jumped down the three cement steps to the runway. Ahead of him, a square of morning light showed the dugout and a section of the left field stands against pink sky.

Bobby came down the steps after him. For an instant, Harvey thought about running up onto the field, but it was Bobby's running shoes against his penny loafers, Bobby's bat against his bare hands. Halfway down the runway, Harvey took a left and pushed open the door to the unused network of tunnels that ran under the stands. He kicked off his loafers in stride and took off into the darkness.

The floor of the tunnel was damp, and Harvey's socks were soaked through within a few steps. The tunnel was about six feet wide, dark green walls with rashes of rust, but then the light from the runway faded, and Harvey was running in total darkness. Behind him, Wagner's shoes slapped soddenly, too infrequently to be a run.

"Take your time, Professor. There's nowhere to go." The voice surrounded him.

Harvey slowed, lowering his feet into the cool puddles on the cold concrete. He reached out with his right hand, felt for the oily wall, and followed its gentle curve. They were behind home plate somewhere, and the tunnel followed the contour of the stands. He had never been in the catacombs. He knew there were connecting tunnels, but couldn't be sure they weren't dead ends. The main tunnel had to feed out somewhere, probably near the visitors' clubhouse under the stands on the third base line. That still wouldn't do him any good; the door to the clubhouse would be locked from the outside. He had been stupid not to run onto the field when he had the chance; there, at least, he could have seen what his chances were.

With his left hand, he reached out for the other wall, hoping to find an alcove, a doorway, anything. The tunnel wasn't narrow enough for him to feel both walls at the same time. For all he knew, he had already missed a connecting tunnel. Maybe he could crouch down against one side of the tunnel and hope that Wagner would walk right past him. Then he could run back to the clubhouse and out to the street.

His foot came down on a piece of paper.

"There you are," Wagner's voice said close behind him, and Harvey broke into a run again, dragging a hand along the wall.

"He was just a punk, Professor. He never belonged in the big leagues." The voice was soft and deep as it reverberated down the passage. "Your roomie was a nothing."

After every two slaps of Wagner's feet came a harder noise, the bat tapping against the concrete.

Abruptly, there was no wall at Harvey's right hand. He moved quickly into the opening and saw a hairline of light ahead. After ten or twelve yards, he found a doorknob that turned, but not easily; it felt as if it would squeak if he twisted it too far. He leaned against the corner of the passageway and caught his breath in a series of silent heaves. He heard Wagner walk past the opening, his bat clicking.

The door probably connected the catacombs to the near end of the visitors' dugout. In that case, the central tunnel would have to end soon, where it met the runway that ran from the far end of the dugout to the clubhouse. Seventy, maybe eighty feet. Wagner would know shortly that he had lost Harvey.

Wagner's footfalls suddenly became faster and louder. Harvey turned the doorknob and pulled on the heavy door. It let out a thin screech. Light flooded the passageway. Harvey found himself where he had expected, at the end of the dugout between the end of the bench and the water cooler against the wall. Just below eye level was Rankle Park's grass. The sky was as soft as tissue, infused with pink over the stands.

Harvey leaped onto the end of the bench by the door

and pressed himself against the back wall of the dugout. Wagner appeared suddenly, carelessly, in the doorway. He took a step toward the dugout steps, where he stopped, like a man whose peripheral vision was burdened. He turned and raised the bat. Harvey jumped off the bench and grabbed the shaft of the bat with both hands and brought his knee up into Wagner's gut. Wagner vomited air and doubled over. When he straightened up, Harvey had the bat and was standing on the grass at the lip of the dugout.

"You tried to kill me, you bastard." Harvey, panting, held the bat over his head.

Below him, Wagner clasped his hands over his stomach. His black hair was matted in wild curls on his forehead. "What happens now, Professor?" he said between gasps.

"Just go home."

"There's nothing in it for me."

"There's nothing in it for you here."

"There's you, Professor."

"The bat's mine now," Harvey said, but Wagner had seen the ball bag near his feet. It was the size of a bowling ball bag, made of canvas, and it was filled with baseballs for batting practice. The Yankees must have left it in the dugout after Saturday's game. Wagner picked it up in his left hand, reached in for a baseball with his right, and started up the steps.

"I used to be pretty good at this," Wagner said, squeezing the ball.

Harvey retreated a few steps, waving his bat. "You're crazy, Wags," he screamed. "I'll hurt you if I—have to."

"You just had your chance."

Harvey backpedaled on the grass in foul territory. "I'll hurt you."

"No, you won't." Wagner bounced the baseball lightly in his right hand. "I'll take this bag of balls against your bat."

Harvey turned and ran toward the infield. From a distance of sixty feet, six inches, any major league pitcher could nail a target the size of a human head; Bobby Wagner could put it right on your ear. There were two ways to go after a batter. If you only wanted to scare him, you aimed the ball directly at his head, because he would instinctively fall away from the pitch. But if you really wanted to hurt him, you would throw your best fastball a foot or so behind his head, and he would fall back into it. As Harvey ran, he saw it happening again and again—the batter involuntarily throwing himself, as if magnetized, into the path of a perfectly aimed beanball. If the batter was lucky enough to get his batting helmet between his cranium and the ball, he'd be able to get up and play ball again. If he wasn't, it was a most unpleasant way to end a baseball career.

Harvey was not wearing a batting helmet. Of course, he was a moving target. But then, he only had thirty feet on Wagner, and Wagner had a bag full of baseballs. Harvey bobbed and weaved as he ran to give Wagner less to throw at.

He was about to look back to see where Wagner was when the first ball combed his hair above his left ear. He heard it sizzle as it flew by and rolled out to right field. Now he looked back and saw Wagner forty feet behind him, running, dipping into the bag for another ball. Harvey veered right. Wagner had to stop to throw again, and by the time he released the ball, Harvey was sixty feet away, near second base.

The ball struck him in the meat of his deltoid behind his left shoulder, and his entire arm went numb. He stumbled forward, managing to keep his balance, and switched the bat to his right hand. He cut to his right, toward the Jewels' dugout along the first base line. It gave Wagner the angle on him, but he had to chance it now; his best hope was to make the dugout, then the runway, the clubhouse, the street, his car.

The electric tingling in his left arm was going away, and it hurt like a bitch; as he ran, he carried it dead at his side. The ninety feet between second base and the foul line had never been so endless. As he tore across the infield, he could see Wagner winding up out of his right eye.

He turned his head, and the ball was coming at it, bearing down, a ninety-five-mile-an-hour Bobby Wagner rising fastball. For a split second that went on too long, Harvey felt transfixed, almost attracted to the ball. He had seen the pitch countless times before, under better circumstances, when Wagner was with Baltimore—the red seams reduced to streaks in the blur of the backspin, less than half a second from mound to plate, the ball taking off in the last twenty feet.

This time the ball was rising toward his head. In that split second, Harvey felt that he and the ball were fated to meet. That was the thing about a good beanball, not a brushback pitch but one meant to change your idea of batting forever: it seemed to pursue you.

Harvey fell forward onto the damp infield grass, and the ball whistled furiously over him. It caromed off the top concrete edge of the dugout and bounced ineffectually into right. He clambered to his feet. There were still forty feet between him and the dugout. He couldn't find enough traction in his socks, and the dugout was not getting any closer.

He was ten feet from the top step of the dugout when the back of his right thigh exploded in pain. His leg gave, and he crumpled to the ground. He heard Wagner breathing coarsely behind him. Harvey tried to get up, but the feeling had gone out of his leg, and he fell back on his seat.

Wagner had caught him just above the back of the knee, and as Harvey clutched his leg in pain, he wondered why Bobby had not simply gone for his head again; it would have been quicker. He was just toying with him now.

Wagner walked slowly toward him off the mound, the ball bag dangling from his left hand. His right hand was caressing another baseball. He came in short heavy strides, looking right at Harvey, and stopped past the first base line, twenty feet away. The two of them were surrounded by thirty-seven thousand empty seats. Harvey did not even try to get up. He still had the bat, though, and from a sitting position, he wound up awkwardly and heaved it at Wagner. It missed him by three feet and skidded along the grass.

The pitcher looked at him. "Nice try, Professor."

"Please," Harvey said.

"It wouldn't take much from here, would it?" Wagner said. "What do you think—one pitch, maybe two?"

"Please," Harvey said again.

"They'd never know it was me."

"Of course they would," Harvey panted. "I've told Linderman everything I know. I've told Mickey. Don't be stupid." Propelling himself with one hand, he inched helplessly away from Wagner. "If you kill me, it'll be murder. It's only manslaughter now. You didn't mean to kill Rudy. Anyway, it was the whirlpool that finished him, not you. He provoked you, didn't he? It's manslaughter, but if you kill me, they'll really put you away."

Wagner looked down at him, chewing his gum. Harvey couldn't tell if he even heard what he was saying. Wagner kept turning the ball over in his hand, like a madman mindlessly practicing his tic.

"You made one mistake," Harvey called out. "Are you listening? You made one mistake. Frances has been making mistakes all summer. Rudy, too. Compared to them, I'd say you look like a prince. Go home. Go home and it's between you and me. It won't do you any good if they know you even came after me, so just go home. You've got to trust me, Wags. I never saw you this morning. You're going to be all right."

Wagner lifted his right hand and wiped his brow with the back of it.

"Go home," Harvey pleaded.

Wagner dragged his forearm across his face, and it made Harvey think of the famous photo of him, after he had no-hit Kansas City in 1978. Bobby was on his stool in front of his locker at Memorial Stadium in Baltimore, his uniform drenched with beer poured over him by jubilant teammates; he had his arm over his face, and he was weeping with joy.

Now, his arm fell away, and there was no expression at all. "You're through, Professor," he said.

Harvey felt his bowels begin to loosen.

Wagner put the ball bag at his feet and cocked his arm.

There was a kind of mechanical fluttering noise and then a great whooshing sound. Harvey looked up.

The entire system of sprinklers set into Rankle Park's outfield turf had gone on. Twelve jets of water rose simultaneously into the air behind Wagner and began twirling slowly in the morning sunlight.

Wagner turned for an instant, and when he did, Harvey scrambled the ten feet to the dugout and dropped onto the wooden duckboards.

Three hundred fifty feet away, a maintenance door in the left field fence opened, and a member of the grounds crew, a tiny figure pushing a wheelbarrow, came out. He spotted Wagner, put the wheelbarrow down, placed his hands on his hips, and yelled "Hey! You!" at the top of his voice.

Wagner looked at the baseball in his right hand as if it were the first one he had ever seen, fixed Harvey with his eyes, then looked over his shoulder at the figure with the wheelbarrow.

He walked in toward the dugout another ten feet, until he could see Harvey cowering on his knees on the dugout floor. He stopped and threw the ball as hard as he could up into the upper deck along the first base line.

Harvey listened to it rattle briefly among the wooden seats.

Then Wagner went past Harvey into the dugout runway and was gone.

The groundskeeper came all the way across the field to the dugout.

"Oh, it's you, Harvey," he said. A tongue of work glove lolled out of his pants pocket. "You threw a scare into me. What in the J.C. are you doing here at this—"

"It's all right," Harvey said, kneading the back of his leg. "I couldn't sleep, so I came out to the park early."

"Pretty early to be at the park," the man began, but Harvey held up a hand.

"It's okay. I get sentimental the last game of the season."

"Your business, I guess," the groundskeeper said, shaking his head with an avuncular smile. He didn't mention seeing a second person; Harvey figured that, from across the field, the groundskeeper had spotted only one. Probably Wagner, since Harvey had hid in the dugout once the sprinklers started up.

"It's just I'm used to having the place to myself at this hour," the groundskeeper went on. "Glad to know it wasn't some kids broke in. Did once, you know. Tore up the infield grass."

Harvey painfully got to his feet. "Do me a favor, will you, and walk me into the clubhouse. I think I might have heard something in there before." It was, among other things, too early in the morning to come up with a more original pretext.

"If you say so."

"Let's just go see. You never know." Harvey pushed the man ahead of him down the runway. At the clubhouse door, Harvey said, "You go first."

Wagner was nowhere to be seen in the locker room. Harvey opened the door leading to the players' parking lot and peered out. An orange sanitation truck hissed and lumbered past. Nothing. Then Wagner's champagne-colored *Jaguar* rolled around the corner onto Roger Williams Avenue. Harvey watched, wondering how long Wagner had been circling the block. As the Jaguar crept past the parking lot, its driver looked in Harvey's direction, and the car sped away.

"Looks all clear, Harvey," the groundskeeper said behind him.

Harvey locked the door. "Good enough. I must've been hearing one of the rats."

"Then I'll get back to work," the groundskeeper said. "By the way," he added, "you know you're not wearing shoes."

Harvey helped himself to a Pepsi from the ice chest. On the team blackboard, Felix had scrawled: "Winning Is Better Than Losing, But Losing With Pride Is Better Than Winning Without It." Underneath, Dunc had written: "Do not take any uniforms home with you. Please clean out all personal possessions from lockers." Harvey quickly went to Felix's office, straightened it up, and phoned Mickey. The clock on the wall said 6:10. His mouth tasted of bile and infield dirt.

He woke Mickey up and told her in the fewest possible words who had killed Rudy and why. "Now look," he told her, "Wags followed me here. He's been following me for a while."

"You sure you're all right?"

"Fine. I've got a little something to show for it, but it could've been worse."

"Where's he now?"

"I don't know. He drove away from here in his Jag a few minutes ago. That's why I want you to get dressed and get out of your apartment. I think he knows he's beaten, but I can't be sure what he'll do. He knows I know, and he thinks you and Linderman know. Don't ask any questions, just go. Doesn't that Burger King down the block open up real early? ... Then hustle down there, sit away from the window, and I'll meet you there in fifteen minutes. I've got to call Linderman."

"Sorry to wake you," he told Linderman a moment later.

"Not as sorry as I am. What is it now?"

"I thought you might be interested in picking up a couple of people. One of them killed Rudy Furth, and the other made the whole thing happen."

"Hold on," he said. "Let me go to the other phone. Shirley's asleep. So am I, I think."

Ten long seconds later, he was on the line again. "Where are you?"

"I'm sitting at Felix Shalhoub's desk at Rankle Park. I've got to talk fast, so listen."

"I listen fast, so talk."

Harvey talked. He told Linderman everything he needed to know and left out the parts that could wait.

"That's a helluva story, Harvey," Linderman said.

"Is that all I get? A helluva story? Whaddya need—a formal presentation with slides? For chrissakes, Linderman, I'm telling you. That's the way it happened."

"It sounds like a lot of neat circumstantial evidence. I've got to have something more."

"You don't need any more, Linderman. This is your lucky day. I got a confession."

"You what?"

"Wagner confessed it to me. And if you get off your ass, he'll confess it to you."

"What do you mean, confessed? Where? When?"

"Right here a few—Just believe me."

"At the park? When, goddamn it?"

"This morning. Don't ask me any more now."

"I hope you're ready to tell it to the judge. Where's Wagner now?"

"I don't know, but he can't be far away. He left here about ten minutes ago in his goddamn champagne Jag. He lives over on the East Side, somewhere off of Blackstone Boulevard."

"Where you going to be?"

"I'm going to pick up Mickey and get some sleep."

"I want you around today, Harvey."

"Where am I supposed to go? We play two against the Yankees today, and by the way, Wagner is scheduled to pitch the second. And Linderman, if I were you, I'd send some of your boys out to Frances's house right away. Just in case Wagner has some crazy ideas. Not that I really give a shit."

"Okay. Now look, Harvey, I know you want to be a hero, but I don't want you to say a thing about this to anybody until I see you later. Got that?"

Harvey removed his wet socks and tossed them in Felix's wastebasket. He put the statistics book back on the file cabinet. He got some shower clogs out of his locker and walked out to the tunnel and found his loafers. Then he locked up the clubhouse behind him, slipped through the parking lot gate, and drove to the Burger King three blocks down from the Beaumont West.

A few men in quilted vests and work clothes, fewer in business suits, and a couple of old women sat at tables strewn with cardboard coffee cups and Styrofoam containers. Two Providence patrolmen in brown nylon jackets were killing time by the window. There was no Mickey.

Harvey approached the service counter and asked a

kid whose face had no color in it if he had seen her. "Mickey Slavin," he said. "You know, the woman who does the sports on TV."

"I don't watch TV," the kid said, wiping off the side of the computerized cash register with a rag. "But hey—I know you."

"Look, maybe you saw her. Red hair, about five-eight."

"No, man. But then I don't look at the customers much. You're Harvey Blissberg, aren't you? How 'bout an autograph?" He ripped a napkin from a dispenser and plucked a pen from behind his ear.

Harvey wearily obliged him, then went to the cops near the window and described Mickey.

"Buddy," the smaller of the two said, "where'd you spend the night, in a sewer?"

Harvey looked down at his damp clothes. The armpits of his blue shirt were arced with sweat. His pants were streaked with grass stains. He had lost a button, and he wasn't wearing socks. "Look," he said, "could you just help me out?"

"Redhead?" the small cop said.

"Yeah."

"Sort of tall, with fullish red hair?" He wriggled his fingers on either side of his head.

"Yeah."

"Does the sports on channel four?"

"That's her."

"Haven't seen her." The cop laughed. "And here's some advice. Say you really got a date with Mickey Slavin at this hour of the morning, then I'd suggest you go home and take a shower first. You smell like hell."

"Gimme a break," Harvey said.

The bigger cop looked up from his cup of coffee. "Something you don't like about us, buddy?"

Harvey caught sight of Mickey coming in the door in a purple sweat suit. "There's plenty I don't like about you," he said to the cop. "Unfortunately, my date's just arrived and I don't have time to discuss it."

He ran over to hug Mickey. "I was worried about you," he said, burying his face in her blowzy hair.

"Those cops over there," she said. "Did Linderman send them?"

"Hardly. And where've you been? I thought I told you to get out of your apartment immediately."

"I was on the phone."

He didn't seem to hear her and dragged her down into a booth by the door. "I love you," he said.

"I love you, too, Bliss." She smiled for a second before it drained off her face. "How could Rudy do it?"

Harvey thought about it for a second. "Love and money," he said. "I don't think he would've gone for it if he hadn't somehow loved Frances, or really thought he did. That's how bad the guy needed to love someone."

"Poor, poor Rudy," Mickey said.

"I'll say this for the guy, though. He took the money because he was stupid and lonely and he loved her and he was afraid of what would happen if he didn't take it, but he knew the money was no good. He had to get rid of it. A sports jacket for me, a stereo for you, the trip to Maine. Typewriters for the orphanage."

"It doesn't make sense," Mickey said.

"Of course it doesn't."

"No, Bliss, I mean there was too much of a chance it wouldn't work. Some wealthy baseball owner might have been dying to get his hands on Wagner, no matter how poor a season he had with the Jewels. Someone could've outbid Levy, no matter what. Also, Wagner could've simply called it quits after a frustrating season, and the scheme would've worked too well for its own good."

"But you're forgetting one thing, Mick. It wasn't that the scheme was foolproof, which it wasn't, but that it satisfied that thing in Frances—that need to have people where she wanted them. That she might not be able to keep Wagner with the Jewels next year just because she wanted him—that was a personal insult to the woman. At all costs, she had to have the edge." Harvey tried to rub out the pain in the back of his shoulder. "It's all so goddamn stupid, Mick. And Frances paying Rudy off at the park on the night of the game he's just thrown? It's almost like she wanted to be caught. And Rudy keeping the money in a bank, instead of a sock? Of course, if he hadn't—"

"That's right, Bliss. If he hadn't been that dumb, we'd never have known anything. Think of it as his last act of friendship. He left you a faint trail of bread crumbs."

"Yeah, what are friends for?" Harvey said sourly. "You know"—he stopped, feeling the whole thing seep in—"I keep thinking about what he said the night Wagner killed him. He came in from the bull pen to pitch for Wagner, and I walked with him part way to the mound. I asked him how his arm felt, and he said something like, 'I can't get my fastball to go where I want.' And I thought, 'Poor guy, he's not having the kind of year he deserves.'" Harvey dropped his head into his hand for a moment. "Mick," he suddenly said, "Who'd you call?"

"Huh?"

"When you came in, you said you were late 'cause you were on the phone. Who'd you call at six-thirty in the morning?"

"I called Stanley L. Brolund. I thought you'd never ask."

"Who's Stanley L. Brolund?"

"Stanley Brolund," Mickey said, "is the gentleman Frances Shalhoub sold her public relations company to."

As she talked, Harvey forgot about his throbbing shoulder and leg. When Mickey finished, she leaned over the table to wipe some dirt off of Harvey's fore-

head. "Now will you tell me what just happened between you and Wagner at the park?"

Harvey looked at her. "It was just a couple of guys
playing with a bat and some balls. You know, the
great American pastime."

The Yankees crushed the Jewels in the opener of the doubleheader that afternoon, 12–5. With one game to go in the season, New York and Boston were tied for first place, Providence and Toronto for last.

Between games, the public address announcer informed over twenty-three thousand fans that the scheduled starting pitcher for the nightcap, Bobby Wagner, would be replaced by rookie left-hander Eddie Storella. The actual decision had been made several hours earlier, when Detective Linderman explained over the phone to a bewildered Felix that Wagner would soon be indisposed by handcuffs.

So far this had proven wishful thinking on Linderman's part; Wagner had eluded both the state and city cops who were fanning out across Rhode Island.

"Find him, damn it," Harvey told Linderman, when he had phoned him from Felix's office. "I've got another goddamn game to play, and I'm crapping my pants."

"Don't worry, Harvey. We're looking," Linderman said. "We've got a net over the state. He can't go too far."

Harvey exhaled loudly into the mouthpiece. "Did you tell Felix about Frances?"

There was a pause on the other end. "I didn't have the heart yet. Besides, you know all we've got is circumstantial evidence."

"I've got more than that, Linderman. Mickey—"

"Save it for later," Linderman said abruptly. "Harvey, you haven't told anybody about this, have you?"

"Just a reporter named Mickey Slavin who's going to break the story tonight at six and eleven. So don't start having any ideas about being nice to Frances Shalhoub, Linderman."

Fifteen minutes before the second game, Harvey anxiously walked the grass in front of the Jewels' dugout, where ten hours before Wagner had tried to kill him. He would have loved to get his hands on Frances now, but she hadn't turned up at the park, in or out of custody. There was nothing to forgive in her; she had turned a triple play, taking Rudy, Wagner, and herself out of baseball, and all on the off chance of paying a twenty-seven-year-old pitcher $250,000 a year instead of letting someone else pay him half a million. Bobby Wagner would go down in history as the first major leaguer to kill a teammate. Rudy would be remembered mainly as Wagner's victim, and, by those with exceptional memories, as a victim of Frances. Poor Felix. The whole thing seemed to have gone right by him, splattering him with mud. In all likelihood, the Providence Jewels themselves would be the answer to a fairly difficult baseball trivia question in twenty years. Harvey felt sick to his stomach again.

"Hey, Professah, ova heah, Professah."

Ronnie Mateo was a few feet away from him in a first-row box seat. He was wearing a black sports jacket with white stitching around the lapels and pockets, and a yellow knit shirt with red and black diamonds running up the left side.

"Professor," he said, "I bet you don't have a tape deck in that jalopy of yours."

"You win," Harvey said.

"I've got overstock on some first-class ones. Nice merch. Nice price, too."

"Get lost."

"But, Professor, you can't lose when it's the music you choose."

"I said get lost."

"I'm doing you a favor, Professor," Ronnie said.

Harvey closed the distance between them and put his face where Ronnie could get a good look at it. "You wanna do me a favor?" he said in a low voice. "Then take those tape decks, pop in some music you like, and shove the whole thing up your ass."

Ronnie's mouth opened slightly and showed his tiny teeth. "Sure thing, Professor," he said, his palms up in front of him. "Sure thing." He looked past Harvey at the diamond. "Sure hate to see the season end, Professor, don't you?"

When Harvey turned toward the dugout, he started. Thirty feet away was Bobby Wagner, in uniform, on his way to the bull pen. He walked quickly with his head up and with an air of distracted calm.

Harvey stood motionless, watching him for several seconds, then ran into the clubhouse and picked up the phone in Felix's empty office. He got through to Linderman almost immediately.

"Wagner's here," he told the detective. "What's wrong with you? He's here, and he's in the bull pen warming up."

"Don't kid me, Harvey."

"I'm not kidding, Linderman. Get your ass and the ass of every cop you've got down here."

"Harvey, don't do anything foolish till I get there." Linderman said. "In fact, don't do anything at all."

Harvey returned to the dugout. Wagner's head and shoulders were visible over the bull pen fence as he warmed up with Happy Smith. After two minutes, the bull pen gate opened, and Felix came out alone and began the long walk back toward the dugout.

Harvey returned to the clubhouse. It was empty except for Dunc, who was wiping off the tables in the trainer's room. Harvey was about to ask him about

Wagner's unexpected arrival when Linderman burst in the door from the players' parking lot. Behind him were four uniformed Providence policemen, and Frances Shalhoub. In one arm she cradled the clipboard she used for charting pitches, and she was tapping a silver pencil against it.

"Where is he?" Linderman said to Harvey.

"In the bull pen," Harvey said, "and in a couple of minutes, he'll be on the mound."

Linderman motioned two of the cops toward the runway. "Get him," he said.

"You want us to just walk right across the field?" one asked.

"I just want you to get him," Linderman said.

The two cops moved for the runway. Felix stood at the mouth of it, blocking them. He passed his hand nervously across the green Jewels logo on the front of his uniform. "Wagner's pitching," he announced.

"The hell he is, Felix," Linderman said. Behind him, Frances posed with the two other cops.

"Let him pitch, Linderman," Felix said."It's the last time he will."

"He killed a man, Felix."

"I don't care what he's done. Right now he's my starting pitcher for the second game. Then he's all yours."

"I'm sorry, Felix; he's coming with us." There was a touch of sadness in Linderman's voice.

"Look," Felix tried again. "He's not going anywhere. You've got cops crawling all over the park. I saw them out there. I'm not going to let you arrest the man in front of twenty-five thousand people."

Linderman couldn't have told Felix where Frances fit in; if he had, Felix wouldn't be making this stand.

"Wagner's not going anywhere yet," Felix said.

"Neither am I, Felix," Linderman replied. He turned back to Frances. "And neither are you, I'm afraid."

"I'll be glad to help you any way I can, Detective,"

she said, tapping her silver pencil against the clip-board. She had on the black dress she had worn at the barbecue she and Felix had held in May.

"You'll help by making yourself available for questioning."

"And what answers would *I* have?" she said.

"For starters, why you paid Rudy Furth to pin a few losses on Bobby Wagner." The words sounded rehearsed.

Felix's shoulders twitched. "What's that supposed to mean?" he said to Linderman.

"You've got quite an imagination, Detective," Frances said.

"Was it because you couldn't stand the thought of losing Wagner after this season?" Linderman asked her. He still didn't sound like his heart was in it.

"You haven't told me the whole story, have you?" Felix said to Linderman.

"No, Felix," Linderman said. "And neither has your wife. Isn't that right, Frances?"

"Frances?" Felix began.

Linderman coughed lightly. "The money in Rudy's clothes the night he was killed, the payments he kept depositing in his special little account—that was your money, Frances."

"I don't know about any money except what you found that night, and I can assure you it wasn't mine." She exhaled. "I have no idea why I'm bothering to dignify this whole ridiculous conversation. Detective, am I mistaken or are you trying to accuse me of something?"

"I'm sorry, Frances, but—"

"Then you better have some proof, Linderman."

Linderman glanced at Felix, then back at Frances. "You had a"—he rubbed his jaw—"a relationship with Rudy."

"Well, let's say I did," she snapped. "So what?"

The four cops in the clubhouse stared straight ahead into space.

"Proof," Frances said. "Proof, Linderman, or the next thing you know you'll be working a desk job in traffic."

The detective's head retracted slightly into his neck.

Harvey took a step forward. "Excuse me, Detective, but I think what Frances is referring to is the proof a gentleman by the name of Stanley Brolund will provide."

Frances's thin silver pencil slipped from her hand to the locker room floor.

At Burger King, Mickey had explained to Harvey why she had asked for Sharon Meadows's name at the batting cages a week ago. She and Harvey had been trying to figure out where Frances fit in, and Mickey figured that if Frances did pay off Rudy in cash, she needed a lot of cash that didn't leave a paper trail. She couldn't just withdraw it from her bank account, or sell off some securities without it being easily detectable. She needed someone who owed her a lot of money. On a hunch, Mickey called Sharon Meadows, posed as one of Frances's former clients, and got the name of the man who bought Frances's firm from her. Mickey tried to reach Brolund, but he was out of the country on business. So she forgot about it; it had been a long-shot hunch anyway. She forgot about it until Harvey left her bed to go to Rankle Park at four in the morning. Mickey had asked him if Frances *was* behind it. When Harvey had said yes, she knew she had to get hold of Brolund. But she had fallen back asleep as soon as Harvey left, and only when Harvey called at six did Mickey gather her nerve and try Brolund again. She woke him up out of a sound Sunday morning sleep, told him she was associated with Frances Shalhoub in Providence, and was calling on behalf of her accountants, who desperately needed some financial information. She told Brolund they didn't have any record of some payments he had made to her. Did he recall anything irregular?

"Brolund?" Linderman was saying to Harvey now.

"Stanley Brolund purchased Frances's public relations company," Harvey said, looking right at Frances as he spoke. "I don't know how much he paid her up front, but a little birdie told me he pays her about ninety-five hundred dollars a month, and he was kind enough to make two of those payments in cash over the summer, at Frances's request. Seems she told Brolund she needed thousand dollar bills for a team promotion. It was all the same to him."

Frances had still not bent down to pick up her pencil. Harvey felt Felix's incredulous gaze on him.

"Two times ninety-five hundred, Linderman, was more than enough to cover her expenses with Rudy."

The two cops near Frances instinctively moved closer to her.

"Like any good businessman," Harvey continued, "Mr. Brolund kept records of those cash transactions, and I'm sure he's more than willing to share them with you. Of course, in the time it's taken me to tell you this, Frances has probably come up with some other reason why she needed almost twenty grand in cash."

For a moment, no one said anything. Through the open door to the trainer's room, Harvey watched Dunc busy himself with some dirty towels. The sound of the Rankle Park crowd drifted down the runway and into the clubhouse. Several pairs of eyes were on Frances, none more intently than her husband's.

Harvey broke the brief silence. "Linderman, I have a feeling Frances is about to tell you her sad story. Aren't you, Frances?"

"You have no idea what you're talking about," she said, too bravely.

"It's too late for your bluffs, Frances," Harvey said. "It won't work anymore."

Frances looked wildly around her. "I won't stand here and be abused," she said.

No one said anything for a moment; then Linderman said to her, "I'm afraid you're going to need your lawyer, Frances."

"You might also consider a good public relations agent," Harvey said, and regretted the remark when he looked over at Felix. The manager stood stunned, watching his own feet.

"I think we should have a little talk," Linderman said to Frances. "I wonder if your husband will mind if we use his office. Felix?"

Felix didn't appear to realize that Linderman had addressed him. When the detective repeated the request, Felix finally looked up and nodded heavily.

Harvey watched Linderman and Frances disappear into the manager's office, then turned to Felix. "C'mon, Felix," he said. "Let's go out and win this game."

For six innings that afternoon, Bobby Wagner and Lou Gunning of the Yankees threw nothing but smoke. Wagner's money pitch, his rising fastball, had more hop on it than at any time in the last four months. By the seventh inning, the fall air had grown sharp, but the big dark green 52 on the back of Wagner's uniform was outlined with a wide border of perspiration. He had given up only one hit, a single in the first. The Jewels had only two meaningless singles off Gunning. The game was scoreless.

The Jewels had company in the dugout—two Providence cops who sat restlessly on the bench. One paid special attention to Wagner, who, when Providence was at bat, sat hunched over in the corner of the dugout, filing a callus on the index finger of his pitching hand with an emery board. The stands were dotted with more cops, at least fifty of them.

In the bottom of the seventh, the Jewels got lucky. Rapp singled and then went to second on Byers's groundout. Salta fanned for the second out, and Manomaitis walked. Gunning then worked Harvey to a count of two-and-two with sliders and a curve, then showed him a fastball tailing away. It was a smart pitch—away from Harvey's strength, but too close for him to ignore. Harvey flung his bat at it, got most of the ball, and had enough wrist behind it to drive a groundball between first and second into right field. It wasn't pretty, but Byers scored easily. After Battle struck out, Providence took the field for the top of the eighth with a 1–0 lead.

Wagner was working deliberately now, savoring each pitch. When he fanned Rumpling for his tenth strike-out of the game, the electronic scoreboard blinked "WAGNIFICENT" on the screen above the out-of-town scores. Boston was leading Baltimore 5–2 in the eighth inning of their second game, and Seattle led Toronto 6–3 in the seventh of theirs. If nothing changed there, or at Rankle Park, Boston would win the division championship, the Jewels would escape a last-place finish, and Harvey, who had scratched out two hits against Gunning, would end the year at an even .300.

Wagner retired the next two Yankees on pop-ups to end the top of the eighth. While the Jewels went down quickly in order themselves, Wagner filed away at his callus.

When Wagner walked out to the mound for the ninth, the crowd started clapping rhythmically. Wagner took his warm-up pitches slowly, bringing his long left leg up under his chin and kicking it out toward home plate. Even from his position in center field, Harvey could see that more cops were now congregating in the aisles and on the exit ramps of the grandstands around the infield. The clapping spread from section to section. Wagner removed his cap and drew his sleeve across his forehead. Then he tucked his glove in his armpit and turned around to gaze out toward center, looking at the charcoal sky, or maybe at Harvey, or maybe just at the scoreboard. The crowd noise swelled suddenly as Boston's 5–2 defeat of Baltimore was posted. Seattle had increased its lead over Toronto. If the Yankees didn't score on Wagner in the ninth, Boston would go to the play-offs.

Hazelwood, the first Yankee batter in the ninth, grew tired of waiting and stepped out of the batter's box. He stood there and watched as Wagner now revolved to his right, his eyes panning across the crowd in the right field pavilion and the grandstands along the foul line. The fans responded to this attention by clapping even louder. When Wagner faced home plate again, he put his glove on, peered in for Randy's sign, nodded, exhaled, and smoked a fastball strike over the inside corner. Hazelwood fouled off the next fastball. Wagner followed with an off-speed curve. Hazelwood waved helplessly at it and strode back to the dugout, shaking his head.

Corley, the next batter, tapped the first pitch back to the mound. Wagner fielded the ball and lobbed it over to Battle. The applause rolled out over the field. There were two outs in the ninth.

Wagner paused again on the mound with his glove in his armpit. His head was turned up toward the stands. Fifty Providence cops looked back.

Carlos Bonesoro was at the plate, waiting outside the batter's box with one proprietary toe on the chalk line. The umpire, both arms in the air to call time out, advanced toward the mound and said something to Wagner. The pitcher picked at the sleeve of his sweat shirt, almost daintily, like a woman removing stray hairs. The umpire settled himself behind the plate. Bonesoro stepped in. Wagner stroked the bill of his cap and performed a deep knee bend. Finally, he mounted the rubber, took Randy's sign, nodded, breathed once, twice, his shoulders heaving, rocked, and delivered.

Harvey lost the ball momentarily against the backdrop of the crowd, then began sprinting back to his left, tracking it. Out of the corner of his eye, he was aware of Wilton gliding over from right.

"Yours! Yours!" Wilton shouted before fading from Harvey's field of vision, leaving him alone with the ball. He put his head down, listening to his own grunts.

The right center field wall was closing in, but it wasn't on him yet, and as he got another look at the ball, he knew it didn't have enough to make the fence. He pushed off the spongy turf, extended his body, left arm out; it was so simple and predetermined, the ball drawn into his glove, a soft silent impact, Harvey sliding on the grass, keeping his glove aloft to show the second base ump there could be no question about the catch.

For a minute, he lay where he was, on his side, 20 feet from the 447-foot sign painted on the wall. Wilton was handing him his hat, saying, "Can of corn, Professor, can of corn." Far away, twenty-three thousand people were on their feet cheering. Circus music poured out of the public address system. Harvey finally climbed to his feet and, ball in glove, started in.

The Jewels were all out of the dugout, swarming around Wagner on the mound, pounding his back. Behind them, two ragged ranks of Providence policemen closed in along either base line. The park's regular security men were chasing a few young fans who had vaulted onto the field.

As Harvey jogged in, he spied Mickey up in the press box over home plate. She looked down at him, smiled, and waved once with an economical gesture. Next to her, Bob Lassiter was bent over his portable; Harvey knew he was hammering out the final paragraphs of his story. Harvey thought, Tarnished Jewels Pitcher Bobby Wagner Hurls Gold-Plated Complete Game Gem in Season Finale.

In the visitors' dugout, the second-place Yankees collected their jackets and gloves and bats and filed into their runway. The circus music stopped, and the announcer read the totals in a booming voice: "For the Yankees . . . no runs, one hit, no errors. . . . The losing pitcher, Lou Gunning. And for the Providence Jew-els . . . one run, six hits, one error. The winning pitcher . . . with twelve strikeouts and the fifth one-

hitter of his career ... Bob-by ... Wagner.... Time
of the game ... one hour and fifty-nine minutes....
Ladies and gentlemen ... on behalf of the players and
management of the Providence Jew-els ... thank you
and good night ... and please drive safely."

When Harvey reached the infield, Wagner was still
in the clutches of a few teammates. Angel Vedrine
had his arm around him while Campy pumped his
hand, chattering, "Hey, babe, way to be, where you
been all year, babe?" The two rows of police had come
to a halt on the infield grass, forming a V. There was
nowhere for Wagner to go now. Just as Wagner noticed Harvey behind him, two cops came up, and each
took hold of one of Wagner's arms.

Harvey came around in front of Wagner and opened
his glove. Wagner looked at him, then reached in to
take the game ball.

"Helluva catch, Professor," he said quietly, observing his share of the ritual. "Just like picking cherries."

Harvey said nothing, but before he could move away,
Wagner reached out for his arm. "Professor," he said,
"they got Frances, didn't they?"

"Sure," Harvey said. "They got her."

The two cops guided Wagner to the dugout, where
Linderman stood with one foot on the top step, hiking
up his pants. Harvey started in ahead of them. He
wondered if, to the fans still cheering Wagner's one-
hitter, there would seem anything unusual about a
bunch of cops protecting one of the American League's
premier right-handers.

"Easy on the arm, boys," he heard Wagner say behind him. "It just threw a one-hitter."

## About the Author

Richard Rosen won the 1984 Edgar Allan Poe Award for Best First Novel for *Strike Three You're Dead*. His second Harvey Blissberg mystery, *Fadeaway*, will appear in 1986. He is a three-time New England Emmy Award winner for his work in public television, and the author of two nonfiction books, *Psychobabble* and *Me and My Friends, We No Longer Profess Any Graces*.

The Suspense just might kill you . . .

(0451)

**Buy them at your local
bookstore or use coupon
on next page for ordering.**